We hope you enjoy thi
renew it by the due da

D0505223

You can renew it at www.norfolk.gov.uk/libraries or
by using our free library app.

Otherwise you can phone 0344 800 8020 -
please have your library card and PIN ready.

You can sign up for email reminders too.

4 10 18   ß w

LADY OLIVIA AND THE INFAMOUS RAKE

Janice Preston

MILLS & BOON

First Published in Great Britain 2018
by Mills & Boon, an imprint of HarperCollins*Publishers*
1 London Bridge Street, London, SE1 9GF

© 2018 Janice Preston

ISBN: 978-0-263-93306-2

Printed and bound in Spain
by CPI, Barcelona

To Ian.

Thank you for understanding
when I disappear into my own little world.

Chapter One

❧❧❧❧

'**W**here have you *been*? Do you know how long we've been waiting? We were about to give up.'

'It's not my fault,' Lady Olivia Beauchamp retorted to her brother, Alexander. 'Do you even *know* how hard it is to sneak out without bumping into a servant? They're everywhere. And what do you mean…*we*?'

'Never mind that now.' Alex grabbed her arm and bundled her unceremoniously towards the waiting hackney. 'Hurry up. If anyone should catch us, there'll be hell to pay.'

Huffing at his cavalier treatment of her, Olivia clambered inside, then stopped short at the sight of a figure already seated within. Alex put his hand between her shoulder blades and shoved. 'Move. It's only Nev. He's come to help me keep you out of trouble.'

Olivia sprawled inelegantly on the seat opposite Neville Wolfe as her brother leapt in behind her and slammed the door. Immediately, the hackney rocked into motion, causing Olivia, by now half-upright, to tip over once more.

'Alex,' she wailed.

Neville's hand covered his mouth, but he failed to muffle his snort of laughter. Olivia glared across the carriage at him.

'Oh, God,' Alex muttered, as he reached across and hauled her upright. 'Tonight is bound to be a disaster.'

Neville passed a flask to Alex, who drank before handing it back.

'Can I have a drink?' Olivia asked.

'No, you cannot,' Alex retorted. 'That's all I need…you half-cut!' He eyed Olivia sternly. 'Two hours and not a minute longer, d'you hear? We've got better things to do tonight than dance attendance on a troublesome chit like you.'

The carriage passed under one of the new gas street lamps at that moment and Alex's eyes widened as the light caught the ruby and diamond bracelet on Olivia's gloved wrist. He reached across and grabbed her hand, holding it up to examine it.

'That's from Mama's parure. What the devil are you about? What else have you got on?'

He yanked down the hood of her cloak, revealing the pair of exquisite eardrops and the matching necklace she wore. The set had been a wedding gift from their father, the Duke of Cheriton, to their late mother. Olivia fingered the neck-lace—remembering how beautiful Mama had looked, all dressed up and wearing the parure—before battening down the guilt that stirred her conscience. She stuck her nose in the air.

'They belong to me, not Rosalind.' Rosalind was their new stepmother and Olivia was finding it hard to adjust to calling her Stepmama, although she took care not to call her Rosalind to her face. Or in front of her father. 'Papa said that Mama would have wanted me to have them.'

'He *also* said you're not allowed to wear them. They're totally unsuitable for a chit in her first Season.'

'Exactly! So when people see a masked lady tonight, wearing such fine jewellery, it will help my disguise. No one will guess I am your younger sister. They will think I am your light o' love.'

'*That's enough.* Where *did* you hear such lan-guage?'

'From you,' she retorted.

Really! Alex is such *a hypocrite!*

'God's teeth, Olivia, you'd try the patience of a saint. How did you get the jewels, anyway? I thought Father kept them locked up in his safe.'

'He does.' But she also knew where Papa kept the key.

'What do you imagine he'll do when he dis-covers they're missing, you little idiot? He'll have the Runners out.'

'Idiot yourself! I'll have them back long before he returns from Birmingham. He'll never know.'

'Well, you be sure to keep them covered up at Vauxhall. You'll be a magnet for every finger-smith and gallows bird there tonight. I must have rocks in my head to ever agree to such a madcap stunt as this.'

'Well, you did not agree. I won our wager fair and square and—as you always tell me, Brother dear—gambling debts are debts of honour, so you had no choice. *We* had a bet and *you* lost!'

Alex muttered something that sounded suspiciously like *spoilt brat* before lapsing into a sullen silence.

A minute later, out of the dark, came a mocking, 'Good evening, Lady Olivia.'

Olivia—miffed at having been betrayed into such unladylike behaviour in front of Alex's friend, even though she had known him for years—responded with a hissed, 'And if you tell a *single soul* about tonight, Neville Wolfe, your life will not be worth living.'

They crossed the Thames by boat and her first sight of Vauxhall Gardens utterly enchanted Olivia as they entered via the water entrance. Papa was exceedingly unfair to refuse to allow her to come to here—apart from one *very* fleeting visit, with him and Rosalind—early one evening, before it was even dark enough to fully

played, the music struggling to be heard above the chatter and laughter of the crowds dancing, strolling and finishing their supper in the many supper boxes.

As they continued to stroll, arm in arm—Neville still ambling along in their wake—a female voice called Alex's name. They turned as one and Olivia sensed her brother's sudden tension. She had no difficulty in recognising the lady who had hailed him—Lady Shelton, the beautiful widow of Baron Shelton of Rutland. She indicated a supper box—in which several ladies and gentlemen were already seated—and beckoned Alex with a smile of enticement that set Olivia's teeth on edge. She'd never been introduced to Lady Shelton nor, she realised as she scanned the occupants of that box, to any of the others, apart from Lords Clevedon and Sudbury. They were of an older set than the young gentleman and ladies she normally socialised with. A shiver chased down her spine. She chose to interpret it as a shiver of excitement rather than apprehension. At last she would experience a little of *real* life...the life outside the confined world of debutantes and chaperons and balls and Almack's.

'You don't mind if we join them, do you, Livvy?' Alex said, his eyes glued to Lady Shelton.

'Beatrice! I'm *Beatrice*, remember?'

'What? Oh, yes, of course. But you don't mind, do you?'

Neville stepped forward and cleared his throat. 'Alex. Have you forgotten what you said?'

'What?' Alex tore his gaze from the buxom blonde and stared at Neville.

Neville's jaw firmed. 'It's no good givin' me the evil eye. You said on no account was I to be tempted to join up with any of our pals while your sister is under our protection. We was to walk around a while, have a bite of supper if it's not too late—'

'Well, it *is* too late, 'cause *she* kept us waiting for ever.'

'And then take her straight home.' Neville spoke over Alex's grumble. '*That's* what you said. And they—' he indicated the occupants of the box with a flick of his head '—ain't even our pals. And they ain't fitting company for your sister, neither.'

'Oh, never mind that now,' said Alex. 'We shan't stay above five minutes—ten, at the most. Do try not to be so faint-hearted. You'll be all right, won't you, Liv—Beatrice? We'll both be with you. There's no need to be afraid.'

'Afraid? Why should I be afraid? Don't be so stuffy, Neville. Really, you are as bad as Papa, fussing over every little thing. How can there be any risk? They'll never recognise me.'

They approached Lady Shelton.

'Lord Alexander, Mr Wolfe,' she purred. 'How lovely to see you both. I hoped I might persuade you to join our little party tonight?' She indicated the box behind her and the neighbouring box. 'Just a few select friends gathered here to celebrate Lord Clevedon's birthday.' Her gaze skimmed Olivia, who detected curiosity, but also a touch of scorn, in her ladyship's blue eyes. 'Will you introduce your companion?' She leaned closer and her strong perfume wafted up Olivia's nose, making it twitch. She held her breath, desperate not to sneeze. Lady Shelton fingered the edge of the hood covering Olivia's head. 'There really is no need to be bashful with us, my dear,' she added, with an amused smile. 'You will be among friends. We do not judge.'

'Oh, this is Beatrice…er…well, just Beatrice,' Alex said, dismissively, as he handed her into the less crowded of the two supper boxes. 'She's… er…well, she's here incognito as a wager. Yes, that's it. A wager.'

Olivia sat down, fuming. Really, Alex couldn't dissemble convincingly if he tried. No one, listening to him, would believe she was his lady-love now. And that might cause them to wonder who else she might be. She might be willing to rebel now and then, and to take a few risks, but she had no wish for her behaviour to become common knowledge. She knew very well what was expected of her and, in public, she was every inch the perfectly behaved young aristocratic lady. She inched along the bench and smiled invitingly at

Neville as she patted the space next to hers. He would do as a decoy. He eyed her warily and then, with a shrug, he sat next to her while Alex squeezed in next to Lady Shelton with a triumphant grin.

'You gentlemen will already be acquainted with my companions,' Lady Shelton said, 'but, for Beatrice's sake, allow me to introduce Lady Sale, Lords Clevedon and Sudbury, Lord Hugo Alastair, Mr and Mrs Bartlett and Mr Douglas Randall.'

A whisper of caution warned Olivia that these people were very different from those she was used to. She scanned their faces again, suddenly anxious, but there was nothing she could do... having accepted her ladyship's invitation she could not now ask Alex to leave without drawing attention and speculation. She drew in a steadying breath. Ten minutes, he had said. She could manage ten minutes.

A glass was placed before her and a male hand, a ruby ring on one finger, tipped liquid from a jug, filling the glass. She raised her gaze, which had been fixed to the white tablecloth—soiled with crumbs, bearing witness to the supper recently consumed—and met the dark gaze of Lord Hugo Alastair. She felt the blood rush to her face as she forced herself to hold eye contact...there was something about his challenging scrutiny that attracted her and yet made her nervous at the same time…tingles of awareness chasing along every nerve in her body, urging her to flee. Or to find out more. His perfectly shaped mouth curved in a smile.

'What is this drink, sir?' Olivia raised the glass, eyeing the amber liquid.

'Arrack punch. Not too potent for you, is it?' There was a barely perceptible pause and she caught the twitch of his lips before he added, 'Beatrice.'

She swallowed a sudden swell of nerves. He couldn't possibly know her identity. Could he? She raised the glass to her lips, conscious the whole time of Lord Hugo's scrutiny. She'd never tried arrack punch before. She sipped, and barely prevented her nose from wrinkling. It *was* strong. But she would not allow this…this…mocking *coxcomb* the satisfaction of believing her weak. Or lacking in experience.

'It is delicious, thank you.'

She tilted her chin. He was as bad as her brothers…all her life she'd had to prove herself to them—prove herself capable of matching whatever they could do. She drank again. It tasted better this time and she felt the warmth hit her stomach, reminding her that she'd been so excited about tonight she'd barely eaten a thing at dinner and now—she glanced around the table— they were clearly too late for any supper here. She was conscious of the weight of Lord Hugo's gaze upon her. She knew him by sight, but they'd never been introduced—he was not the sort of man who attended come-out balls or who frequented Almack's. In fact, he was exactly the sort of man her Aunt Cecily would warn her to avoid: a disreputable rake and definitely an unsuitable acquaintance for a young lady in her first Season. She glanced at his lordship and saw his attention had been diverted by Mrs Bartlett, his head cocked towards her as she spoke into his ear. He smiled at her words and from looking rather dangerous—with his dark, sardonic good looks—his features were transformed. He looked much younger as his eyes crinkled—lines fanning out from the corners—and his lips parted to reveal strong white teeth. His right hand rested on the white tablecloth, his fingers moving—drumming lightly, as though he was restless—and that ruby ring on his third finger caught the light.

Olivia found her gaze riveted to those reflected darts of colour as she drank again and she realised, with a sense of shock, that she had drained the whole glass. Lord Hugo's hand moved, picked up the jug and refilled her glass. Startled, she met his gaze again and a curious shock rippled through her. Again, she recognised nervousness and excitement all tangled up together. And something more. Something…deeper and slightly thrilling.

Anticipation?

His smile turned arrogant. Knowing. She recognised the look from that of her brothers when
they were being particularly annoying—convinced they knew her better than she knew herself. Her brows twitched into a frown and she
wrenched her eyes from Lord Hugo. Across the
table, Lady Shelton was draped all over Alex,
so Olivia avoided looking at them, too, embar-
rassed by their lack of shame in behaving in such
a way in public—kissing and…and…*fondling* like
that. Even Neville was taking no notice of her;
he was too busy flirting with a gaudily made-up
woman—clearly no lady—who had paused outside their box. She was starting to wish she had
never goaded Alex into that wager. This was not
as much fun as she had thought it would be.

'Oh!'

Lady Shelton's gasp brought Olivia's attention
back to her.

'Oh, heavens.' Lady Shelton fanned herself vig-
orously. 'It is so very hot. I wonder, Alexander,
would you be an absolute angel and escort me
outside for some air?' Her free hand disappeared
beneath the table. 'Perhaps we could dance…or
something?'

Alex leapt to his feet, his cheeks flushed. 'It
would be my pleasure, ma'am.'

He helped her from the box, then appeared to
remember Olivia, for he leaned across Neville and
whispered, 'I shan't be gone long. You'll be safe

enough here with Nev. Just don't be tempted to wander off. With *anyone*.'

And he disappeared into the crowd, Lady Shelton on his arm. Soon afterwards, Lord Sudbury, Mr and Mrs Bartlett and Lady Sale followed them, leaving Olivia alone with Lord Clevedon, Mr Randall, Lord Hugo and Neville. She edged closer to Neville, even though he was still flirting with that same woman. The prickles of awareness chasing over her skin warned her that Lord Hugo's attention was once more upon her, so she studiously avoided looking in his direction. In doing so, however, she inadvertently caught Mr Randall's eye. He was a bulky man of around five-and-thirty and he immediately moved, coming to sit on her side of the table, sliding along the bench until he sat right next to her, his thigh pressing against hers as he twisted his upper body to face her and fingered the edge of her hood.

Then his hand swooped down to land on her thigh and she squeaked a protest, knocking his hand away.

'Just a bit of fun, darling,' he whispered into her ear. 'Why not?'

'Randall.' There was a note of warning in Lord Hugo's voice.

'Alastair?'

'The lady does not appear to welcome your attentions.'

'What business is it of yours?'

Mr Randall then fell silent as Lord Clevedon rose to his feet. Olivia did not know whether to be relieved or alarmed. She was acquainted with Lord Clevedon, having met him at several functions—so he was clearly a respectable gentleman—but she was anxious he did not recognise her and this was drawing far too much of his attention. Up until now he had been too busy talking with Lord Sudbury to take much notice of anyone else. His gaze wandered casually over Olivia.

'My guest is clearly a lady, Randall. You will oblige me by treating her as such at *my* birthday party.'

'My apologies,' Randall muttered. He was so close Olivia could smell the spirits on his breath and his cheeks were flagged with hectic colour. He shifted away until he no longer crowded her and she smiled at his lordship.

'Thank you, my lord.'

His eyes narrowed slightly. Then he bowed, a smile playing on his full lips.

'The pleasure is all mine, my dear.' He gestured at Lord Hugo. 'I shall leave it to you to ensure our glasses are kept topped up, Alastair. I cannot have it said that I am an ungenerous host.'

Lord Hugo—with a sardonic grin—obliged and, because she was overly warm in her velvet domino, Olivia continued to sip the punch. She dare not remove her domino, for that would uncover her hair—distinctive with its blue-black sheen—and she was now desperate not to be identified. She reached for the bow at her throat and pulled it loose, parting the front of the cloak to allow some air to reach her skin, but still leaving her head covered. As she did so, she glanced across the table at Lord Hugo.

Dark eyes lazily surveyed her chest area, then rose to linger on her lips and she trembled. She'd thought this would be an adventure. Now, it just felt dangerous and she felt very foolish and very inexperienced. She broke out in a light sweat even as her mouth dried and she snatched up her glass again and drank thirstily. She might never have been introduced to Lord Hugo, but she knew his reputation as a devil-may-care rake. A shiver tiptoed down her spine as she recalled some of the tales she had heard…stories she could well believe of the man who lounged opposite, a mocking edge to his hard gaze as he drank liberally and refilled the glasses on the table—including hers—at frequent intervals.

Uneasy at being alone in the box with the four men—even though one of them was Neville—Olivia distracted herself by drinking as the men chatted idly and made pithy comments about the people passing by. Gradually, though, she relaxed and she regained her normal, bubbly spirits, giving her the confidence to join the conversation.

Chapter Two

Some time later, Lord Clevedon produced a pack of cards from his pocket and he smiled at Olivia. 'May I challenge you to a few hands of piquet, my dear? I cannot offer an alternative game, for I only have the reduced pack here.'

Olivia had often played piquet with her family, and prided herself on her skill, but she hesitated, knowing that playing cards in a public place was not at all the same as playing cards at a private function. Neville dug his elbow into her ribs at that point and muttered, 'Not at all the thing, La—Beatrice' under his breath.

Olivia glared at him. Then stuck her nose in the air. If she wished to play a hand or two of cards with Lord Clevedon, why should she not? Nobody knew it was her, except Neville, and he did not count.

His lordship shuffled the cards before fanning them between long, elegant fingers. 'Do not concern yourself, Wolfe. We shall play the classic game—the first to gain one hundred points wins. Your…er…*friend* has already proved herself admirably bold, venturing here with two escorts, neither of whom, I'll wager, are members of her family.'

His words reassured Olivia that he had not guessed her identity and, ignoring Neville's desperate grimaces, she said, 'Very well, then. I accept your challenge, sir.'

At that point, Mr Randall exited the box after mumbling an excuse. Olivia was pleased to see the back of him—she just wished Lord Hugo would also leave, with his unsettling gaze that seemed to penetrate deep inside her to winkle out her secrets.

'What stakes shall we say?'

Olivia bit her lip. 'I have no money with me with which to wager.'

'No matter, my dear. Let us hope Lady Luck will smile upon you and, if she should not, I will happily accept your vowel, you know. Of course, if you fear to take the risk, we can play for a penny a point. I am sure one of your two cavaliers will be happy to cover any losses.'

Olivia—discovering in herself a sudden desire not to risk her money on a skill she suddenly doubted—thought a penny a point might be just the answer. Before she could accept Clevedon's offer, however, Lord Hugo, his deep voice an amused drawl, said, 'A penny a point? My dear Clevedon, you insult the lady.'

Olivia glared at him. The sight of that mocking smile fired her anger, egging her on, and she elevated her chin.

'My thoughts exactly, sir. Why, a penny a point is hardly worth bothering with. What do you say to…to…?' Frantically, she tried to decide what would be deemed a reasonable wager without her having to risk *too* much.

'A guinea a point,' Lord Hugo said, with a lift of his brow.

She held his gaze defiantly. 'Perfect.'

'Deal the hand, Clevedon,' Lord Hugo drawled. 'I have an extraordinary desire to see the outcome of this game before I take my leave.'

Light-headed from the effects of the punch and with the enormity of what she had agreed to, Olivia frowned as she forced her somewhat fuzzy attention on her hand. She won the first deal, but she was soon out of her depth. Clevedon played ruthlessly and Olivia was left reeling at the speed at which his points stacked up. Neville, his face grimmer by the second, shot her an encouraging smile.

'I'll go and find Alex.'

He stood and, none too steady on his feet, left the box. Olivia watched him go until he was absorbed into the crowd, then turned her attention

to the remaining two men in the supper box and
to the new hand dealt to her.

'I… I think I would rather not play any more,'
she said, her stomach churning.

'Such a shame you have suffered an unfortu-
nate run of cards,' Clevedon said, smiling. 'But
we cannot stop now—we are *so* close to the finish. One more deal should do it.'

Pride alone stopped her from refusing to finish the game. She lost as, deep down, she had
known she would.

'Never mind. Perhaps, if we play on, your luck
might change, Beatrice, my dear.'

The breath left Olivia's lungs in a whoosh. *Beatrice*. She had forgotten. She felt the blood drain
from her face as she realised the dilemma she
faced: she could not give Clevedon her vowel. She
was here incognito. She could not risk this escapade becoming common knowledge—it would
destroy her reputation and her father…

Sick dread pooled in her stomach. *She* would
be in trouble, yes, but that was not the worst of it.

*Oh, dear God. What have I done? Papa will
blame Alex and then—*

She thrust aside that frantic voice inside her
head as Clevedon raised the pack of cards, his
brows raised, waiting for her reply.

'I…no. I do not care to play again, thank you.'
She sucked in a shaky breath and continued, 'I
will pay you your money by the end of next week,

my lord, if you would be so good as to give me until then to settle my debt?'

'But of course, my dear. Just give me your vowel and then I shall call upon you—shall we say next Saturday evening—and you can repay me. I shall, of course, need your address.'

Panic threatened to overcome her, squeezing her lungs until she could barely breathe. 'I... I... I cannot give you my vowel, sir. But I give you my word that you will be paid on time.'

Clevedon's smile was sympathetic, but there was a hard edge to it now. And how could she blame him? He had no idea of her identity. Why should he trust her? She scanned the people thronging the square.

Oh, where is Alex? Or Neville? Why have they not returned?

'I am sorry, my dear, but...a debt of honour, you know. And an unknown adversary. I am afraid that I must insist on a signed vowel or—perhaps—payment of a different kind?'

Her throat constricted. Her gaze flew without volition to Lord Hugo, but he was staring out across the square, seemingly taking no notice of their conversation.

'D-different kind? I do not understand.'

Clevedon proffered his hand and, as if in a dream, she took it and rose to her feet.

'Come walk with me, Beatrice. A kiss. Or two.

That is all I ask. There are private nooks aplenty in the Dark Walks.'

His eyes lowered to her décolletage. She snatched her hand from his and pulled her domino tightly across her chest, her hand at her throat.

'I...no. I should rather not. Thank you, sir.'

'Your address, then? Or how shall I know where to apply for my winnings?'

Beneath her fingers was the hard outline of Mama's necklace. In a panic, she slid her hands inside her hood and reached behind to unclasp the necklace. She tugged it free and almost flung it on the table.

'There. You may take that as my promise to pay my debt. And, when I do, you must return my necklace.'

A low whistle reached her ears. Lord Hugo's eyes had widened at the sight of the necklace. Belatedly, Olivia recalled she could have offered the bracelet or even the eardrops—either would have covered the amount she owed and both were worth far less than the necklace.

And Papa is far more likely to notice the necklace is missing than he would the others.

But it was too late to change her offer now for Clevedon had already pocketed the necklace, saying, 'A pledge? Hmmm... I should have preferred a kiss, but very well. I accept your pledge. I shall still require your address, however.'

'No! Why?'

His brows rose. 'No? But how, my dear, are you to pay my winnings and how am I to return your necklace? Unless…but of course. You may call upon me at my house in Dover Street. If you wear your domino, then it is unlikely you will be recognised. Shall we say, Saturday evening at seven o'clock? Bring the money—and your delightful self for dinner—and I shall return the necklace.'

'Dinner? No. I could not possibly—our agreement was for me to pay my debt, nothing more.'

'There is the little matter of interest payable, my dear. I shall hold the necklace for you until Saturday, but should you fail me I shall have no choice but to sell it to defray expenses. You do understand, I trust? Don't be late.'

She could stay there no longer. Sick at heart, she fled the box, stumbling a little in her haste, and plunged into the dense mass of people thronging the square, desperately searching for Alex or Neville.

Lord Hugo Alastair watched the mysterious Beatrice vanish among the crush of people, who were growing rowdier by the minute, and he hoped she would quickly find safety with Beauchamp or Wolfe—he'd wager she was younger than she'd tried to appear, but she was without doubt a lady. He bit back a cynical smile—yet another young wife, unrecognisable in her hooded domino and lace-edged mask, out with her lover, proving yet again that matrimony was for fools. Hugo had had his fair share of disenchanted wives on his arm in the past. Although—now he considered it—neither Beauchamp nor Wolfe had paid her much attention. If either of those young greenheads was her lover, they weren't making a very good fist of it.

He scanned the densely packed square and disquiet threaded through him. A female on her own would prove an easy target for the many predators prowling the Gardens—thieves, pickpockets… and worse.

He frowned, recalling the way Beatrice had taken fright at Clevedon's suggestion of a kiss or two. That was not the reaction of a married lady out with her lover. And, now he came to think about it, neither was Clevedon's suggestion one that Hugo would ever have expected of the man who was now examining that ruby and diamond necklace with a look of pure satisfaction on his face.

'Care to enlighten me as to who the mysterious Beatrice is, Clevedon?'

Clevedon smiled smugly. 'My salvation, dear boy. My future wife.'

'Your *wife*?' Hugo's astonishment was perhaps too overt and Clevedon looked up with suddenly narrowed eyes.

'Why ever not?' he said, evenly. 'A man in my

position must marry eventually. The Beauchamp chit is as good as any.'

Hugo racked his brain to come up with a mental picture of Cheriton's daughter. Their paths rarely crossed; young ladies in their first Season held no appeal for him and he, as a younger son with no prospects, held even less appeal for them. Or for their parents. Lady Olivia Beauchamp. He remembered her now: a true beauty, with a willowy figure and the same black hair and silver-grey eyes as her sire. And utterly innocent. Anger stirred, deep in his gut.

What the hell is Beauchamp about, bringing his sister here and then abandoning her?

'I never had you down as the marrying kind, Clevedon.'

Hugo had always suspected the other man's proclivities, but that was a delicate—not to say, illegal—matter and not one he could even mention, although he was aware Clevedon was not the first man to prefer the company of other men and neither would he be the last. He could see now that Clevedon's suggestion of a kiss in payment for the debt had been an elaborate ruse... Clevedon had known damned well that the Lady Olivia Beauchamp would never consent to walking down those shady pathways with him. He had well and truly hooked her in.

Clevedon shrugged. 'It is not by choice, dear boy, but I find myself in need of a wife with a wealthy father. And they don't come much wealthier than Cheriton. Besides, our marriage would be one of pure convenience. My life need not change.'

Distaste mushroomed in Hugo's gut. Lady Olivia might be a spoilt little rich girl who wanted for nothing—and a foolish chit for taking the risks she had tonight—and yet he could still find sympathy for a young girl who would marry with high hopes only to find her dreams dashed by the indifference and neglect of her husband.

His face must have revealed his feelings because Clevedon laughed out loud.

'Scruples, my dear Hugo? Surely not.'

Hugo stood up. 'I don't approve of playing games with innocents.'

'Needs must, dear boy. Needs must. It would not be my choice were things different, but her dowry will compensate for the inconvenience. And, of course, there will be the added bonus of marrying into such a powerful family.'

'You think you can force Cheriton into agreeing to a marriage?'

Clevedon shrugged again. 'Why not? When a juicy plum like the Catch of the Season drops into one's lap, it would be remiss not to take advantage. And now, with this,' he held the sparkling necklace aloft, 'I have the means to exert a little additional persuasion, shall we say.'

Hugo tried to mask his revulsion at what Clevedon had in store for the girl. Marrying money was one thing. Ruining a girl's reputation and innocence in order to force a wedding was beyond the pale, particularly when the man had no taste for female flesh.

'Look here, Alastair. It was her decision to come here, presumably against Cheriton's orders.' Clevedon shrugged. 'If she wants to play with the grown-ups, she must accept the consequences, as must her fool of a brother. He, too, will get his comeuppance very soon, if I'm not mistaken.'

His words resurrected a memory from earlier that evening—Sir Peter Tadlow cajoling Marie Shelton, *'Please, Marie'*, until Marie, with an irritated huff, had flounced out of the supper box and intercepted Beauchamp, Wolfe and their female companion. Tadlow had followed Marie from the box and not returned. Not that that was any loss—Hugo never had taken to the man. But he had wondered at the time why Marie—mercenary to her core—was bothering with Lord Alexander Beauchamp, whose pockets always seemed to be to let, even with a father like the Duke of Cheriton, who was rich as Croesus. Why had she draped herself all over Beauchamp and plied him with punch before enticing him away from the supper box? And where did Tadlow fit in?

'What was Marie up to, with young Beauchamp?'

Clevedon's eyes gleamed. 'What do you think?

Use your imagination, Alastair, do. I declare, you are growing dull of late.'

'Yes. But why?' Watching young Beauchamp had put Hugo in mind of his younger self—a young man on the path to self-destruction. 'And where did Tadlow disappear to?'

Clevedon sighed. 'You are like a dog with a bone, Alastair.' He slipped the necklace into his pocket. 'Tadlow,' he said, with exaggerated patience, 'was keen to avoid being seen by Beauchamp. He's got some scheme or other planned.'

'Scheme?'

Clevedon shrugged. 'Something about revenge on Cheriton—seems he interfered in some plan Tadlow had to wed Bulbridge to Lady Helena Caldicot. Tadlow's her uncle on her mother's side.'

Sir Peter Tadlow and Viscount Bulbridge—and Bulbridge's cousin, Douglas Randall—were recent additions to Hugo's circle and he could not like any of them. All three were the sort of dissolute fellows that should serve as a stellar warning to unwary young bucks: *Look closely, lads, for here lies your future.* An unwary young buck such as he had been at the age of seventeen when he had set out to squeeze every last drop of pleasure from life without regard to the consequences.

Dear God. That was nine years ago!

'Anyway,' Clevedon continued, 'Cheriton stuck his nose in, as is his wont, and put a stop to it so they're out to bleed him through his son. Tadlow reckons Cheriton owes him. And young Beauchamp can look after himself—it's no different for him than it is for his silly sister. If they come out to play with the adults, they must be prepared.' He smiled wolfishly. 'Now, much as I enjoy your oh-so-charming company, Alastair, old man, I think I shall join the others next door. Coming?'

Hugo could stomach no more tonight.

'No. I'm off to my club. I'll say goodnight.'

He left the box and plunged into the crowds, sick with disgust as he wondered why the hell he was still hanging around with Clevedon and his ilk, with their louche, care-for-nothing ways. Hugo might have always been wild and reckless, but he would never deliberately ruin an innocent girl for the sake of money and he would never stoop to using a young man to wreak revenge on his father. It was almost as though a veil had lifted from his eyes and he saw for the first time some of their true characters.

He had only attended tonight because it was Clevedon's birthday, but he'd already decided it was time to stop socialising with this crowd altogether. In the past year or so he had gradually clawed his way out of the swamp of vices that had held him captive for so long, but he was aware it would be all too easy to slide back into the mire. A few too many drinks, and judgement and common sense were pissed down the gutter along with the alcohol.

Anger at the way the two youngsters had been targeted by Tadlow and Clevedon continued to gnaw at Hugo as he strolled through the hordes gathering to enjoy the fireworks display. Of the two, Clevedon was the most dangerous because he was welcomed almost everywhere in the *ton* and far more readily than Hugo himself was accepted. Parents fawned over him, eager for a title for their daughters and, if his plan to compromise her succeeded, he was the sort of man Cheriton might very well accept as a husband for his daughter.

Even though he told himself he would not put himself out—it was none of his business, after all—still Hugo found himself watching out for a figure in a midnight-blue velvet domino.

She'd said she had no money. Had she found her brother? Or Wolfe? They'd both been well on the way to being foxed anyway, as had Lady Olivia. And guilt mixed in with the disquiet as it continued to spiral through him—guilt over his own part in topping up her glass, time after time. It made no difference to tell himself he wouldn't have done it if he'd realised who she was...how young she was...how innocent. He still felt responsible.

And it is my *doing that she lost so heavily. I provoked her into agreeing those high stakes.*

He stopped dead. People jostled around him, loudly complaining, but he ignored them. Then he cursed, fluently, beneath his breath. It went against the grain, but he felt compelled to look. To at least try to make sure she was all right... that she had found her brother. He gazed around. But how on earth could he locate her in this heaving mass of humanity? Where would she go? He bit back another curse as realisation dawned. She would stay near the supper box, in the hope that either her brother or Wolfe would return for her. He turned and shoved his way back through the crowd, until Clevedon's box was in sight, and... *there*.

'Bloody hellfire!'

She was close to the box, but not close enough to be visible to the occupants, and she was surrounded by several young men. One of them had his arm around her shoulders and was trying to pull down her hood, but she was fighting him off—verbally as well as physically, from what Hugo could make out. The lads surrounding Olivia were not gentlemen—probably clerks or some such, out for a good time—which was just as well because by the time Hugo reached them, Olivia's hood was down, her hair was awry and her face unmasked. Her eyes were huge in her pale face, but they nevertheless fired ice shards at her tormentors as she berated them. As he came within hearing distance, Hugo bit back a grin to hear her spitting a variety of insults.

'You vile worms! Churls! Scabs! Sodden-witted knaves! Leave me alone, or I'll kick you so hard you won't remember your own name for a month!'

The surrounding youths were laughing at her... mocking...and Hugo could see the effort it cost her to hold tears at bay.

He stepped into the fray.

Chapter Three

'Enough!' He faced the lad who was taunting Olivia by waving her mask above his head, its ribbons dangling and dancing. He held out one hand. 'I'll take that.'

The lad exchanged looks with his friends. 'And who might you be? The little tart gave it me as a tro— *Argh*...'

Hugo's fingers tightened around the youth's throat, causing his eyes to bulge.

'I said... I. Will. Take. That.'

A ragged but muted cheer sounded from some of the onlookers as Hugo continued to hold the youth high, by the neck, allowing just the tips of his toes to scrape the ground. It took no time for the lad to capitulate. He thrust the mask into Hugo's face. Hugo took it, releasing him, and, as her tormentor slumped to the ground, Hugo faced Olivia. She was shaking, her eyes suspiciously luminous, but she held herself straight, her nose in the air, as she accepted the mask, tied it back in place and pulled her hood over her head.

'Thank you.' She began to walk away.

For God's sake! Where does *she think she is going?*

With two strides he caught up with her and grabbed her by the arm, spinning her around to face him. She wrenched her arm free.

'Leave me alone.'

'How do you mean to get home?'

'I shall find my brother.'

'And if you don't? And if you get accosted again? The next men might not be inclined to leave it at teasing.'

She elevated her nose. Again. Really, she was beyond hoity. He was almost inclined to leave her to it, if she was this stubborn.

Almost.

'I shall escort you home.'

She was slowly but surely backing away from him. With a growl that originated deep, deep inside him, Hugo followed her and grabbed her arm again.

'Let go of me.'

Those amazing eyes of hers shot icy slivers at him. What would they look like, fired with passion rather than fury? Would they—? He batted those errant thoughts aside. She was eighteen years old…had only just made her debut in society.

'With what will you pay a jarvey to drive you home, Lady Olivia?'

He used her name deliberately, so she would know he recognised her. Her eyes flared.

'You have no money, or you would have paid Clevedon,' he reminded her.

She gasped at that, her worry palpable. 'D-does Lord Clevedon know it was me? What if he tells my father?'

'No. He does not know.' The urge to soothe her took him unawares. Besides, there was no point in her fretting when he knew damned well Clevedon would never tell her father about tonight.

'So, how will you get home if you don't find your brother?' he went on, ruthlessly. 'Will you pay your fare with your bracelet?'

He raised her arm and the jewels caught the light, winking ice and fire.

'Or maybe an eardrop?'

He slid his hand under her hood, skimming the satin-soft skin of her neck, and found her earlobe, tugging at it gently. Her breath quickened, her bosom heaving, and he snatched his hand away before he gave in to his instincts…the ones clamouring at him to haul her into his arms and to kiss some sense into her. He grasped her wrist. Firmly.

'You're coming with me,' he rasped out and began to stride in the direction of the water gate, towing her along behind him.

'Wh-where are you taking me?'

The fear in her voice had him slamming to a halt. He clenched his jaw.

'Home,' he gritted out. 'And, before you ask, yes...*your* home.'

'I... I won't go without my brother.'

'Your brother? Well, and where is he?' Hugo flung his arm wide, almost knocking a passing gentleman's hat from his head. 'If he is supposed to be looking out for you tonight, he's making a poor fist of it, that's all I can say. I am not spending all night searching for your ramshackle brother when he clearly doesn't give a da—hoot that he's left you on your own in among this sort of crowd. I'm taking you home. Then I can return to my own plans for the evening.'

With that, he whirled around and set off again, his hand still clamped around her wrist.

He did not dare to slow his stride—she would only argue again. The sooner he delivered the troublesome minx home, the sooner he could forget all about her and her risk-taking, and her luminous, hypnotic eyes that reminded him of the moon and were fringed by the thickest, darkest, longest lashes he had ever seen.

Temptress eyes.

They soon reached Vauxhall Stairs and the water gate. A boat was already waiting and they embarked, along with several other passengers, some of whom Hugo knew. He nodded a greeting, but then pointedly directed his gaze across the river to discourage conversation. If any of them should recognise Olivia...his stomach clenched. She would be well and truly compromised and there was no way he ever intended to wed, not after the wretched example of his parents' union.

'But what—?'

'Be quiet,' he growled, glaring down into those wide eyes that glittered at him from behind her mask. 'We'll talk later.'

He ignored her loud puff of exasperation, concentrating instead on the dark ripples of the Thames slipping past the boat as the oarsmen strained to reach the opposite bank.

They disembarked, still in silence. Olivia stumbled and Hugo steadied her, wrapping his arm around her waist.

'Oops,' she said, stifling a giggle.

She straightened and pulled away from him, but her progress was erratic as she made for a waiting hackney. Hardly surprising, given the number of times he had refilled her glass—and her readiness to drain it every time. Hugo instructed the jarvey to take them to Grosvenor Square, where Beauchamp House—the Duke of Cheriton's London residence—was located, then he handed Olivia up the step and climbed in behind her.

'Why did you stop me from speaking in the

boat?' Her voice quivered with indignation. 'Who are you to tell me what to do?'

Hugo shifted on the seat so he was half-facing her, and folded his arms across his chest.

'I am the man who is saving you from the results of your own folly.'

She pushed back her hood and tore off her mask. 'Hmmph. Some saviour you are. I should not be alone with you like this. It is scandalous.'

Her pert little nose was in the air again—she really was the most infuriating wench he had ever met.

'More scandalous than you getting drunk and wandering around Vauxhall unescorted?'

'I am *not* drunk. And I am masked. No one could recognise me. I know your reputation, Lord Hugo Alastair. You are the sort of man my aunt always warns me about. Well, you need not think you may take advantage of me, for I shall fight you and scream *very loudly* if you try to touch me.'

Her words might be full of bravado, but Hugo did not miss the way she shrank back into the corner of the hackney as she spoke them and the intermittent illumination from the street lamps as they passed revealed her hands gripping one another so tightly they shook.

He sighed. 'I have no intention of touching you, Lady Olivia. I prefer my ladies willing. And experienced.'

Her eyes flashed at that but, thankfully, she remained silent.

'I was impressed by your vocabulary back there,' he said. Talking would, surely, help take her mind from their situation. And his. 'Where did you learn such insults?'

'Shakespeare,' she replied, haughtily. 'I am surprised you did not recognise them. I presume you did study his works at school?'

Impertinent little... He swallowed his irritation. 'I did. Although I believe it is sodden-witted *lords*, not knaves.'

She glared at him. 'Why would I call them *lords*? I was insulting them.'

'They are not the typical words one might expect from a young lady.'

She shrugged. 'I've heard Alex use them.'

Her brother again: Lord Alexander Beauchamp...younger son of the Duke of Cheriton and as wild as they come. Although what *his* excuse might be, with such a decent and supportive father, unlike Hugo's—

He clamped down on that memory there and then. He would not allow himself to remember his childhood or his brutal father. It was shut up tight in a dark corner of his memory—a corner he refused to revisit.

'Your brother should have more sense than to utter such words in your hearing.'

'You sound just like Dominic. That's what he

always says. But Alex…you do not understand. Alex is…'

Her smooth forehead furrowed as she chewed her full bottom lip. Hugo waited, loath to say anything that might distract her from the confidence he sensed she was about to share. Her earlier tension had gone, to be replaced by agitation. Her hands now writhed in her lap. Hugo was certain he was not the cause this time. This was connected to her brother.

'Alex has always been troubled,' she said, eventually, her voice subdued. 'He… I do not understand why, but he has always had a difficult relationship with Papa. Ever since…' Her voice dropped to a near whisper and Hugo got the impression she had almost forgotten his presence. Then she drew in a hasty breath, and straightened. 'Well, never mind that. The family look out for him. That is all.'

The family. Did she realise how fortunate she was to have such a tightly knit family to support her? And yet the silly chit risked disgrace and worse by this foolhardy escapade.

'Your father will not be happy when he learns of your antics tonight.'

Her gaze flew to his. '*No.* You cannot tell Papa.' She grabbed his hands. 'Please. You cannot.'

'He needs to know the danger your brother put you in.'

Hugo marvelled at the words coming from his mouth. Him…the wildest and most reckless of them all…ready to test any boundary for the sake of having fun. And now here he was, attempting to imbue some common sense into a troublesome young lady like Lady Olivia Beauchamp.

'Please. Do not tell Papa. Not for my sake, but for Alex's.' Her eyes searched his. 'Please?' Her hands tightened their grip.

He locked in the words '*persuade me*'. Reined back his sudden urge to seize her mouth, taste her lips. He extricated his hands from hers, suddenly uncomfortable…too viscerally aware of her nearness, the way she gazed up at him with parted lips. And those eyes…

He twisted to look out of the window. Piccadilly. They would soon reach Grosvenor Square.

'Why should I care about protecting your brother?'

'Alex…he is difficult, I know. He drinks. He gambles. He fights. But he is unhappy. At least, everyone *else* thinks he is upset by what happened. *I* believe he's angry. But I do not understand why.'

It was the second time she had said that. Curiosity stirred within Hugo…what had happened in the Beauchamps' past? He made a mental note to quiz his mother.

'The only thing that takes him away from all those…those *vices* is horses. He adores horses and they adore him. He has an almost magical connection with them. Give him an untameable horse and he will gentle it until it follows him around like a puppy.'

'That does not explain why I should not tell your father.'

'But you cannot. Not when Alex finally has a chance to settle down…when he has the chance to have something of his own that will make him content.' She chewed at her lip again. 'It is not yet common knowledge, but Papa has purchased Sir William Rockbeare's estate in Buckinghamshire. Do you know Sir William?'

'I know of him.' Everyone knew Rockbeare's cattle were the best riding and carriage horses in the country. 'I heard he'd sold up.'

'Well, Alex got into trouble while Papa was away in Buckinghamshire. And Papa told him if he could stay out of trouble for the rest of the Season, then he could move to Foxbourne and run the stud and training stables. If he proves himself, in a few years Papa will sign the estate and all the horses over to him. Do you not see?'

She sat forward, her silver gaze intent upon his, sending strange impulses quivering through him. Not the impulse to seize and to take this time, but…the desire to protect. He frowned, dragging his attention away from his feelings and back to her words. Too much thought about his feelings always made him fidgety and out of sorts. That's why he was usually careful to avoid such namby-pamby nonsense.

'It is a wonderful chance for Alex and he wants it *sooo* much, and he has been trying so hard to keep out of trouble and if Papa finds out about tonight...' She hung her head. 'It was all my fault.' He caught the sound of a tiny sniff. 'I won a bet and Alex lost which meant he had no choice but to take me to Vauxhall. But it was not a fair bet. I *knew* I could not lose, because Uncle Vernon had already agreed to allow me to drive his blacks in the Park, but Alex didn't know that, and he thought it a safe bet because Vernon never allows *anyone* to drive his blacks.'

Hugo frowned, trying to make sense of her jumbled tale. 'Then why did your uncle allow *you* to drive his blacks?'

He knew the pair she meant and he knew how proud and protective her uncle, Lord Vernon Beauchamp, was of them.

'Because I tricked him. He upset Aunt Cecily—he was teasing her and she was in a snit with him, but he needed her to do him a favour because Lady Slough was pursuing him relentlessly, he said—'

'Lady *Slough*?' An image of the lady in question—short, stout, fifty if she was a day—formed in Hugo's head. 'Lady Slough was pursuing your *uncle*?'

Lord Vernon Beauchamp was one of the most

eligible bachelors in the *ton*—much sought after and very popular with the ladies.

'Well, not for *herself*, of course.' She tutted. Hugo could barely contain a chuckle. She really was an entertaining miss—an unexpected mixture of naivety and shrewdness. 'For her *daughter*. Anyway, Uncle Vernon needed my Aunt Cecily to seat him as far away from Lady Slough and Amelia as possible when they came to dinner—'

'But…why would they be invited to dinner?'

'Because Lady Slough is my stepmama's aunt—even though she used to disown Stepmama but now she is toadying up to Stepmama for all she is worth—and she really believes Uncle Vernon will marry her spotty daughter. Which he won't, I can tell you, because Uncle Vernon will *never* get married, he says.'

Hugo had every sympathy with that point of view.

'Anyway, I was telling you all about my bet with Alex…so, Uncle Vernon *begged* me to persuade Aunt Cecily not to sit Lady Slough or Amelia next to him—because she threatened to do exactly that—and *I* said I would persuade her, but that he would owe me a favour. And he said, *Anything*. And then, the next day, when I reminded him he tried to wriggle out of it, but Papa was a witness and told Uncle Vernon he should be more careful about making such vague promises. So Vernon had already agreed, but Alex didn't know…and Dominic is right! I *am* a horrid, manipulative creature.'

'Dominic?' It was the second time she had mentioned this Dominic.

'Avon.'

'Of course.' Dominic, Lord Avon, was Olivia's eldest brother and heir to the Dukedom. 'So you don't get on with Avon?'

She pouted. 'Well, I do. He is nice enough when he's not teasing me. But he does take himself and his position as Papa's heir exceedingly serious. He is opposite to Alex. Poor Alex.' She slumped back into the corner. 'I shall *never* forgive myself if he loses the chance to have Foxbourne because of me.'

'Why do you care so much?'

She stared. 'He's my *brother*. Of course I care. I *love* him.'

Envy stirred. Everyone knew the Beauchamps were a close family. What must it be like, to have complete and utter faith and trust in your own father? Hugo had never known such security, even though his mother had tried her best to protect him and Lucas, his older brother, from their violent father. Neither of them had returned to Rothley Hall, the family estate up in Northumberland, after they left university. Lucas had made his home in London and Hugo had spent more time with Lucas than at Oxford, finding his elder brother's life of excess and debauchery much more exciting than a life of study. They had been wild years—until Lucas had been betrayed by the woman he loved and a man he thought his friend and had left London abruptly, a bitter man. Later, following their father's death, Lucas had become the Marquis of Rothley and led the life of a joyless recluse.

Since then, Hugo had been on his own, continuing with all those same rakish excesses and vices until this past year or so, when that way of life had begun to pall, almost without him realising it. He had even—God help him—invested some of his recent winnings in government bonds. *That* was the influence of Sir Horace Todmorden, his new stepfather, whose seemingly unshakeable faith in Hugo was beginning to change him.

'What are you thinking about? You look…sad.'

The soft query jerked him from his thoughts. 'Nothing.' Then, at her crestfallen expression, he gentled his voice. 'I was thinking about my father and how fortunate you are in yours.'

Her hand covered his. 'You must miss him dreadfully.'

'Hardly.' He huffed a laugh. 'He was a brute.'

'Oh.' Her fine, dark brows drew together as she withdrew her hand. 'But…you still have other family, do you not?'

'My mother and my brother, Rothley.'

He'd said enough. She could have no real interest in his family. Once he had delivered her home, their paths were unlikely to cross very often. But their conversation had stirred hope within him, for not only had Mama married Sir Horace last year, but Lucas, too, had now wed. He and Mary, his new wife, and Mary's two young children, would arrive in London very soon for a prolonged visit. And then...pleasure glowed deep inside at the thought that, maybe, he would finally be part of a close-knit family himself.

He shook all thoughts of his family from his head as the hackney rocked to a halt.

'We're here.' Hugo glanced up at Beauchamp House. Belatedly, he realised he should have instructed the jarvey to stop around the corner. 'Put that mask back on and pull up your hood.'

Olivia stared at him, an unfathomable expression on her face before, with yet another pout, tying her mask in place. Hugo jumped from the hackney. The front door of the house now stood open, a footman silhouetted within the frame. Hugo waved him away.

'Wrong address,' he called.

The man raised his hand in acknowledgement and retreated into the house, closing the door behind him. Hugo leaned back inside the carriage.

'How did you intend to get back inside?'

'Around the back. There's a window... Alex makes sure it's unlocked whenever he goes out at night and doesn't want anyone to know.'

'And he told his younger sister about it?'

'No. Nobody ever tells me *anything*. But I usually find out anyway.'

The hint of pride in her tone made him smile. Again, he thought of her as an odd mixture of naivety and intuition, but that didn't mean she was up to snuff when dealing with the darker aspects of life…or of society, for that matter. He held out his hand and she took it to climb down to the pavement. Without volition, his fingers closed around hers and he had to force himself to release her.

'Wait for me,' he said to the jarvey. 'I won't be long.' Then to Olivia, he said, 'Come. Show me. But if your father appears, I'm off.'

'Papa's away,' she replied. 'He and my stepmother left yesterday, with her grandfather. They're going to Birmingham to collect his belongings, although…' She frowned. 'I *think* they're meeting Uncle Vernon somewhere first. He wrote to Papa, only Papa would only tell me it was nothing to worry about.'

Yet again, Hugo found himself biting back a smile—this time at her disgruntled tone. She clearly prided herself on knowing everything that was going on within her family. They had reached the corner and turned into a side street. There was a low bark, the click of claws on the pavement, and an enormous dog launched itself at Olivia. Hugo's heart thundered as he threw his arms around its neck, dragging it away.

'Hector!' A tall, slender man, supporting him-self on a crutch, lurched towards them.

'Hector!' Far from being petrified, Olivia's squeal was one of delight.

The dog squirmed, its tail waving, as Hugo held it fast.

'You know this monster?' he panted.

'Of course I do. It's Hector. My stepmother's dog and…oh! F-F-Freddie.'

The man had reached them and, with a fero-cious scowl at Hugo, he reached out and tugged the hood from Olivia's head.

'What do you think you are doing?' He kept his voice low as he scanned the surrounding street. 'And who the de—who on *earth* are you?'

Chapter Four

Olivia clutched at the man's sleeve. 'Oh, Freddie! *Please*. You must not tell *anyone* you have seen me.'

'Livvy, how can I keep this a secret? I enjoy my work for your father—he trusts me to be honest with him.' He pushed her behind him and glared at Hugo. 'I asked who you are, sir. And you can release the dog. He will not run off. Nor attack you—unless I tell him to.'

Hugo released the huge hound. 'I'm Alastair. And you, sir?'

'Frederick Allen. The Duke's secretary.'

'Allen? You are connected to the new Duchess?'

'Her brother.'

'Well, before you imagine the worst, Allen, let me assure you that I am merely escorting Lady Olivia home from Vauxhall Gardens where, unfortunately, she became separated from her brother, who originally took her there.'

'It's true, Freddie. Alex disappeared and I had no money to get home and Lord Hugo very gallantly offered to escort me so I would not come to any harm.'

'No harm? There will be no end of harm if anyone should spot you.' Freddie glanced around again. 'We must get off the street.' He tugged Olivia towards a flight of steps leading down to the basement area, where a door stood ajar casting a patch of light on to the flagstones. Freddie jerked his head, indicating that Hugo should follow.

Once they were hidden from view, he growled, 'How can you have come to no harm when you're out at this time of night, unchaperoned, with a strange man? Does Nell know?'

'No. I did not wish her to be obliged to lie on my behalf, so I did not tell her. But you must not tell Papa, or Rosalind, or…or…*anyone*. You *know* Alex will get the blame and then he will lose Foxbourne, and he will be devastated and then he will disappear again like he did before, and no one will know where he's gone, and—'

'Olivia!'

She clamped her mouth shut.

'You cannot possibly know what might happen in the future, so please stop imagining the worst all the time.'

Olivia stuck her pert little nose in the air again. Freddie caught Hugo's eye and rolled his eyes and Hugo warmed to the man, who looked to be a similar age to himself.

'Olivia, if you do not wish me to tell your father about this, I suggest you go inside and get to bed, *now*. And take Hector with you. If anyone sees you, tell them you came outside with me and Hector but, for goodness' sake, keep your gown covered and hide that mask. You and I will have further words in the morning, after church.'

Olivia clutched Freddie's arm. 'But what about Alex? What if he's in trouble?'

'Leave Alex to me. Goodnight, Livvy.'

Her lips firmed. 'Very well,' she said, with a pout and a sigh. 'Goodnight, Freddie. Goodnight, Lord Hugo. And thank you for bringing me home.'

Hugo bowed. 'It was my pleasure, my lady. Goodnight.'

She stared at him—slightly resentfully, he thought, but he could not fathom why that might be—then she swung around and, with Hector at her heels, she vanished inside the house. Hugo found himself the object of Freddie's scrutiny.

'What happened?'

Hugo told the other man how Lady Shelton had persuaded Alex, Olivia and Neville to join them.

'You have no idea where he went?'

'No. Only that he wandered off with Lady Shelton on his arm. But that's not all.'

He revealed Tadlow's plan to wreak revenge on the Duke through Alex.

Freddie's brow furrowed. 'That wretch,' he said, in disgust. 'He is my stepsister's uncle. A nasty piece of work. I must warn Alex to beware of him and just hope he'll listen to me. Silly young chump,' he added. 'Let us hope he's not courting more trouble than he can handle.' He sighed. 'I must away to Vauxhall, then. See if I can find him and warn him. Although if he's been drinking he may well be in no mood to listen.'

'Does he not have an incentive to mend his ways now?'

Freddie raised his brows.

'Lady Olivia told me about Foxbourne and how much it means to Alex.'

Freddie nodded. 'It means the world to him, but Alex is young and impetuous. A bit like his sister,' he added with a grin. 'And with both his father and uncle out of town, it's too easy for him to fall back into his old habits. If the Duke finds out Alex took Olivia to Vauxhall against his expressed wishes—let alone that he left her alone with such an unsuitable group of people, if you'll pardon my bluntness—then he will have little choice but to follow up his threat to put a manager into Foxbourne.'

He began to climb the area steps. Laboriously.

Sympathy stirred in Hugo's heart, and also something of a feeling of shame—whatever reasons he'd ever had for self-pity, at least he was fit and able. He followed Freddie up to the street.

'I shall come with you,' he said. 'I have a hackney waiting in the Square.'

'There is no need. You've done enough.'

'I intended to return anyway. I'll help you find Beauchamp first, then I have business of my own to attend to.'

Lady Olivia might have forgotten her reckless wager, and the price Clevedon intended to extract, but Hugo had not. Not only was there a wayward brother to track down, but he also had a necklace to retrieve.

Olivia clung on to Hector's collar as they climbed the stairs. After the terror and excitement of the evening, tiredness all at once swamped her. Her legs felt cumbersome, as though they belonged to someone else, as she attempted to move quietly. The familiar surroundings appeared to be somehow distant from her—as though she was viewing them through thick, somewhat distorted glass. She realised she was a touch drunk.

All I need to do is get to my bedchamber without anyone seeing me.

A single candle burned in a wall sconce opposite the head of the stairs, as it did every night, and she resumed her climb up to the second floor and her bedchamber. She stumbled over the final stair as she gained the second landing and she swallowed down a giggle.

'Shhh,' she said to Hector. He looked up at her, somewhat reproachfully, she thought. She weaved a little as she headed along the corridor towards her bedchamber. 'We must not wake Aunt Cecily. Or Lady Glen… Lady Glenlo… Lady G.'

She grimaced at the thought of meeting Nell's formidable aunt, who had been living at Beauchamp House for the past few months, ever since Papa and Rosalind's betrothal and their subsequent marriage.

Without warning, her throat thickened and her eyes blurred. She stopped walking and frowned.

'But I *like* Rosalind… I mean, Stepmama,' she said out loud. 'Why do I feel like crying?'

The click of a door latch roused her and she turned, her heart thumping, afraid it would be Aunt Cecily. Her aunt would never swallow some cock-and-bull story about going outside with Hector. She would see right through Olivia. She released her pent-up breath as Nell peered from her bedchamber.

'I thought you were my aunt,' Olivia said.

'But Cecily's bedchamber is nowhere near here, Livvy,' Nell said. She stepped out into the passageway, a frown creasing her forehead. 'Why are you dressed? You retired hours ago, with the headache.' She scanned Olivia from head to toe.

'Have you been *out*? Where did you get that bracelet? What have you been up to?'

Olivia's stomach somersaulted.

The bracelet. Mama's necklace. *Lord Clevedon.*

How could I have forgotten?

'Livvy?' Nell's voice was laced with concern as she grabbed Olivia's arm. 'Are you ill? Shall I fetch someone?'

Olivia wrenched her horrified thoughts from that dreadful game of piquet. 'No. But I'm in such trouble. Oh, what am I to do, Nell?'

'Shhh.'

Nell dragged Olivia into her bedchamber and thrust her towards the bed, where the rumpled sheets were—Olivia discovered as she slumped to the mattress—still warm. Nell lit a candle on her bedside table and then sat next to Olivia, her arm around her, as Hector padded across to flop down on the fireside rug.

'What is it, Livvy? What happened?'

Olivia tugged at the ties of her domino and let it slide from her shoulders as her hands went to her neck, exploring the bare skin in the vain hope that the entire episode had been a dream— or a nightmare—and, somehow, miraculously, her mother's necklace would reappear. Tears stung her eyes again.

'Oh, I am a wicked, wicked girl.'

'Livvy! You are frightening me. What has *happened*?'

Nell shifted away from Olivia and, grabbing her by the shoulders, she shook her.

'Please. Tell me, Livvy. It cannot be so very bad, but I cannot help if you do not tell me.'

Olivia sunk her head into her hands, her thoughts muddled and sluggish as she tried to remember it all. Slowly, disjointedly, she told Nell about her wager with Alex, their trip to Vauxhall and that disastrous card game with Lord Clevedon.

'Lord *Clevedon*? I am shocked. I thought he was a gentleman.'

'He is. But he did not know it was me. He thought I was a *floozy*. He probably thought I only got what I deserved…but…oh, *Nell*! I could have asked Lord Hugo for help… I am certain he would have helped me. But I forgot all about it because I was so certain he would try to kiss me in the hackney and when he did not—' Olivia sniffed and rubbed her eyes. 'He is as bad as Dominic and Alex. He thinks I am a s-s-silly child and not even p-p-pretty enough to steal a kiss. I was at his mercy, and he…he…'

He was kind.

He listened.

And I…oh, no…

'I told him all about Alex and Foxbourne and

everything. Why did I tell him? I did not mean to, it just all poured out.'

'But… Livvy…who is Lord Hugo? How is he involved?'

'Lord Hugo Alastair.'

Nell gasped. 'Livvy! Do not tell me you were alone with *him* in a hackney.'

'Yes,' said Olivia, miserably. 'And he did not even *try* to kiss me.'

'But where did you meet him? Where was Alex? Surely Alex did not allow you to go off alone with a rake like Lord Hugo?'

'Alex was not there. He went off with that strumpet Lady Shelton,' Olivia said, tartly. 'He left me with Lord Clevedon and Lord Hugo. But then, after I lost Mama's necklace, I went to look for Alex and Lord Hugo rescued me and he brought me home.'

'Well, it is Alex's fault. Let him retrieve the necklace.'

'I cannot. He already scolded me for wearing it. And he's like to go off and challenge Lord Clevedon to a duel or something. You know how hot-headed he is.'

'We shall confide in Freddie, then. *He* will know what to do,' Nell said.

'Freddie already knows, but he does not know about the necklace and I cannot tell him, because then he will feel he *has* to tell Papa and then he will cast Alex out and it will all be my fault. Oh,

Nell. What am I to do? Papa will be home in a few days and he is bound to see it is missing.'

'Well…' Nell frowned, clearly thinking. 'Well. I suggest we sleep on it. I am sure we'll think of something in the morning.'

Progress was slow when Hugo and Freddie arrived back at Vauxhall Gardens. Hugo matched his pace to that of his companion as they turned down yet another path, searching the faces of the numerous young men in the dimly lit thoroughfare, seeking Alex. Hugo curbed his impatience—Freddie could not help being slow, and Hugo was keen to help him find Alex. Everything he had learned tonight about the Duke's son had reminded him of his younger, wilder self.

And then there was this weird, completely out-of-character compulsion to help Olivia—he made it a rule in life not to burden himself with unnecessary responsibilities—but there was something about her spirit that drew him to her. And the odd glimpse of bewildered child beneath the bold front she exhibited to the world roused his normally well-concealed protective instincts. The decision was made. If he could help the two of them, he would do so.

Hugo scanned the couples they passed, but there was still no sign of young Beauchamp. Freddie was noticeably struggling to cope with the crowds and the distance they needed to walk.

'I have an idea.' Hugo halted as they entered the main area near to the rotunda. 'We could walk around for hours and keep missing Alex. Why do you not wait here…' he indicated a nearby bench '…and I will search the pathways. That way, you will see him if he should happen to pass.'

'And it will take much less time,' Freddie said, with a rueful smile.

Sweat beaded his upper lip and he took out a handkerchief to dry it. Out of nowhere, three youths sped past, knocking him back. They snatched the handkerchief from his hand. Hugo grabbed Freddie to prevent him falling and, as soon as he was steady on his feet, he spun around, ready to chase the thieves.

Freddie held him back. 'Leave it. They have gone.'

Sure enough, they had melted into the crowd.

'Are you hurt?'

Freddie shrugged. 'Only my pride, but I am accustomed— Hoi! Alex!' He had straightened, craning his neck to see over the crowd. 'I saw him, Alastair. Over there.'

Hugo dashed in the direction he pointed and, sure enough, there ahead of him was Lord Alexander Beauchamp and Neville Wolfe.

'Beauchamp,' he roared.

Alex swung around, searching the faces near to him. As he neared, Hugo could read the desperation in his eyes, the tightness in the set of his lips.

Alex grabbed Hugo's arm. 'Do you know where she is? You were with her. Neville here saw you both, but he lost you in the crowd. Where did she go, Alastair? What have you done to—?'

'Hold hard there, Beauchamp.' Hugo wrenched his arm from Alex's grip. 'Do not throw any accusations at me that you are not prepared to back up.'

He held the younger man's gaze. Saw the leap of muscle as Alex clenched his jaw. Then Alex's amber eyes widened and his jaw went slack. 'Freddie? You here? Where's Livvy?'

Neville Wolfe nudged Alex. 'Not Livvy! Beatrice!'

Oh, God, they can't even get their stories straight. Was I ever as wild and stupid as this pair of buffoons?

'Lady Olivia is safe at home, no thanks to you pair of numbskulls. What the devil were you thinking, bringing your sister here and then abandoning her like that?'

Hot colour swept Alex's face, but he scowled nevertheless.

'There's no harm done,' he muttered. 'I didn't want to bring her…you don't know what she's like…kept going on about debts of honour and the word of a gentleman. I didn't think there'd be any harm in it. She was *supposed* to stay put. She's safe at home now, you say?'

'Yes, thanks to Lord Hugo here,' Freddie said.

Suspicion clouded Alex's face. 'You were alone with her? In a carriage?'

'You would rather I had left her here? Alone and vulnerable?'

'Clevedon said she went off to look for us. He didn't say anything about her leaving with you.'

Hugo tamped down his irritation at young Beauchamp's accusatory tone. He was well into his cups, by the smell of his breath. And it wouldn't help to keep this escapade quiet if they had a stand-up argument here, with so many eyes and ears around.

'I left later. I happened to come across her being accosted by some youths.'

Alex hung his head at that. 'I know I shouldn't have left,' he mumbled, 'but, well… Marie Shelton! You know how it is…'

Hugo did. That was the problem. He knew exactly how it was for Alex because, not so many years ago, that had been him. Only he didn't have an impetuous and, seemingly, fearless younger sister to watch out for.

'You should take care around Marie,' he said. 'She was put up to it by Sir Peter Tadlow, some scheme to get at your father through you. Did you meet up with him again, by chance?'

Alex's flush deepened. 'What if we did?'

'What happened, Alex?' Freddie asked. 'What did Tadlow want?'

'We had a friendly game of hazard, after…

after…when we were on our way back to Cleve-don's box. And we were all to go on to a gaming club together, only then I remembered Olivia and I came back for her. It's not *my* fault she took it into her head to wander off alone, is it?'

'You stupid young pup,' Hugo growled. 'Stay away from that pair and from Marie Shelton. They'll fleece you for all—'

'What is it to you?' Alex's eyes blazed as he thrust his face close to Hugo's. 'It's none of your concern what I do and who I do it with. I can take care of myself. C'mon, Nev.'

He pivoted on his heel and stalked away through the crowd. Neville, with an apologetic shrug, followed. Hugo heaved a sigh.

'That,' he said, 'is an unhappy young man.'

Freddie's brows rose and he gave a rueful smile. 'He is. He is…difficult, far too ready to fly up in the boughs. Even his father struggles to get through to him at times. He heeds his aunt, Lady Cecily, and sometimes his uncle, but seems to harbour some deep-rooted hostility towards the Duke. The trouble is… I was asked to keep an eye on him while the Duke and my sister are away, but I simply cannot go to all the places he can.

'That is why I feel I must tell the Duke about tonight, despite what Olivia wants. *Someone* must keep watch over Alex.'

'What about Avon? Surely he is better placed than you.'

Freddie huffed a laugh. 'They're brothers. They get on well enough, but if Dominic tries to tell Alex what to do, Alex is just as likely to do the opposite. He can be like it with his father, too, only not so overtly—he has no choice but to accept *his* authority most of the time, especially now with the carrot of Foxbourne dangling in front of him.'

'I'll help you to keep an eye out for him,' Hugo said, before he could censor his words.

'You?' Freddie eyed him with suspicion. 'Why would you want to do that?'

Why indeed?

Hugo had made it his business in life never to put himself out for anyone and yet here he was…

'He reminds me of myself at his age.' That much was true, at least. 'And it offends me that a man such as Tadlow would use a young man to punish his father. I should like to at least protect him from that. Only until his father returns, of course.'

'In that case, I shall accept your offer with pleasure. The Duke should be back by midweek so it will be a weight off my mind if you can help me watch over him until then. Thank you. You will alert me if there is anything you feel I should know?'

'Of course.'

Freddie bowed and then limped away, leaving Hugo to return to Clevedon's birthday celebrations, which were still in full swing, but without the guest of honour. Nobody could tell Hugo where Clevedon had gone, or how long ago he had left, leaving Hugo with no choice but to resolve to speak to him the next day.

Tadlow and Marie were both there and Hugo joined their conversation. They already trusted him and he hoped to discover their plans for Alex, but Tadlow was too foxed to make much sense and, when his head sank to the table and his eyes closed, Hugo admitted defeat. He would have to try again when the man was sober. He tried to recapture the party spirit, but within half an hour he was stifling yawns and casting a jaded eye over the rest of the company as he wondered idly what the devil he was doing still there. His wandering gaze paused on Marie as her full lips stretched in a come-hither smile, one brow arching in invitation and her blue eyes aglow with promise. Hugo, however, felt not the smallest urge to respond. Instead, a pair of wide, black-fringed silver eyes materialised in his mind's eye.

This time it was a curse he stifled. He drained his glass and stood up. Marie reached out, slipped her hand beneath his coat, and curved her hand around his buttock, squeezing, but Hugo sidestepped, out of her reach. Unsettled, and with a quiet anger humming through him, he could not wait to get away. He was in no mood for more of these people. They could go to hell as far as he was concerned.

'Goodnight,' he said abruptly and walked away.

Chapter Five

Olivia awoke the next morning with a woozy head and a vile taste in her mouth. She grimaced and cranked open her eyes. The maid had been in to open her curtains—she must have slept right through that—and the bright sunlight stabbed at her eyes. She screwed them tight and groaned. Then, as memories of the previous evening filtered into her consciousness, a feeling of sick dread settled in her stomach.

Mama's necklace.

She rolled on to her side and curled into a ball, her head in her hands, fingers rubbing her temples as she tried to think of a solution.

All she could think was: *Thank goodness Papa is away.*

But would Freddie notice the necklace was missing?

She shot up into a sitting position, ignoring the nauseous roil of her stomach, and forced her eyes open. There, on her dressing table, were the bracelet and eardrops. She hadn't even had the sense to put them in a drawer last night when she took them off. Had the maid noticed them? If she had, hopefully she would not realise their significance.

Olivia swung her legs out of the bed and levered herself to her feet, wincing as pain speared her temple.

How much punch did I drink last night?

And she had Lord Hugo Alastair to thank for that. Lord Hugo Alastair...legendary for his exploits, according to Alex and to the gossip of her friends. There had been much giggling and whispering behind their hands on the few occasions his path had crossed that of the young innocents out in society for the first time. And the most recent on dit—that his older brother, Lucas, was due back in town for the first time in six years—had stirred not only much excitement among some of their older sisters, but also the retelling of the most lurid tales of the infamous Alastair brothers—tales intended to act as a dire warning to beware of Lord Hugo and his ilk, but that instead merely intrigued.

No woman was safe, they had been told.

Hmmph. No woman is safe...except me.

She had been ready to fight him off in the hackney, but he had shown no inclination to even flirt with her, let alone *kiss* her.

I prefer my ladies willing. And experienced.

She *supposed* he had acted the gentleman, but it still rankled. She had become accustomed to young men courting her and paying her compliments, not ignoring the charms that others praised. He had scolded her and treated her like his sister. All her life she had striven to prove she was good enough for her brothers, only to be dismissed, time and time again, as a mere female and, even worse, a child. But Alex was only two years older than her, and Dominic three—that wasn't so big a difference. Not like Papa and Uncle Vernon and Aunt Cecily, who was a full *ten years* younger than Papa.

Olivia went to the dressing table and scooped up the jewellery, a sharp memory of her mother rising from the past as she stared down at the rubies and diamonds.

Mama…seated at her dressing table as her maid clasped the necklace around her neck. The rubies had looked like drops of blood and the diamonds like chips of ice as they sparkled in the candlelight.

It was Olivia's last clear memory of her mother—being pushed impatiently aside as she tried to touch the jewels…her mother snapping, *'Oh, do get the child away from me. She will crease my dress…'* The maid scurrying to the door and calling for Nurse…being bundled from the room in tears at yet another rejection from her mama.

No matter how hard Olivia had tried to be the perfect daughter, Mama had been…uninterested. That was the word. She had been proud of *her boys*, as she had called them—although Olivia couldn't recall her spending much time with her sons—but the only love and approval Olivia could remember from her childhood had come from her father, her uncle and her aunt.

Her throat thickened and she swallowed past the painful lump that had formed. Not long after that memory, she had been told her mother was dead. She had been just five years old…she barely understood at the time but, as she had grown, she had finally understood that she would never now have the chance to make her mother proud of her.

The sound of her door opening shook her from her memories and she quickly opened the drawer in front of her and flung the jewellery inside. She would put them back in the safe later.

'How are you this morning?' Nell's violet eyes were wide with sympathy.

'I am very well.' Olivia ignored the pounding of her head. She did not deserve sympathy. She crossed to Nell and took her hands. 'I am sorry for disturbing you last night, Nell.'

'I do not mind, although I should have preferred it if you had told me your plans. *Mayhap* I could have persuaded you not to go…that it was a mistake.'

The mischief in Nell's smile suggested she was

well aware that Olivia would not have listened to her and, despite the guilt and worry causing Olivia's stomach to alternately clench and roil, she laughed. They had been firm friends ever since their first meeting at the start of the Season, even before Nell's stepsister and Olivia's father had met and fallen in love.

'Have you thought about how to get the necklace back?'

'No.' Olivia rang the bell for Hetty, her maid. 'But I am sure I shall find a solution.'

'And Freddie definitely does not know about the necklace?'

'No. You have not told him, have you?'

'No, not about the necklace, but I did tell him we spoke last night because he looked so worried I was almost afraid he would speak to Lady Cecily about it and she, of course, would be duty bound to tell your papa when he returns.'

'Did Freddie find Alex?'

'Yes, although he stormed off when Lord Hugo scolded him for putting you at risk. Freddie was quite impressed by his lordship... He has promised to help Freddie watch out for Alex until your papa comes home.'

Impressed?

Olivia pictured those lazy, mocking eyes and that hard edge to his smile as he goaded her into agreeing to a guinea a point. Now her head was no longer fuddled with the effects of punch, she realised Lord Hugo had seemed like two completely different men the night before. She had no trouble reconciling the Lord Hugo Alastair of notoriety with the bored, cynical man in the supper box, but the man who had come to her rescue, and who had escorted her home…safely… and who had, according to Nell, agreed to help Freddie watch over Alex…*he* was less easy to define. Which was the real man? She trusted Freddie's judgement, but…what if it was an act and, somehow, Lord Hugo meant Alex harm? She'd told him things last night she would never normally reveal to anyone outside her family. Was he the sort of man who might use those revelations against Alex? One thing was for sure. Somehow, she must contrive to speak to Lord Hugo and try to make sure Alex was at no risk.

It is a pity I cannot so easily deal with Lord Clevedon—unless I reveal all and throw myself upon his mercy.

At the moment, that was her only hope. She had been scared last night by his insistence that she dine with him when she redeemed her necklace but now, having thought it through, she realised her disguise as a female of lax morals had prompted his treatment of her. Clevedon was a respectable and well-respected nobleman—if he knew Beatrice's real identity, he surely would not still insist on her dining with him. Would he?

*But...if I reveal to him that Beatrice was me,
will he keep my secret? Or will he tell Papa?*

Maybe, if she prayed most devoutly at church
later, God might show her another way.

The door opened and Hetty came in with a jug
of water. Nell squeezed Olivia's hand.

'I shall see you later.'

Reluctance slowed Hugo's steps as he neared
the Bruton Street town house where his mother
resided with his new stepfather, Sir Horace Todmorden. His lack of enthusiasm did not stem
from any disinclination to see his mother—he
loved his mother and, despite his initial doubts
about their whirlwind courtship and marriage last
year, he had to admit Mama and Sir Horace were
happy together. And having Mama living closer
to hand—instead of at the far end of the country
at Rothley—had proved more agreeable than he
had anticipated.

No. His reluctance was entirely due to the fact
that Mama was nobody's fool. He inhaled deeply
and then released that breath with some force. He
must do this. He could not leave things as they
stood. It was his fault Olivia had ended up playing
to such high stakes and had been forced to pledge
that necklace and it behoved him to set her mind
at rest. He walked on with renewed purpose and
rapped on the front door.

'Good morning, Stape,' he said as the door opened. 'I've come to escort my mother to church.'

The butler's eyes widened slightly, then he stepped back and bowed as Hugo strode past him into the house.

'I shall inform her ladyship of your arrival, my lord, if you would care to wait in the salon?'

Not ten minutes later the door opened and Mama swept in, already dressed for church in a dark blue pelisse and matching hat.

'Hugo?' She crossed the room in her normal brisk fashion and placed both hands to his chest. 'You *are* real.' Her dark eyes twinkled as she looked up at him. 'I felt certain Stape had made a mistake. I almost accused him of helping himself to the brandy while dear Horace is away.'

'Mama. Looking as beautiful as ever, I see.'

Hugo kissed her cheek, then gave her a hug, feeling his heart lift.

'But what is this nonsense? You? Escort me to church? Stape must be mistaken about that.'

'There is no mistake, Mama. With Sir Horace away, I thought to offer my services, that is all.'

His stepfather had been called back to his estate near Brighton and was not expected to return until Tuesday. Mama tilted her head to one side, making her look more than ever like a bright-eyed, inquisitive bird.

'Well, I am delighted to accept, my dear. In fact, nothing would give me greater pleasure than

to walk into St George's upon your arm, but…'
her eyes narrowed '…I *know* you. You are up to
something. And I shall be watching you.'

She smiled, wagging her forefinger at him, and
Hugo—who was already wondering how on earth
he might contrive a private word with Lady Olivia Beauchamp without setting the gossips of
the *ton* on fire—knew that his own mother, with
the sharpest eyes of anyone in his acquaintance,
would be the first to notice any particular attention. And, worse, she was the *only* person with
enough nerve to interrogate him about it.

'Watch all you like, Mama. If a son cannot do
his mother a service without an ulterior motive,
then what *is* the world coming to?'

Mama smiled serenely as she pulled on her
gloves. 'As you say, my dear. Come then. Shall
we walk, as it is such a lovely day?'

Hugo bowed and proffered his arm.

As they crossed Hanover Square on their way
to St George's he saw her, alighting from Cheriton's town coach. She was with her aunt, Lady Cecily, as well as her eldest brother, Avon, Freddie
Allen—the Duchess's brother—and the Allens'
stepsister, Lady Helena Caldicot. She and Olivia
made a striking pair, both tall and willowy, but
as different in colouring as it was possible to be,
with Lady Helena's silver-blonde locks contrast-
ing with Olivia's raven-black hair. No sooner had
the pair set foot on the pavement than a pack of

eager young pups clustered around them: bowing, proffering their arms, clearly striving to be the favoured one. Hugo bit back a derisive snort at the sight. At least he had never made a complete cake of himself over a woman like that.

No. You have made very certain never to risk your heart.

He dismissed that snide inner voice as he watched Olivia laughingly refuse all offers, instead linking arms with...Nell, she had called the other girl last night. They sashayed up the few steps to the church door—two young ladies with the world at their feet: beautiful, well connected and no doubt with generous dowries. It was what the *ton*...the Season...society...was all about. He stared at the pups dogging their footsteps. At least they were a better match for her than a cynical, world-weary man about town such as Clevedon. Or himself.

Which of them will she favour?

He wrenched his attention from the group, irritated by his random thoughts, the last of which he mentally amended to *Which of them will they favour?*

Last to emerge from the town coach was Lady Glenlochrie, handed down by Avon. She leaned heavily on her stick as the remainder of the party made their way slowly into church.

'Hugo?'

Startled, he looked down at his mother. Saw

the interest in her small, dark eyes. And cursed his inattentiveness that had slowed their pace to a near crawl as he had become absorbed in watching the Beauchamps' arrival.

'My apologies, Mama,' he said smoothly. 'I found myself wondering why Lady Glenlochrie was with the Beauchamps, but then I remembered her connection with the Caldicot chit.'

Mama's lips thinned. 'Chit? Really, Hugo, I do wish you would not use such words. It is most ungentlemanly.'

At his nonchalant shrug of his shoulders, he saw the interest in his mother's expression fade into one of disappointment. She had made her ambition very clear. Since his brother, Lucas's, nuptials at the end of last year, her one wish was that Hugo would meet a nice young lady and settle down. He huffed a silent laugh. Never. He wasn't the marrying kind and, besides, no *nice young lady* would ever consider him as suitable husband material. But their exchange had reminded him...

'I came across young Alex Beauchamp last night at Vauxhall. He struck me as being an unhappy man. Any idea why?'

His mother's eyes twinkled. 'It amuses me to hear you describe him as such, my son. He is not so very different from you at that age.'

'I am aware of that. I, however, had good reason with the father I had.'

Guilt and pain fused in Mama's expression. 'You did and I am more sorry than you know for not protecting you and Lucas more.'

'Mama.' He put his arm around her shoulders for a quick hug. 'You did everything you could to protect us and we're both more than grateful for that.' The memory of his mother taking the blows intended for her sons reared up and impotent rage raked his gut. His father had been dead three years and was way beyond any revenge or retribution. Hugo hauled his thoughts back to the Beauchamps. 'Someone hinted at something in the past that affected young Beauchamp. I don't believe I've ever heard the story.'

'It was his mother. She was murdered and Alex discovered her body. He was only seven years of age and it affected him really badly. And for some reason—no one quite knows why—he seems to blame his father.' Mama shot a quick look around, then lowered her voice. 'Far be it from me to speak ill of the dead, but it was a release for both the Duke *and* his children. Their mother had no time for them...they were far better off being raised by Lady Cecily. *She* is like a mother to the three of them and has devoted her entire life to them. They are very fortunate to have her.'

So that was what Olivia had alluded to in her jumbled tale of the night before. To know your mother had been murdered—even if she wasn't the perfect mother—must have affected Olivia as much as Alex.

They continued on into the cool interior of St George's.

Olivia squeezed her eyes tight shut as soon as they settled into the Beauchamp family pew at St George's and prayed for a flash of inspiration. She waited, but none came and, finally, she opened her eyes to find her aunt frowning at her.

'Are you unwell, Livvy?' Aunt Cecily took her hand. 'You are very pale. Are you in pain?'

As Olivia opened her mouth to protest her good health, she was distracted by the sight of a tall, dark-haired gentleman walking up the aisle with a tiny, older woman upon his arm. He turned his head, scanning the congregation already seated in the high-sided box pews and, even though she was seated furthest away from him, his gaze lingered on Olivia, a smile tugging at his mouth. She felt her eyes widen.

What is he doing here? What does that look mean? What is he doing with Lady Tod—?

Her thoughts stumbled and tripped over one another as Lord Hugo Alastair handed Lady Todmorden—his mother, who had been Lady Rothley before, Olivia now recalled—into a pew. Never had she seen Lord Hugo attend the church, although Lady Todmorden attended every week and, as she and Aunt Cecily were on friendly

terms, they often exchanged a few pleasantries if
they met at a function, or in passing on the street,
or—and Olivia's heart gave a racketing thump before it began to race—after church.

'Livvy? What is it? You look as though you
have seen a ghost.' Aunt Cecily now chafed
Olivia's hand between hers.

'I am perfectly all right.' Olivia forced her gaze
back to her aunt, praying she hadn't noticed her
interest in Hugo. She elevated her nose. 'I was
merely indulging in pious reflection. This *is* a
church, is it not?'

The bells ceased ringing just as Aunt Cecily
tutted and it sounded extraordinarily loud in the
sudden, solemn hush inside the church. Olivia cast
a sidelong look of reproach at her pink-cheeked
aunt because that is precisely how Aunt Cecily
would expect her to react, but inside she was a
mass of seething conjecture. Alex rarely attended
church—he claimed to prefer the services at St
James's Church, on Piccadilly, but Olivia was certain he had never set foot in the place. So Hugo
was not here today to see Alex, which meant he
had come to speak to her. Hope blossomed. Had
he recovered her necklace already? She had prayed
for a miracle; perhaps this was it.

And, in among that hope was…another emotion she did not recognise. She could put no name
to it, but it prompted the frequent urge to slide her
gaze sideways until she could just see, from the

corner of her eye, his lordship. And, every time, a little jolt of…something…sped through her, making her feel, somehow, more alive. Excitement. But not just any ordinary, everyday excitement. This was…fizzing, bubbly, high—the feeling she always got at her first sip of freshly poured champagne. It made her heart feel somehow hollow and yet full at the same time. She could hardly bear to sit still as the vicar droned on or as she bent her head in prayer. She snatched another glance at Lord Hugo among the kerfuffle as they all stood to sing, drinking in his tall, broad-shouldered frame and the firm line of his jaw.

Olivia waited in a fever of impatience for the service to end, even though she could not see how she could snatch a private word with Lord Hugo. She might enjoy occasional acts of rebellion, but she was not reckless enough to talk openly to a man of his dubious reputation. She was well aware of the behaviour expected of a young lady and she took care to behave with perfect propriety in public.

As the congregation left their pews and moved slowly towards the church door—the Reverend Hodgson prided himself on greeting every one of his parishioners at the door after Sunday service, and always exchanged a few words with each— Hugo caught Olivia's eye with a meaningful look. Her pew steadily emptied and she moved along, behind Aunt Cecily. As they neared the end, she tapped her aunt's arm.

'I've left my reticule behind,' she said.

'I'll wait while you fetch it.'

'There's no need. I shan't be long. I shall see you outside.'

Olivia waited to make sure Aunt Cecily kept moving towards the church door. A surreptitious glance confirmed Lord Hugo also lingered in his pew even though his mother was already halfway to the church door. Olivia went back to fish under the pew for the reticule she had nudged out of sight with her foot.

As soon as the majority of worshippers had exited the church, Olivia made her way back along the pew, emerging into the aisle at the exact time Lord Hugo passed.

Chapter Six

'Why are you here?'

One brow elevated. 'Good morning, Lady Olivia. I trust you suffer no ill effects from last night?'

'Shhh! What if someone was to hear?'

One corner of his mouth quirked as he held her gaze, that infuriating brow still arched enquiringly. Olivia quashed her huff of impatience as they began to walk, slowly and side by side, towards the door at the back of the church.

'Yes. I am very...that is, my head pains me somewhat, but that is of no significance.'

'I wished to set your mind at rest about the necklace. I shall return it to you as soon as I am able to.'

'Oh.' She felt guilt now at her abruptness. 'Then I am most grateful. Have you already spoken to Lord Clevedon?'

'Not as yet, but I shall. Do not worry. I shall deal with him.'

She clutched at his sleeve, forcing him to halt. 'Papa will be home soon. Possibly by Wednesday, my aunt said. It is important I get it back before then.'

He patted her hand, his expression indulgent, firing her indignation as she recalled his gentlemanly behaviour last night in the hackney.

'I shall do my best, but you must be patient.'

Like an adult placating a child.

He was nothing like the Lord Hugo Alastair of legend. Or did he simply not find her attractive? On impulse, Olivia stepped closer to him and gazed up into his eyes.

'You are very kind. How shall I ever repay you?'

She dropped her gaze, but a peek through her lashes caught him in a purely masculine appraisal of her that was completely at odds with his words, telling her that—however much he tried to disguise it—he was absolutely aware of her and attracted to her.

'Consider it my good deed for the year. You had better leave ahead of me.'

He feathered the back of his fingers along the line of her jaw. Her stomach tightened at his touch and, feeling her cheeks heat, she turned and headed for the church door. Outside, Aunt Cecily was quietly conversing with the Reverend Hodgson.

'I am sorry to keep you waiting, Aunt,' she said airily, as Hugo emerged behind her and then sauntered over to stand with his mother, who was chatting to a group of older ladies.

Olivia was relieved to see their coach already waiting at the kerb. Freddie was occupied with assisting Lady Glenlochrie up the steps and would hopefully have missed the coincidence of her and Hugo both leaving the church last, after the events of last night. All she had to do now was wait until Hugo returned her necklace and then all would be well.

'You must be patient, Livvy,' said Nell.

Olivia paced the salon and, for the umpteenth time since Sunday, she said, 'Where is he? Why has he not returned it?'

The suspicion was growing that, perhaps, she should not have put so much trust in Hugo's promise to retrieve the necklace. She'd heard nothing from him—not one word—and here it was, Tuesday already, and Papa would be home any day. In fact, she counted her blessings he was not already here. At least Freddie had noticed nothing amiss, even though he had access to Papa's safe, but she could not fool herself that Papa would miss its absence.

'What if he thinks it has been stolen?'

'Who?' Nell's fair brows bunched, crinkling her forehead. 'Lord Hugo? I do not—'

'Not Lord Hugo! Papa!' Olivia flung herself down on the sofa next to Nell. 'He will notice it is gone. He—'

She fell silent as the salon door opened and she looked around, almost expecting to see her father there, the empty jewel case in his hand, with a face of fury. The air whooshed from her lungs in a relieved gasp as Aunt Cecily hurried in, a letter in her hand. And then Olivia forgot her own troubles as she took in her aunt's expression. She jumped to her feet.

'Aunt? What is it? Not…it is not bad news?'

Her heart nearly seized in her chest as she mentally reviewed every member of her family—where they were, what disaster might have befallen them. Papa and Rosalind and Mr Allen on a long journey—carriage accidents did happen, as poor Freddie, maimed as a baby, knew to his cost; Uncle Vernon heaven knew where, having left last week on a sudden visit to Worcestershire to look for some boring long-lost cousin; Dominic—he was here in London, and she was confident *he* would be in no trouble…which left…

'Is it Alex? Is he in trouble?'

'No. It is not Alex.'

Aunt Cecily looked—and sounded—most peculiar. Olivia helped her to a chair and, as her aunt sat, she caught a glimpse of the letter, recognising her uncle's dark, sprawling script. Her pulse steadied. If he was well enough to pen a letter, he was not ill. Or—and it was her greatest fear for any member of her family—dead. She did not know whether it was because of the early loss of her mother, but her family meant everything to her and the thought of losing any one of them could send her spiralling into panic.

'It is your Uncle Vernon. I can hardly credit it but…he is getting married.'

'Married? Uncle Vernon?'

Aunt Cecily nodded. 'On Friday. Near to a place called Stourbridge, in Worcestershire.' She jumped to her feet. 'There is so much to do. I must send word to Dominic and Alex. They shall escort us. If we leave early tomorrow, we should be there in time.'

'But…who is he marrying? Is it someone we know?'

Whoever she was, Olivia was already half-inclined to dislike her. Their stable home life—already irreversibly altered by the addition of Rosalind and her family to their household—would now be changed even more. Even though she liked Rosalind and her family, Olivia had still found the recent changes difficult. As the youngest, and a girl, she had always felt she must struggle for her fair share of attention, but now her place in this new, enlarged family seemed even more insecure.

At least Papa still lived at home, but if Uncle Vernon married he would want to live on his own country estate in Devonshire instead of at Cheriton Abbey with the rest of the family and they would hardly ever see him. Resentment squirmed inside her, even though she knew she was being unreasonable. She knew she could not expect everything to remain the same for ever—and, hopefully, she would herself one day marry which would mean she must leave to have her own family—but for both her father and her uncle to marry in the very year of her own come-out into society was just moving too fast.

She felt a little as though she was in a carriage drawn by runaway horses, speeding towards a cliff edge, but she needed a pause while she caught her breath.

'It is a Miss Dorothea Markham, and...' Cecily frowned as she re-read the letter '...he does not say much about her, other than that she is adorable.'

Her brows rose as she exchanged a look with Olivia.

'It sounds,' she added, in a faint voice, 'as though your uncle has fallen in love.'

The dread inside Olivia grew throughout that interminable day until she felt utterly consumed by it. The appearance of Alex midway through the afternoon prompted an idea: she would not see Hugo if she sat waiting meekly at home, but she might very well see him in the Park.

'Alex, dearest, *dearest* brother of mine.'

He eyed her with suspicion. 'What are you after now, brat?'

She let the insult go. 'Will you escort Nell and I to the Park? Please? Aunt Cecily is too busy with the arrangements for the journey tomorrow and Lady G. is having her nap. And, besides, if we go with her, we shall be obliged to go in the carriage. And it is such a lovely day. I long for a little exercise. *Please?*'

'Ask Avon. Walks in the Park are more his style than mine. I've got more important things to do.'

'Dominic has gone to Westfield to tell them he will be out of town for a week or so,' said Olivia.

Westfield School was an orphan asylum and school in Islington that Dominic supported both financially and in person.

'And I thought we might ride to the Park,' she continued. They could cover more ground that way. 'After all, we shall be stuck in the carriage for the next two days or more, so—'

'Not me,' interrupted Alex. 'I'm not going.'

'Not going? Why not?'

'It's only a wedding, isn't it? I shall meet the bride soon enough, when they come to London. No need to go all the way up there—sounds a dead bore to me. With Papa, Aunt Cecy, you and Avon all there to represent the family, I shan't be missed. And I have commitments here, y'know.'

Olivia frowned. 'What commitments?'

He grinned and tweaked her cheek. 'Never you mind, Livvy. Nothing for a young miss to trouble herself about, you can be sure of that. It's men's business.'

Olivia tamped down her irritation. Men's business indeed.

'*Please*, Alex. You can spare an hour or two, surely? Nell and I are bored with sitting indoors. Our callers have been and gone…' with two eligible and attractive young ladies in the house there was never any dearth of eager male callers '…and now there is nothing to look forward to but dinner and bed.'

Aunt Cecily had already sent their apologies for the soirée they had been to attend that evening.

'Oh, all right,' said her brother, with bad grace. 'I know you…you will go on and on, so I might as well agree now as later.'

Olivia squealed and clapped her hands before tiptoeing up to press a kiss to Alex's cheek. '*Thank* you. I shall send word to the stables and run and get changed.'

Now she must pray that Hugo would be there and that she might contrive to snatch a word with him.

Lord Hugo Alastair strode away from Grosvenor Square after watching young Beauchamp disappear into Beauchamp House. Hopefully he would stay out of mischief for a short while at least. Hugo now had a greater understanding of why indolence was his preferred state of being. What the devil had possessed him to promise Freddie he would keep an eye on Beauchamp? At least the Duke should be home some time tomorrow. He hoped. That was what Olivia said on Sunday.

And that was another thing… Olivia. Her and that blasted necklace. In between watching over Beauchamp—and he could not believe that young pup's resilience. Had he ever been that energetic? On the go morning, noon and night?—he had been trying to locate Clevedon, but he'd gone to ground. No one had seen him since Saturday night and even calling at his house had elicited no further information other than that his lordship was out of town and they did not know when to expect his return.

At least he would be back by Saturday. Of that Hugo was grimly certain. But his promise to Olivia weighed upon him. He knew she must be anxiously waiting for news, but a man such as he could not call upon an innocent miss without inviting gossip and ill-founded conjecture—he was not the sort of man who called upon young ladies and neither would such a social call be tolerated by the parents of said young ladies. And although he had met up with Freddie, despite there being nothing, as yet, to report on Alex's activities—if Tadlow really did have a plan, it seemed he was in no hurry to implement it—he could not pass any message to Olivia through Freddie because he clearly knew nothing about that necklace. As far as Freddie was concerned, Olivia's escapade was done and dusted and there was nothing further to worry about.

And therein lay Hugo's main worry. From what he had learned about Olivia on Saturday evening, she was not the sort to sit around and simply wait. She was more likely to meet trouble head on and that made it more than probable that she would take matters into her own hands before Saturday came around, which is why that bloody necklace was niggling away at Hugo. He needed to get word to her before she did something stupid. But how?

Now Alex was safely home, Hugo had nothing to do until this evening, when he had accepted an invitation from Tadlow to a card party. He knew from past experience it would be high stakes. He suspected Lord Alexander Beauchamp would be on the guest list. Until ten o'clock, then, he was a free man as far as Beauchamp was concerned. He could relax; shrug off the responsibilities he had so unthinkingly taken upon his shoulders and, to that end, he was heading for White's to see who was about.

His steps slowed as he realised that idea held little appeal. He was unusually restless...the mantle of unfinished business pressed down upon him until he could not bear the thought of sitting around and talking of inconsequential matters. With a muttered curse, he halted. He had just left Berkeley Square via Berkeley Street and now he retraced his steps, past the end of Bruton Street—he was in no mood to face one of his mother's inquisitions: she had a way of winkling out how a man was feeling, even though he had no wish to talk of such namby-pamby nonsense—and rounded the next corner into Bruton Place. Since his marriage to Mama, Sir Horace—an ex-cavalryman and a decent enough cove, now Hugo came to think of it—had generously shouldered the expense of stabling a riding horse for his new stepson. A ride in the Park would surely shake some of these fidgets out of his system.

At the stables he found his stepfather, looking tired and dishevelled, unlike his usual dapper self, and deep in conversation with his head man.

'Good afternoon, sir,' he said. 'You just arrived home?'

Sir Horace straightened into his customary upright stance, squaring his shoulders and straightening his coat, looking every inch the ex-military man. 'Indeed, m'boy. Bennet and I were just discussing that new mare I bought at Tatt's last week.'

'Is there a problem with her?'

'She kicked out at one of the lads the other day and broke his arm. And she's a biter. Bennet said some of the lads are chary of going in the stall with her now.' Sir Horace frowned, his side whiskers bristling as he pursed his lips. 'I must decide what to do with her. I cannot, in good faith, sell her on, but neither can I reconcile myself to destroying her...not until we have tried everything to calm her down. I suspect she was doped for the sale. She was docile enough before I left for Helmstone.'

Sir Horace had been called back to Helmstone—his country estate, situated just outside Brighton—on urgent business on Saturday.

'Who sold her? Can you not return her?'

'*Caveat emptor*, m'boy,' said Sir Horace. 'The animals were sold "as seen". Besides, she really does have exceptional conformation.'

'And *I* reckon she's been ill-treated, milord,' said Bennet. ''Twouldn't be right to send her back, even if we could.' He glanced at Hugo. 'Was you intending to go out on Falcon, milord?'

'Yes.'

'I'll get him saddled and bring him out for you.' Bennet disappeared into the stables.

'I shall have to put my mind to what to do about that mare,' said Sir Horace, a deep frown furrowing his brow as he watched Bennet go. 'I can't have her injuring my lads.'

'Was your trip satisfactory?' asked Hugo in an effort to distract his stepfather. He didn't like to see the old man so troubled. 'Is everything in order at Helmstone?'

'Indeed it is, m'boy. The harvest looks promising…' His voice tailed into silence and he tugged at his whiskers—a sure sign he was agitated, so Mama said.

'Is something else troubling you, sir?'

Even as the words left his mouth, Hugo silently cursed himself. Didn't he already have enough to worry about without adding more? But the old boy looked pretty grey and Hugo was quite fond of him, really. He'd made Mama very happy and that, in Hugo's book, was everything.

'Nothing for you to worry about, son. Nothing you can do—' The old boy's jaw closed with an audible snap as a calculating light dawned in his shrewd grey eyes. He grasped Hugo's arm and steered him to a quiet corner. 'As it happens…' he said, slowly, 'there might be…' His bushy brows bunched over the bridge of his nose. Then his frown cleared. 'Thank you, my boy!'

It was Hugo's turn to frown. 'Why are you thanking me?'

'Why, you offered to help, did you not?'

Hugo thought back. He was almost certain the word *help* had not crossed his lips. A warning rumbled deep in his gut, like the distant growl of thunder on a summer day. Now what had he let himself in for? His eyes narrowed.

'What do you have in mind?'

'Well, I must think this through…but it could be just the solution for the both of us.'

'The both of us?'

This was sounding more and more ominous and caution screamed through him. He owed his stepfather who, to his credit, had never dismissed Hugo as a worthless rake as the rest of society did. Sir Horace, himself childless, had taken time to get to know Hugo when they had first met in the spring of last year and had sought his advice on running his estate—discussing new agricultural developments, as though Hugo knew anything about *them*—and shown every sign of valuing Hugo's opinions. So much so, that Hugo had found himself reading up on such matters in the news-sheets and the periodicals at White's.

And that was another thing. Sir Horace had pulled strings and made certain that Hugo's membership of White's was approved, even though it raised a few eyebrows. So now, for the first time in his life, Hugo was a member of the most respected of gentlemen's clubs and, he realised, he was frequenting it more and more often.

His stepfather slapped him on the back, jolting him from that sudden realisation of how much his life was in a state of flux. Satisfaction now gleamed in that shrewd gaze and a heavy weight settled in Hugo's stomach. Somehow, he had embroiled himself in something else that would interfere with his life of idle pleasure. But... curiosity stirred nevertheless.

'Well, well, my boy. I am suddenly feeling much brighter. Yes, indeed. I haven't time to go into the detail now, but I shall see you later. Are you free to come to dinner this evening?'

'Indeed I am. I have a commitment later in the evening, but will dine with you with pleasure, sir.'

'Good, good. We will speak then. For now, though... I am eager to see your mama and I suspect you were on your way elsewhere so I shall detain you no longer.'

With a cheery wave, Sir Horace disappeared from sight. Hugo blew a puff of air from his cheeks as the clatter of hooves on cobbles announced that Falcon, Hugo's bay gelding, was ready.

What the devil *have I let myself in for now?*

Before long Hugo was turning in through the gates to the Park. He turned on to Rotten Row and immediately nudged Falcon into a trot and then— where the carriages thinned out—into a canter, in no mood for conversation as his thoughts leapt forward to that night's card game and what Tadlow might have in store for young Beauchamp. He'd ridden almost the entire circuit when he heard his name.

Chapter Seven

'Hugo!'

Hugo stifled a curse as he looked over his shoulder, but he soon forgot his irritation when he identified the man who had called his name. He reined Falcon to a halt.

'You are not due in town until tomorrow.'

Lucas grinned, and clasped Hugo's outthrust hand in a hard grip. 'We made good time on the journey. We arrived earlier this afternoon. Then Sir Horace came home and told me you'd just ridden out here, so I thought to join you.'

Hugo eyed his brother's mount. 'That's his favourite horse. You *are* honoured. Did you leave Mary and the children in Bruton Street?'

'I did. She and Mama are catching up on all the news from Rothley and Mary isn't keen to leave the children—they've both been asleep since we got here and she doesn't want them to wake up in a strange place alone.'

Lucas's wife, Mary, had been married before and Lucas was now stepfather to her two children—Toby, aged six, and three-year-old Emily.

'Who would have thought it—the original Infamous Alastair, a doting family man.'

The two men turned their horses and rode on side by side.

Lucas laughed. 'I'd forgotten all about that old nickname.' He nodded at two fashionable young matrons, whose wide eyes and slack jaws followed the brothers' progress as they passed by. 'No wonder we are attracting such attention.'

'The Infamous Alastairs ride again,' said Hugo, with a grin. 'How long is it since you were last in London?'

'Six years now. It seems a lifetime ago. I was two years younger than you are now, Brother. Speaking of which, is it not time you thought about settling down?'

Hugo grimaced. 'You sound just like Mama. In fact, I'll hazard a guess she has already begged you to help her in her campaign to see me wed.'

Lucas smirked. 'She might have mentioned it a time or three. And, as a good dutiful son, I am simply obeying her wishes.'

'She has become impossible since your wedding. I only manage to silence her by pointing out I have nothing whatsoever to offer a bride, apart from a jaded reputation and a courtesy title.'

'But from what I have been hearing, that is no

longer true. You are a member of White's. You have investments. You are *almost* respectable.'

Hugo frowned, then forced a laugh. 'Almost, but not quite, eh?' He knew it would take more than that to banish the *ton's* memory of his hedonistic past. 'I should probably have accepted the younger son's lot a long time ago and gone into the army instead of going to Oxford. God knows I spent little enough time there.'

Lucas laughed. 'That's true. You spent more time with me in London than you did at university.' Then he slid a sly sideways look at Hugo. 'Or you could have gone into the church. I can just see you—in the pulpit every Sunday, preaching to the worthy.'

Hugo tipped his head back and laughed, but when he straightened and directed his gaze forward again, he felt the laugh slide from his face. Olivia, atop a dainty chestnut, her slim figure elegantly clad in a dark blue riding habit with military-style trim, was riding towards him. Hugo wrenched his gaze from her to take in her two companions—her brother, Lord Alexander, and Lady Helena Caldicot.

This would have been an ideal time for Hugo to snatch a word with Olivia and put her mind at rest except that—as the Beauchamp party drew closer—Hugo could read Alex's scowl as he glared at him and he could *feel* the frostiness of Olivia's silver-grey gaze as it swept over him, her hoity nose in the air and her lips set in a tight line. With Lucas at his side, there was no way he would risk an encounter with those two in their current moods.

He stifled a sigh. Alex clearly hadn't forgiven him for Saturday night and Olivia wouldn't know that Clevedon was out of town—she would only wonder why Hugo had not yet returned her necklace as he had promised. He tamped down his frustration as he tipped his hat to the trio and rode on past without as much as a *good afternoon*.

'Care to share, Little Brother?'

Hugo snapped his gaze to meet Lucas's arched brows. The knowing curve to his mouth suggested his perceptive brother hadn't missed the chill in the atmosphere.

'Are you still breaking the hearts of the ladies of the *ton*? I have to say, that dark-haired one was a beauty, but maybe a touch too feisty for comfort. And—' he swivelled in his saddle to look behind them '—I should have thought a touch on the young side for a dalliance with a man of your age and…er…tarnished reputation.'

Hugo felt the growl build in his throat. 'There *is* no dalliance.'

'Could've fooled me,' drawled Lucas. 'Must be losing my touch—been out of the game too long, I dare say. But, seriously, if not a dalliance, there is definitely something between you. And if I can tell, so will countless others, mind. Never forget the first rule of a satisfactory *affaire*, my lad. Don't get caught. Who is she?'

'*They* are Lord Alexander Beauchamp, his sister, Lady Olivia, and their new step-aunt, Lady Helena Caldicot. Her stepsister has just married Cheriton.'

Lucas whistled. 'Cheriton's brood? My…you *are* mixing with the elite. And why, pray tell, are the Beauchamps looking daggers at you?'

Anger flared. He answered to no one—particularly not the brother who had abandoned him in London at the tender age of twenty. 'I suggest you ask them if you are so curious.'

Hugo dug his heels into Falcon's flanks, pushing him into a canter. Lucas kept pace with him until, his rage subsiding, Hugo slowed. He was behaving like an idiot. He had long ago forgiven Lucas for his abrupt departure from London and he should know better by now than to let his brother's ribbing provoke him. He smiled ruefully at Lucas. His anger was at the situation in which he had found himself, not at his brother.

'Very well. You are right. There is more to it, but it is not what you think and I am not at liberty to tell you more.'

Lucas winked. 'Soul of discretion, eh? I see you haven't forgotten *all* of your lessons.'

'Did you see that?' Olivia ripped off her York tan gloves and dashed them on to her bed. She had managed to contain her fury all the way home, but as soon as she and Nell were alone she let fly. 'Not even the slightest attempt to speak to me and to set my mind at rest.'

'But… Livvy…you heard Alex. He forbade you to stop and speak to Lord Hugo in any case.'

'Pooh. That is no excuse for his *lordship* to not even *try* to talk to me.'

'Who was the gentleman riding with him, do you think, Livvy? Do you think that is Rothley? There was a distinct resemblance, do you not agree? They made a striking pair.'

Olivia waved her hand dismissively. Who cared who he was, when her whole life was in ruins? Anyway, she had barely noticed the other man. She'd had eyes only for Hugo, trying to convey her fury with just one look. For all the good it had done her. He'd not even acknowledged her other than a tip of his hat.

'He does not even know yet that Papa isn't coming home as planned because of Uncle Vernon's wedding.' Her throat was so tight she could hardly breathe. 'Who does he think he is—promising to help me and then brushing me aside like a…a…bothersome fly?'

Nell snorted with laughter and Olivia glared at her. 'Do not laugh at me, Nell. And as for Alex… of all the high-handed, interfering—Oh! I could throttle him! Ordering me about like a…like a…'

'Like a bothersome fly?' Nell spluttered.

'Hmmph!' Olivia threw herself on her bed, her mind whirling with indignant thoughts. 'I'll show him that I don't need him and his…his…top-lofty opinion of himself. I don't need his help. You see if I don't.' Then, gradually, the whirl slowed and steadied, until… 'Oh, Nell!' Hot tears scalded her eyes. 'What am I to do? W-w-w…' She gulped, then sucked in a deep breath. 'We leave in the morning. We won't be back until next week. And Lord Clevedon threatened to sell Mama's necklace if I don't go to his house to pay my debt.'

Nell sat next to Olivia and patted her shoulder. 'I am sure he will not do so, Livvy. Why do you not write to him and explain? I am sure he will wait until you are back in town.'

Olivia rolled on to her back. 'But he does not know it is me, Nell. I did think about telling him the truth, but how could I trust him to keep my secret? What if he feels honour bound to tell Papa? Then Alex won't get Foxbourne and he will never forgive me.'

With Papa and Uncle Vernon both with new wives, her brothers would be even more important to Olivia. 'Oh, what am I to do?'

Nell chewed her bottom lip. '*I* am not going to the wedding. I suppose I c-could always go to L-Lord Clevedon's house and retrieve the necklace.'

Olivia stared at Nell, her heart swelling as she recognised the fear in her friend's eyes, but also the determined set of her mouth. She sat up and flung her arms around her.

'No, you will not,' she declared. 'This is my mess and I shall deal with it. I'll prove to Lord Hugo that I can manage my own affairs. All I ask of you, dearest Nell, is that you back up my story to Aunt Cecily.'

'What is the matter, Livvy? You have not eaten a single morsel of your dinner.'

'I feel unwell, Aunt.' Olivia allowed her shoulders to slump. She had powdered her face earlier, to ensure she looked pale, and rubbed a little soot from the fire under her eyes to add to the illusion of sickness. 'I cannot face eating anything. I am sorry.'

'You did complain of the headache when we returned from the Park,' said Nell. 'Has it worsened?'

Olivia nodded, then winced, raising her hand to her temple.

'You do look peaked, now I come to think of it. Oh, dear. I am so sorry, Livvy. I have been in such a fluster preparing for our journey tomorrow, I did not notice. Perhaps you should retire early? A sleep will do you the world of good. Grantham?'

The butler bowed. 'Yes, milady?'

'Alert Hetty that Lady Olivia is unwell and is in need of her assistance in her bedchamber, if

you please. Goodnight, Livvy. You will no doubt
feel better in the morning.'

Grantham left the dining room and a footman
came forward to draw back Olivia's chair and
allow her to stand. Olivia averted her gaze from
her dinner plate as she did so. It was lobster, her
favourite, and her empty stomach groaned a protest. She stiffened her resolve. A hungry night
was a small price to pay for being able to remain
in town and redeem Mama's necklace.

Some time later, Nell slipped into Olivia's
bedchamber. She carried a plate piled with fruit,
bread and cheese.

'I went to the kitchen and told Cook that I was
still hungry.'

'Oh, thank you, Nell. I am *starving*.'

As Olivia ate, she became aware of Nell's gaze
on her. 'What is it? Why do you stare at me so?'

Nell's fair brows drew together into a frown.
'Lord Hugo.'

Olivia put her half-eaten peach on the plate.
'What about him?'

'Oh, Livvy. We are friends, are we not? It is
only… Today is the first time I have even seen
him close to. He is very handsome.'

'He is completely unsuitable for you, Nell. He
is a *rake*.'

Olivia cringed inside as she saw the light of
laughter in Nell's violet eyes.

'I was right. You *have* developed a *tendre* for him, Livvy. It is as plain as the nose on your face.' She sobered. 'But…if he is not suitable for me, neither would he be suitable for you, Liv. Your papa—'

'I do not have a *tendre* for him, Nell. That is ridiculous. Of course he is unsuitable.'

Utterly unsuitable.

'But he is very handsome,' Nell murmured, teasingly.

And exciting.

'Those eyes—' Nell's voice was dreamy '—so dark and, somehow, soulful.'

His eyes…

Olivia felt again the weight of his gaze in the hackney. The glitter as they passed beneath the streetlamp…as deep and fathomless as a lake in the moonlight. She shivered. Then, to mask her reaction, she picked up her peach and began to eat again.

'What nonsense,' she declared, around her mouthful of fruit.

Hugo presented himself at Sir Horace's town house in Bruton Street for dinner that evening, as promised. He would dine with his family before heading over to Tadlow's place for his card party, where he would keep an eye on Alexander Beauchamp—hopefully not a waste of time, even though it might prove impossible to dissuade that young hothead from getting in over his head yet again.

'Hugo!' Mama hurried towards him, her hands outstretched and her face creased with delight. 'Horace said he had invited you, but I did not allow myself to hope you would come. You lead such a busy life.'

Only Mama could describe my life of idle pleasure as busy.

Hugo bit back his smile as he took her hands and bent to kiss her cheek. Mama: ever supportive, ever loving, ever protective. She would never hear a word against either of her sons, even during the years when their wild behaviour had set society on its ears. Her loyalty was what made her the wonderful mother she was. Mary was the same—utterly loyal to Lucas and yet unafraid to stand up to him, discreetly, if she deemed him wrong. It was the trait Hugo would seek in a wife, were he to ever to wed. An image of Olivia arose in his mind's eye. She had that same quality. Loyalty. For Alex. For her entire family.

He thrust aside her image and such ridiculous thoughts.

He had no intention of ever marrying—his parents' example had been enough to put him off marriage for life and, besides, what if he should turn out like his father? A violent, foul-tempered husband and father? He glanced across the room to where Lucas was assisting Mary to her feet.

He showed no sign of their father's traits. Since Mary and the children had come into his life he had turned into, as Hugo had jokingly said earlier, a doting family man.

Irritated by such thoughts, Hugo shook them away. If ever by some miracle he changed his mind, it wouldn't be to saddle himself with a troublesome minx like Olivia Beauchamp, no matter how those luminous eyes of hers tempted him.

He focused again on his mother.

'Mama, I always have time for you. You know that. Besides, I am all eagerness to renew my acquaintance with my sister-in-law and her delightful children.'

'The children are in bed already, I am afraid.' Mary smiled at him as she came to greet him, her neat figure clad in a gown the exact same shade of blue as her eyes. 'They are quite exhausted with the long journey, poor wee lambs. Say you will come to visit us tomorrow—they will be so excited to see you. Toby has spoken of little else than his Uncle Hugo since we left Rothley.'

'I will do my best,' said Hugo.

He kissed Mary's cheek. She was just as he remembered from her wedding to Lucas—in fact, she appeared to have bloomed in the months since. She—in fact, they both—radiated happiness and contentment and, although Hugo was pleased for them, their love for one another on top of his mother's obvious joy in her own wedded bliss with Sir Horace only served to remind him that he was, essentially, alone.

It is my choice, he reminded himself irritably.

He shook hands with both Lucas and Sir Horace.

'And do not forget we have that matter to discuss, my boy,' said Sir Horace. 'In fact, if you are in agreement, we can talk it over now, before dinner is served? Bad form to discuss business at the dinner table with ladies present and I believe you said you have a prior commitment later tonight, so you will not wish to linger afterwards, I dare say.'

'I do indeed, sir. Very well then.' Better to know the worst now, perhaps, than have it hovering over him throughout the evening. 'Do you wish to discuss it here or in private?'

'Oh, no, m'boy. No need for privacy. Your mother is in full agreement and as it will—in a manner of speaking—affect Lucas and Mary as well as you, I should like them to stay.'

Lucas's brows rose. 'Shall we all sit then?'

'Yes. Yes. Do, please.' Sir Horace took up a stance in front of the unlit fireplace and clasped his hands behind his back. 'Now, as you boys know, I do not have children of my own. Never found a lady I wished to spend my life with, until I met my wonderful Lucy here.' He smiled at Mama, then harrumphed loudly, clearing his throat. 'Well, I am getting on in years now and not only do I find my energy beginning to wane, but also I find myself wishing to spend more of my time with your mother and less time on business.

'With that in mind, Hugo, m'boy, I have a proposition for you. If you will take on the role of my right-hand man and help me with managing the Helmstone estates, then I shall name you as beneficiary in my will. None of my properties are entailed and I should as soon they went to you as to anyone.'

Hugo stirred in his seat. 'But… I know you have no children, but surely you have *some* family, sir?'

He exchanged a glance with Lucas, wondering how his brother would feel about being left out in this way. As the eldest, he had inherited Rothley Hall along with the title, but years of depredation by their father had left the estate in a perilous state. Lucas had spent the three years since their father's death working hard to repair the damage.

'None that I would recognise if I met them in the street,' said Sir Horace. 'No, you and your mama are my family now and I wish to see you right.'

'But what about Lucas?'

'I have the Rothley estates. You have nothing.'

'And I do not intend to neglect your brother,' said Sir Horace. 'I am impressed with what your mama has told me of your dedication and hard work, Lucas. You are a father now and, we hope, you will expand your little family in time. I am a wealthy man and I want for nothing. I have a tidy sum of money in Government Bonds and I, with your mother's blessing, have decided to gift that sum to you to make reparations to the Hall and to put your land in good heart.'

Lucas leapt to his feet. 'Sir! I don't know what to say…really, there is no need…we can manage…'

Sir Horace raised his hands, palms out. 'I know, I know, my boy. Of course you can manage. But allow an old man the chance to help where he may, I beg of you.'

Mary had also risen and now she put her hand on Lucas's arm and said, 'We both thank you from the bottom of our hearts, Sir Horace. We have been managing and we would have continued to manage, but there is no denying this will help. It is most generous of you, sir.'

Sir Horace's cheeks turned pink. 'Good. Good. That is settled then. Well, Hugo? What say you to my idea? You will need to spend much of your time at Helmstone, but it is not so very far from London, so you need not be entirely cut off from your friends. And there is a tidy little house at Cedar Lodge—only six bedrooms, it is true, but big enough, I'll wager, for a young man looking to set up his nursery.'

'My *nursery*?' Hugo ignored Lucas's smirk as he glared at Sir Horace. 'What the deuce gives you the idea I am looking to enter parson's mouse-trap?'

Sir Horace looked a little startled. 'But your mother said—'

'Now, Hugo,' said Mama. 'Do not, I beg of you, be difficult. It may have been a little wish-ful thinking on my part—I dare say I should not have given voice to such a hope, but…well…see-ing Lucas and Mary so happy together made me a little sad that you are still on your own. But now, with such an improvement in your prospects I was hopeful you might think about settling down. And just think how wonderful it will be to have grandchildren almost on our doorstep, Horace, my dear.'

'Is this—?'

Lucas tried and failed to hold in his snort of laughter and Hugo scowled at him. All that achieved was to draw a huge guffaw from his older brother.

'Is this a *condition* of your offer, sir?' Lucas ignored Mary's attempts to shush him. 'That my confirmed bachelor brother must set up his nurs-ery? Is there a time limit?' His dark eyes swam with tears of laughter. 'Do you get to approve his choice of bride?'

Hugo gritted his teeth and folded his arms across his chest. He'd rather have nothing than find his life no longer his own.

'No, no, nothing of the sort.' Sir Horace paced

a little, his face anxious. He stopped before Hugo. 'You must not think I intend for this to place any obligation on you, other than to help ease the burden on me and your mother. I only mentioned Cedar Lodge because I did not want you to feel obliged to live at Helmstone with us if you choose not to. I can always find another tenant for it if you prefer?'

Hugo's resentment subsided. 'No. Cedar Lodge sounds perfect.' He stood and thrust out his hand, which Sir Horace took. 'Thank you, sir. I shall be delighted to accept your offer. I won't let you down.'

Chapter Eight

As dinner progressed, Hugo grew steadily more accustomed to this change in his circumstances. By the time Mama and Mary withdrew to leave the three men with their port and cigars, he realised he already relished the idea of having more purpose to his life—quite a turnaround for a man who had spent his entire adult life sidestepping any commitment or permanence. Sir Horace's faith in him brought a lump to his throat and a hitherto rarely felt emotion drifted through him. It took several moments before he identified it as pride, laced with gratitude.

It was not long before Sir Horace left to join the ladies, leaving the two brothers alone.

'So where are you off to later?' Lucas eyed Hugo through a cloud of smoke. 'Is it to be the delights of the flesh or delights of the gaming table?'

'The latter, although I'm not sure I'd describe it as a delight.'

'Why go, then?'

'I made a promise to keep an eye on someone for a few nights. He'll be there and so, therefore, will I.'

'Sounds intriguing. Where is there?'

'Sir Peter Tadlow's place. He's hosting a cards party.'

Lucas tapped his cigar ash into an ashtray. 'That reprobate's still around, then? Never did care for him. Who is it you're watching out for?'

'Alex Beauchamp. Cheriton's spare.'

'Ah, he of the murderous glare. Care to tell me why or are you sworn to secrecy?'

'Sworn to secrecy, I'm afraid.'

Lucas's teeth gleamed in a smile. 'And does this have aught to do with the delectable Lady Olivia?'

Hugo forced a nonchalant smile and rose leisurely to his feet. The conversation was becoming entirely too intimate for his liking. 'It is time I went.'

Lucas's eyes narrowed. 'You always were a deep one, Hugo—hiding your true feelings behind that mask of ennui you cultivate. You are like I used to be—wary of letting anyone close, afraid you'll turn out like our old man but, trust me, you are nothing like him. All that belief gained me was years of loneliness and misery. Give yourself a chance.'

Hugo arched one brow. 'Marriage has turned you into an authority on how I feel, has it?'

'Marriage…love…has opened my eyes.'

Hugo's gut tightened. Lucas was getting as bad as their mother, prying and poking into his private feelings. Well, it was none of their business. He'd managed his life well enough thus far. He could see no reason to change.

'This conversation is irrelevant—your imagination is leading you astray. Now, I must go. Do you care to accompany me? It'll be like old times.'

Lucas tipped his head to one side as he studied Hugo. 'I think not, Brother. I find myself drawn to staying at home with my Mary these days. I did wonder if that might change now we are in town, but—somewhat surprisingly—it seems it has not.' He leant forward and stubbed out his cigar. 'You will have to uphold the Alastair reputation on behalf of us both, I fear.' He winked. 'Enjoy your evening. Goodnight.'

Envy stirred as Hugo left the house after saying his goodbyes to Mama, Sir Horace and Mary. That deep contentment that pervaded both couples…would he ever experience such a thing? A year ago he would not have given a passing thought to that. But now…despite Hugo's denial, Lucas's words had touched a nerve.

He rolled his shoulders as if to shake off that feeling of, somehow, being excluded from a desirable club.

* * *

A couple of hours later he stifled a yawn as he and his companions finished yet another hand of whist at the table set up in Tadlow's salon. There were five tables and around thirty guests, of both sexes, including Beauchamp who, so far, had been playing hazard, rolling the dice with moderate success. Hugo kept watch on Alex from a distance. Tadlow noticeably spent much of his time with the young man, clearly keen to gain his trust, but the game appeared honest.

Just before midnight, Lord Clevedon arrived and paused in the doorway, casting a cautious look around the company before venturing further into the room.

Hugo pushed his chair back and stood. 'If you will excuse me, gentlemen, ladies—I shall vacate my seat for another player.'

His chair was filled immediately as he wandered over to Clevedon, delighted the man was finally back in town. Their friendship might be on the wane, but Hugo had a necklace to retrieve and here was his chance. Then, as soon as the Duke returned to London, Hugo could hand over all responsibility for the Beauchamps and concentrate on his own life.

'I haven't seen you since your birthday, Clevedon.'

Clevedon grimaced. 'Had to beat a strategic retreat, dear boy. Got some nasty types on my tail. Thought m'grandmother might stump up enough blunt to help, but she proved remarkably stubborn.'

Hugo frowned. 'Thought you had more sense than to get mixed up with moneylenders?'

'They're not—' Clevedon snapped his jaw shut as a flush coloured his face.

Hugo's heart sank at the whiff of desperation from the other man—it gave him scant hope Clevedon would easily give up his plan to compromise Olivia.

'What d'you say to a hand or two of piquet?'

Clevedon shook his head. 'I'm in no mood to play—I only looked in to see if Sudbury is here but, as he's not, I'll be on my way.'

Damn! There goes any chance of winning the necklace from him.

Hugo thought fast. He had an idea...not a brilliant one, but it was all he had. 'That plan of yours,' he said. 'The one involving the Beauchamp girl?'

Clevedon eyed him. 'What of it? You're not turning all moral on me again, are you, Alastair?'

'No...but I got to thinking, after you told me about it. It'll never work, you know.'

And it wouldn't. He could see that now. But what could he suggest to Clevedon as an alternative? He still needed an incentive to return the necklace.

Clevedon cast a glance around the room. 'Come into Tadlow's study. It's more private.'

They left the salon, Hugo's brain working furiously as he examined the ramifications of his idea.

The minute the study door closed behind them, Clevedon demanded, 'Why shouldn't it work?'

'Because the scheme was always flawed and you'd know it if you'd bothered to think it through, you fool. Do you really believe Cheriton would force his daughter to marry against her wishes?'

'She will be ruined if he does not.'

'You've given the girl no reason to trust you. She's likely to dig in her heels and refuse to be forced into marriage and—even if her reputation *is* ruined—there are plenty of other fellows out there who would gladly take her on. Think about it, man. She'll have alternatives and, after the way you treated her at Vauxhall, you are the last man she will choose.'

Clevedon scowled. 'I never thought of that. But what am I to do? I'm up to my neck in it, Alastair.'

'What are you up to your neck in?'

Clevedon tugged at his neckcloth, his mouth thinning. 'Nothing.'

Despite himself, Hugo felt sympathy at the stricken look in the other man's eyes but he hardened his heart, remembering Clevedon's plan to entrap Olivia. The thought of a vibrant young woman like Olivia shackled to a man who could never love her…never satisfy her…enraged him.

'But I must get *some* funds,' Clevedon burst out. 'Or…' He paced across the room and back. 'Maybe the *prospect* of money…yes, that might work. Once my name is linked with hers, maybe they'll give me more time.'

Hugo thought quickly. He must, somehow, persuade Clevedon to return the necklace tonight. His idea wasn't perfect, but it was all he had.

'Then why not court her the traditional way?' It was risky, but surely Olivia would not trust Clevedon after their encounter at Vauxhall? 'You know—dance with her; call upon her; take her flowers; speak to her father? You never know… it might work. You have all the qualities a father would look for on his daughter's behalf.'

It was the truth. Clevedon had a title, a decent reputation and he was charming. He was accepted everywhere. He might not be a man who loved women, but that was not widely known.

'Except that daughter now despises me, as you pointed out.'

'Not if she believes you returned the necklace to her out of the goodness of your heart—a magnanimous gesture to encourage her to think well of you. Except…' Hugo paused.

'Except what?'

'Well…' he spoke slowly, as though thinking out loud '…she would know then that you recognised her all along on Saturday night and that you deliberately targeted her. That will do nothing to endear you to her.'

A frown creased Clevedon's forehead and Hugo waited, hoping he would reach the obvious solution.

'Alastair, my good friend. *You* shall return the necklace on my behalf and collect my winnings.'

'Me? Oh, no.' Hugo shook his head, hiding his satisfaction at having hooked Clevedon. 'How would I explain that?'

'You shall tell the Lady Olivia that my conscience has been troubling me as the necklace is so much more valuable than her debt but, as I did not know Beatrice's true identity, I had no way of changing our arrangement. I confided in you and—as *you* had recognised her on Saturday— you offered to return the necklace and to recoup the winnings on my behalf. And you must make *very certain* to tell her that you did not reveal her identity to me. I do not want her to feel uncomfortable in my company.'

'How will that help you to win her hand?'

'Firstly, she will feel kindly disposed towards me and, secondly, I shall take your advice and pay court to her and encourage her to fall in love with me. You'll see. I'll soon have her eating out of my hand.'

His smug smile, brimming with confidence, made Hugo itch to punch him on the nose.

'And if you fail?'

'I shall *accidentally* compromise her. By then I will have gained her good opinion of me and she will be happy enough to accept me.'

Hugo strove to keep his expression blank. Had he inadvertently made matters worse? He would be able to return the necklace, but at what cost? He had relied on Olivia not fully trusting Clevedon, but hadn't foreseen that the Earl might still try to force a marriage. Hugo vowed to stay close to Clevedon for the few weeks left of the Season to make sure he kept abreast of any further mischief.

'How shall you accidentally compromise her?'

'Details.' Clevedon waved a dismissive hand. 'I shall think of something when the time comes, never fear, dear boy, never fear.'

Guilt wormed its way into Olivia as she lay in bed, the covers up to her chin, facing Aunt Cecily the next morning.

'I have been sick three times in the night.' Her voice sounded suitably weak and wavering. 'I cannot face a carriage journey. *Please* say I may stay at home.'

Aunt Cecily frowned, then raised her nose and gave an audible sniff. Her green eyes narrowed.

'Hetty has been in to clear up,' Olivia added hastily. 'Oh, Aunt Cecily... I cannot face the rocking and the lurching of the carriage. And what if my sickness got worse? I should *hate* to be the cause of you missing Uncle Vernon's wedding.'

She also hated the fact that she would miss Uncle Vernon's wedding, but she knew she could not enjoy it with this business of the necklace hanging above her head. The mattress dipped as Aunt Cecily sat beside Olivia. A cool hand caressed her forehead.

'You do feel rather warm.' Aunt Cecily's green eyes softened. 'Mayhap you are right...we shall have to travel at a fast pace if we are to arrive at Stourwell Court in time for the wedding.' The door behind her opened to admit Olivia's maid. Aunt Cecily leant down to kiss Olivia's cheek. 'I hope you feel better soon and, when you are well enough to go out and about, you are to do as Lady Glenlochrie says, do you hear me, Livvy?'

'Yes, Aunt.'

'It is fortunate she has not yet felt mobile enough to move back to her own house, or I should be compelled to stay behind, too.'

Lady Glenlochrie—Nell's aunt—had broken her ankle at the start of the Season, preventing her from chaperoning Nell for her debut and forcing Rosalind to come to London as her stand in. She had moved to Beauchamp House together with Rosalind, Freddie and Nell after Papa and Rosalind were betrothed.

'I have also instructed Alex that, as he refuses to accompany us, he must hold himself available to escort you, Nell and Lady Glenlochrie to whichever evening entertainments you choose to attend in my absence. He was not—' and her green eyes twinkled '—amused, but he did agree in the end.' Aunt Cecily rose to her feet. 'I shall write to let you know when we are due to return, but I cannot see it being before the end of next week. Now, I must go. The carriage will be outside before long. Goodbye, my dear Livvy. And... *behave.*'

Olivia tried to project an aura of innocence. Aunt Cecily shook her head at her, smiled and left the room.

'Hetty.'

Olivia's maid—round-cheeked and pretty—came to her bedside.

'As soon as the carriage leaves, bring me some chocolate and rolls, will you? I am *starving.*'

'Yes, milady.'

Olivia closed her eyes and tried to come up with a plan to retrieve her necklace without putting either her reputation or her person in danger.

Hugo patted his pocket for the umpteenth time, checking that the necklace was still there as he cast an eye over the colourful, glittering mass of people crowding the Charnwoods' ballroom, seeking the raven tresses of Lady Olivia Beauchamp.

Of course it's still there, you fool.

It had been in his pocket all day as he haunted the places a young lady might possibly frequent, hoping he would see her, but to no avail. The Charnwood ball was his last hope. He raised his glass to his lips and sipped. At least the champagne was acceptable. Charnwood had clearly spared no expense.

Trying hard to control his irritation, Hugo scanned the dancers once more. Balls were not his first choice of entertainment. He didn't care for the noise. He didn't care for the dancing. He didn't care for the reminder that he was *persona non grata* as far as many members of the *haut ton* were concerned. He preferred more down-to-earth pursuits, where a man didn't have to be on his best behaviour at all times. Clevedon was here, he noted, and dancing with Lady Helena Caldicot, so that must mean Olivia was present although she wasn't currently dancing and he had yet to spot her.

He glanced around at a sudden tug on his sleeve and the delicious scent of violets assailed him. She was walking away from him, her slim hips—sheathed in ivory silk—undulating in a very feminine, sensual movement. His pulse quickened as she glanced over her shoulder and their gazes connected. With a flick of her brow, she communicated her demand that he follow. Hugo tamped down his natural resistance to being commanded to do *anything* by this minx and he prowled in her wake, up the steps leading from the ballroom. He emerged into the reception hall in time to see her disappear upstairs. He clamped his jaw, and followed. On the landing, he looked around, generations of Charnwoods staring down at him with haughty disdain.

Where the devil...?

A flutter of movement caught his eye and her face peered around a door jamb. She beckoned him imperiously and he stalked towards the door and past her, into the room.

A bloody bedchamber. It would be.

'This,' he growled, crossing the room to put as much distance as possible between them, 'is not wise.' He glanced out of the window before turning to face her. It was still light outside—hopefully he could conclude his business with Lady Olivia and then move on. Except, of course, he couldn't. Alex Beauchamp was here tonight and there was still no sign of the Duke having returned from his journey to the Midlands.

'Never mind that. What have you been doing? Why have you not told me what is happening?' She glided across the carpeted floor towards him, elegance personified, her blunt demands completely at odds with her appearance. 'Do you not understand how frantic I've been? Have you got my necklace?'

She halted in front of him, gazing up at him

with such innocent trust in her silvery eyes that he felt something shift in his chest.

'Do *you* not understand the risk you run by being in here with me?'

She dismissed his query with a wave of her hand. 'No one will find us here. It is Sophie's room.'

'Sophie?'

'Lady Sophie Wray. The daughter of the house. You must know her. It was her debut this year.'

'No. I do not concern myself with young misses straight out of the schoolroom.' Hurt flashed in her beautiful silver eyes, leaving a blend of satisfaction and shame souring his mouth. 'Besides. That is not what I meant.'

Her eyes flared with sudden awareness. She put her hand on his arm. 'But *you* would not harm me. I know you.'

He fought the urge to knock her hand away as he battled to control other, baser urges. That scent of violets was doing strange things to him…baiting him…drawing him down an avenue he knew could only lead to trouble.

'You do *not* know me.'

He stepped back, needing space between them. He reached into his pocket and extracted the necklace, holding it out to her, expecting her to snatch it from him and to disappear back to the ballroom. The necklace that had caused him nothing but trouble. It would be a relief to be rid of it.

She squealed. And the next thing, his arms were full of warm woman and his senses were full of that violet scent. Her arms were around his neck and she hugged him tight, her smooth silky cheek pressed to his, her curves soft and yielding as her body moulded to his.

Chapter Nine

Instinct had Hugo in its grasp before his mind could catch up. He slipped the necklace back into his pocket and then, with both hands free, he stroked down the delicate curve of her spine to the deliciously rounded swell of her buttocks. His demons urged him on, and his grip tightened, lifting, pulling her closer as his hips flexed instinctively. A sensible, sane corner of his mind warned him to release her, but he thrust it ruthlessly aside. This was his reward. She'd had him running around in circles, trying to help her out of a predicament caused entirely by her own impetuous and scandalous behaviour. She appeared to have an unshakeable belief in her own ability to cope with whatever happened, but the sooner she realised there were some situations she could not control merely by the force of her will, the better.

A kiss was the very least he deserved.

His plan—such as it was—was to shock her. Make her wary. Scare her, even.

He pulled his head back and gazed down at her. She tilted her face to his. Her eyes sparkled; her petal-pink lips were stretched in a smile. The joy and trust in those silver eyes nearly undid him. *Hell and damnation.* Why did his normally well-hidden and tightly controlled protectiveness choose now to surface? He released her bottom, sliding his hands back to her waist. But before he could follow through with his intention to move her back, away from him and away from temptation, her arms tightened around his neck, her lids fluttered down—her sooty lashes a fan against her creamy complexion—and she pressed back into him, rising on tiptoes.

Her lips found his. Soft, lush, beguiling. His fingers flexed on her waist, pulling her close once more, and he lost all conscious thought. The only reality was the slide and glide of her lips over his. The kiss was erotic in its innocent, untutored style. She had never done this before—his experience told him that. Her hands moved, rising to either side of his head, her fingers thrusting though his hair. Battening down his deep sense of foreboding, he traced her mouth with his tongue, gently urging her lips apart. A split second of resistance—of tension beneath his hands—and then, with a very feminine murmur, she relaxed, opening her mouth and allowing him in.

Dear God.

It was a kiss. Only a kiss. But a kiss such as he had never before experienced.

He lost himself in that kiss, his fingertips exploring and caressing everywhere her silky-smooth skin was open to his touch—her face, her neck, her arms.

Her scent surrounded him. Filled him. Lured him.

His heart pounded. He was hard. Painfully hard.

He groaned and gathered her closer still, revelling in that yielding of her supple curves as they pressed to the length of his body. The inexorable feeling rose within him that she was part of him… she *must* be part of him.

That stray thought alone caused his throat to constrict. It brought emotions—unfamiliar and nerve-racking—to crowd his brain. Self-preservation reared its head and he forced his lips from hers and—too late—he finally succeeded in setting her away from him. He studied her face: her dazed eyes, heavy-lidded, her swollen lips, the flush that washed her skin a delicate pink. And he battled the craving to kiss her again. To go further.

It was a kiss. Only a kiss. But it was a kiss that rocked Hugo to his toes.

She recovered first. She caught her plump bottom lip between her teeth as her eyes—the pupils huge, reducing that ring of silver grey to a sliver—roamed his face. He fought to keep his expression blank, but any concern that she would turn missish on him was banished as she released her lip and her mouth widened into a smile: a satisfied—even slightly smug—smile.

'I enjoyed that,' she said. 'Do you know that is the first time anyone has kissed me?'

It was Hugo's turn to bite his lip. Against the urge to haul her back into his arms and kiss her all over again. Instead, he turned away from her. Resisting temptation.

'I could tell.'

He heard the whisper of a gasp behind him and instantly felt shame at his brutish riposte. He had intended to frighten her a little…to teach her to be cautious around strange men. Instead, it now struck him that he had merely roused her curiosity. There was none of the maidenly bashfulness he had anticipated.

'Did I not do it properly?'

He faced her again. Slowly. She stared up at him, her fine brows arched. He felt his eyes narrow.

'Do you expect me to score your performance?'

'Why are you behaving so oddly? I merely asked a question. I am curious.'

Hugo thrust his hand through his hair. 'The kiss was…acceptable.'

She pouted. 'Well, I do not think that is a very gallant thing to say.'

'You expect me to be gallant?' He stepped closer and curled his hands into fists to stop him grabbing her and shaking her...or hauling her close again. 'I am not one of your brothers, my dear. Do not expect me to behave as such.'

She stuck her nose in the air, spun around and flounced to the door. Hugo gritted his teeth. Lady Olivia Beauchamp was no longer his concern. He had returned the necklace—

'Wait!' He delved into his pocket.

She pivoted to face him.

'Have you not forgotten something?'

He walked towards her, allowing the necklace to swing gently from one finger. This time she snatched it from his grasp and, opening her reticule, she stuffed it inside.

'Thank you.' She turned to go.

Now he had returned the necklace, assuaging his guilt at having provoked her into gambling at such high stakes. His responsibility for her was over, other than to stay close to Clevedon. Which left her brother. Lord Alexander.

'Is your father home?'

Olivia paused, her hand already on the door handle. 'No.' She twisted again to face him. 'Have you not heard?' Her voice sounded brittle. Her temptress eyes glittered with suppressed emotion.

'My uncle is getting married and Papa has stayed in the Midlands to attend the wedding.'

Married? He masked his astonishment. Lord Vernon Beauchamp…married! That little *on dit* ought to be headline news.

'I had not heard, no.'

'Dominic and Aunt Cecily left this morning to attend the ceremony. *I*—' her eyes were icy now '—had to pretend I was ill because *you*—' she poked his chest with an accusatory finger '—could not be bothered to let me know you had my necklace.'

'We have not been formally introduced, my dear. I can hardly call upon you and whisper secrets in your ear without causing gossip and speculation.'

'Hmmph. You could have… I don't know… signalled to me or something in the Park yesterday. Instead, you just ignored me as though we had never met.'

'As I said, we have *not* met. Not in the eyes of society. I take it you do not wish to provoke a scandal? Besides, I did not then have the necklace. Clevedon has been out of town. I only retrieved it last night.'

And now—his heart sank at the realisation—not only must he continue to pretend friendship with Clevedon, a man he was growing to despise, but he must also continue to dog the footsteps of her scapegrace brother now the Duke would not be home for several more days. He had given his word.

'You had better return to the ballroom,' he said. 'Before you are missed.'

'Not yet.' She dismissed his concerns with a nonchalant wave of her hand. 'Nell knows to cover for me with Lady G.' She moved towards Hugo and every muscle in his body stiffened. 'I wish to know what you said to Lord Clevedon to persuade him to give up my necklace.'

'I appealed to his better nature. He allowed me to redeem the necklace on your behalf as a gesture of goodwill.'

He had offered to pay Clevedon the one hundred guineas and the man had near bitten his hand off in his eagerness to take the money.

'Does he…did you tell him who Beatrice really is?'

'No. I did not tell him.'

He could see no advantage in her knowing Clevedon had been aware of her identity from the start—it would only worry her to no purpose. She would live in fear of Clevedon revealing her escapade to Vauxhall, not realising her secret was perfectly safe because of Clevedon's plan to court her—a plan that made Hugo's blood run cold. Or made his blood boil. He couldn't quite decide which.

Plus, she was too transparent. If he told Olivia the truth, she would never be able to hide that knowledge from Clevedon, who would lose his trust in Hugo, making it nigh on impossible for Hugo to keep track of any more of his plans.

'But you should stay away from Lord Clevedon in the future,' he added.

Her brows twitched into a frown. 'Why?'

'The reason is not important. Please, just stay away from him.'

Her lips pressed together. Then she sighed.

'Well, I am exceedingly grateful to you for returning my necklace, in any case,' she said.

She reached up to brush back a lock of hair that had fallen over Hugo's forehead and his loins tightened at that intimate, tender gesture.

'We must arrange a time and place to meet,' she continued.

He'd thought he was tense before, but now he was as rigid as a marble statue. 'I *beg* your pardon?'

She sank her teeth into that lush bottom lip of hers again, but her eyes smiled at him.

'Why, Lord Hugo. *What* a fearsome frown.' She tapped his arm in coquettish admonishment. 'I merely meant that I now owe *you* a sum of money.'

He might be frowning, but he felt like smiling. She did that to him…she, somehow, lightened his spirit…her *joie de vivre*…the way she had bounced back after such a stressful ordeal. But he could not afford to relax too much around her. It would be too easy to forget who she was. Who he was.

'I do not—'

She put a gloved finger to his lips. 'No. I shall not renege on my gambling debt. It is a matter of honour. That is what Alex always says. Although…' her dark brows met, furrowing her forehead '… I hope you will agree to my paying in instalments? I promise I shall pay it all, as soon as I can. Nell and I were going to pool what's left of our allowances, but I should prefer not to involve her if you do not object. Will you trust me?'

His heart clenched and then felt as though it expanded until his whole chest was flooded with warmth. 'Of course I trust you.'

Their gazes fused and he saw her eyes darken again as her lips parted, releasing a soft sigh. He wrenched his gaze from hers.

'It is time you went.'

He clasped her upper arms and moved her aside, then reached for the handle. A quick glance ascertained the landing outside was empty. She was at his back. He could hear her breathing. Smell those violets. He could *feel* her presence as every single hair on his body stood to attention. He did not risk looking at her…if he did, he would not answer for the consequences. He reached behind him, grabbed her arm and propelled her from the room. He closed the door behind her and, with a shaky sigh, he bent his head and rested his forehead against the door panel.

What had just happened?

Olivia stood on the upstairs landing, glaring at the door Lord Hugo Alastair had just shut in her face. *How exceedingly rude.* She huffed a sigh. She'd thought—although, to be sure, she had no experience—but she'd *thought* their kiss was…oh…wonderful…full of shooting stars and bursts of light and firecrackers exploding. But she was wrong. It had meant nothing to him…he had even…well, *almost*…accused her of being useless at kissing. Although he had appeared to enjoy it at the time. It was only afterwards he had pokered up on her.

She rubbed her tingling lips. Her heart was still racing and skipping. She longed to go back inside the room and…

And what? Accost him? Make *him kiss me again? Prove I can do it better? Hmmph.*

She forced her feet in the direction of the staircase. She wouldn't give him the satisfaction. He was as bad as her brothers, dismissing her as a silly little girl and as someone who could be ordered about and who was too insignificant to warrant a rational explanation. She'd had enough of that throughout her childhood: her brothers had left her out, refusing to let her tag along, accused her of spoiling their games, rejected her.

Like Mama...

She felt tears scald her eyes as that all-too-familiar feeling of never quite being good enough invaded her. Well, no more. She was out in society now and she was a success! She would show them she was more than just an insignificant female who could be brushed aside whenever it suited them. She gritted her teeth, brushed the foolish, self-pitying tears away and marched down the stairs, her back straight and head high.

Inside the ballroom an anxious-looking Nell hurried to her side.

'You have been gone such a long time, Livvy.' She frowned, her violet eyes scanning Olivia's face. 'What happened? Are you all right?'

'Of course I am all right, Nell. Why should I not be all right?'

'Did Lord Hugo have the necklace?'

Olivia nodded. 'And now I have it,' she said, patting her reticule.

'We should return to Aunt Glenlochrie, Livvy. She has been asking for you.'

'I shall go and set her mind at rest.' Olivia linked arms with Nell and steered her around the edge of the ballroom, avoiding eye contact with several young gentlemen vying with each other to attract her attention. She had no intention of dancing tonight. She had used her fake illness as an excuse, claiming a lingering lack of energy, but it seemed some young men still harboured hopes.

Then Lord Clevedon was before them, bowing, and she had no choice but to stop and to acknowledge him. Her grip tightened involuntarily on her reticule and the incriminating evidence within.

'Good evening, Lady Olivia, Lady Helena.'

They both bobbed curtsies. 'Good evening, Lord Clevedon,' they chorused.

'Might I engage your hand for the next dance, Lady Olivia?'

'I regret I must refuse, my lord. I am not dancing this evening as I have been unwell.'

It had taken all her charm and persuasion to convince Lady Glenlochrie that she was well enough to attend the ball this evening, including a solemn promise that she would not tax her strength by dancing, and thank goodness she had succeeded—the weight that had been lifted from her by the return of her necklace was worth the sacrifice of not dancing for one evening.

'I am sorry to hear that, my lady. I trust you will recover your customary vitality very soon. In the meantime, might I escort you to your chaperon?'

Olivia caught sight of Hugo on the far side of the room. He was talking to his mother, Lady Todmorden, his brother and another lady—presumably his brother's wife—but his attention was on Olivia. She could almost *feel* him commanding her to obey his edict even though he had given her no good reason for such an order. Besides, all

Lord Clevedon had done was challenge her to a game of piquet. It was not *his* fault she had lost, or that she had pledged her necklace because she was unable to give him her vowel. And neither was it his fault the wager was so high. No. That was *Hugo's* fault, as was the fact that the arrack punch had flowed so freely. No doubt the strength of that punch had impaired Clevedon's judgement that night as much as it had impaired her own.

How dare he try to dictate how I must behave?

She averted her gaze and bestowed a gracious smile upon Clevedon as she placed her hand on his arm.

'Thank you, my lord.'

See, Lord Hugo Arrogant Alastair! I can make my own decisions and if you *do not find me attractive there are other men who do.*

Clevedon stayed with them for the remainder of the evening: procuring drinks, escorting them to supper and generally being charming. Olivia kept her reticule—complete with the incriminating necklace—in her tight grasp the entire time, her stomach a tangle of nerves in case it somehow came open and spilled its contents. But now 'Beatrice's' necklace was safely back in her possession—and without any strings attached, which was more than she had dared hope for—Olivia did start to feel more magnanimous towards his lordship.

Hugo disappeared after supper and, somehow, the ball lost any further appeal for Olivia. She felt nothing but relief when Lady Glenlochrie complained she had one of her heads coming on and it was time they went home.

Chapter Ten

Olivia tried her best over the following days to block Hugo and that delicious kiss from her thoughts. He clearly still thought her far beneath his notice, judging by the way he had bundled her out of the door afterwards, and he had made not the slightest attempt to see her since. She had looked for him in vain at church yesterday, but his mother had been escorted by his stepfather, Sir Horace. Lord and Lady Rothley and their two adorable children were there, too, but there was no sign of that despicable, untrustworthy rogue. She was clearly good enough for him to snatch a kiss when the opportunity arose, but not good enough to—

And every time her meandering thoughts reached that point, she hauled sharply on the reins and dragged them to a halt. Good enough to what? What was it she wanted...expected...from Lord Hugo Alastair? She knew enough of their world to know he was not a man any young lady in her position could even contemplate as a suitable paramour, let alone hanker after.

And yet hanker she did.

And would it really hurt him to show her a little attention?

The days had passed in an alternating blur of brooding reflection and splendid daydreams in which a certain dark and sinfully handsome lord cast himself at her feet and declared his undying love. At times she could not resist embellishing the reality of what had happened—adding further imaginary encounters and embraces—and then, with the next breath, she was consumed by indignation at his casual dismissal of her.

Doesn't he know I'm the Catch of the Season?

She'd been told it often enough by the young men who fawned around her, vying for her attention. She did squirm inside as the thought popped into her head, however. It sounded so conceited and she would never dream of saying such a thing aloud—or even thinking it, normally—but she could not deny that it did help bolster her mood whenever her spirits dived.

Which happened all too often. Whenever she thought about Lord Hugo Arrogant Alastair, in fact. Which seemed to be all the time.

'Livvy!'

Olivia's head jerked up. Nell's expression was a picture of exasperation.

'You have just agreed to walk to Brighton with me,' said Nell.

'Brighton? *Walk?* Why on earth would I agree to such a silly suggestion?'

'Why indeed?' Nell sat on the sofa next to Olivia and plucked *La Belle Assemblée* from her lap, casting it aside. 'I *knew* you were not listening to me and you have not turned a page in the past quarter of an hour so you cannot claim you were engrossed in the fashion plates. What is wrong? I thought you would be in alt now the necklace is back in your possession.'

Olivia's neck grew hot and the flush crawled up to heat her cheeks. 'I *am* in alt!'

Nell raised a fair brow. 'I thought we were friends, Livvy. Please tell me what ails you. Is it that you have missed the wedding?'

'No. *Yes.*'

'No? Yes? Make up your mind.'

Olivia rubbed her brow. 'I am sorry I have missed it, but…' She hesitated. She longed to speak of her confusion, but was it fair to burden to Nell with the truth? Nell would keep the secret of that kiss if Olivia was to confide in her, but she would suffer under the weight of keeping it secret from Rosalind. And if Rosalind's suspicions should ever be aroused then she, surely, would see it as her duty to tell Papa. And what if *he* then felt honour bound to challenge Hugo?

What then? Olivia's blood ran cold. She could not risk any harm coming to her papa.

'Yes. I am sorry to have missed the wedding, but I have no one to blame but myself and, as I cannot change what I did, I shall try to forget it and pay more attention to you, my dear step-aunt.'

Nell's violet eyes crinkled. 'It never fails to make me smile, to hear you call me that. Now, what I was asking you is this. Sophie Wray has sent round a note asking if we should like to accompany her and her mama on their shopping expedition this morning, as Lady Cecily is away. *I* should like to go—I must confess to feeling unaccountably restless today and I have discovered in myself an urgent desire to fritter some money away on fripperies.' They had been unable to visit the shops since Aunt Cecily's departure as Lady Glenlochrie's ankle was not strong enough to walk very far.

Olivia was delighted by the opportunity to escape her ever-circling and increasingly brooding thoughts. She jumped to her feet. 'I should enjoy that—I shall run and change my gown.'

Half an hour later, the Earl of Charnwood's barouche drew up outside Beauchamp House. A liveried footman leapt down to open the door and let down carriage steps as Olivia and Nell approached and Sophie—her smiling face framed by dusky curls and a charming rose-pink bonnet—waved.

'Livvy! Nell! I am so pleased you decided to accompany us.'

Lady Charnwood—a slim, stylish woman who bore a startling resemblance to her daughter— said, 'Sophie. Do try for a little more decorum, my dear. Such displays of enthusiasm are entirely unbecoming in a young lady.'

'Oh, Mama. It is only Liv and Nell. You *know* I am the perfect young lady when there are important people within hearing.'

Olivia and Nell exchanged a grin as the footman handed them into the barouche.

'A young lady should curb all tendencies to excess at *all* times,' said her mother. 'That way, the correct behaviour will become second nature and mistakes are less likely to occur. Good morning, Lady Olivia, Lady Helena. I trust you are both well?'

'Yes, thank you, ma'am,' they chimed in unison.

Bond Street was a-bustle with shoppers when the carriage drew up at the kerbside and anticipation stirred inside Olivia. She had yet to become blasé about all the attractions London had to offer after having spent most of her life on Papa's estate in Devonshire. She still could not get enough of the sights, the sounds, the smells—although the latter often left much to be desired—and the entertainments, in which she included the shops and warehouses. The carriage drove away—leaving the footman behind to carry their purchases—the coachman having been given instructions to collect them in an hour and a half, to take them to Gunter's Tea Shop, as Lady Charnwood had promised to treat the girls to ice cream after their shopping excursion.

Nell, Sophie and Lady Charnwood all managed to find some essentials that they could not resist purchasing, but Olivia found herself unable to muster any enthusiasm for shopping now they were actually there. Not one item tempted her to buy—and telling herself that she must save her allowance to pay back Hugo simply made her feel more wretched. She had agreed to the shopping expedition to forget about that heartless rogue and still she could not banish him from her thoughts. Still, she smiled and enthused about the other three's purchases as they piled them in the footman's arms and she was certain nobody would suspect there was aught amiss. Finally, after a very thorough examination of the stock at the premises of Messrs Harding, Howell & Co., the barouche returned to collect them and they set off to Gunter's Tea Shop.

Large plane trees grew in the centre of Berkeley Square, providing welcome shade for those customers of Gunter's who chose to enjoy their ices from the comfort of their own carriages. The Charnwood barouche drew up beneath the canopy of one such tree and a waiter hurried across the road to take their orders. The three girls settled very quickly for their favourite strawberry-flavoured ice cream and it was as Lady Charnwood was deliberating, at some length, between peach- and pistachio-flavoured ice cream that Olivia's idly wandering gaze alighted on Hugo, who was leaning against a run of railings close to the carriage in front. He was talking with his brother, Lord Rothley. They were an eye-catching sight—both tall and dark, with a slight air of danger surrounding them that made her heart flutter alarmingly. And she was not the only one captivated by the pair of them together—they attracted plenty of attention from people strolling through Berkeley Square, especially the females, who eyed the two men surreptitiously as they passed them by, she noted with an inner *hmmph*.

As though he sensed her gaze, Hugo turned his head and looked directly at Olivia. He winked as his lips curved into a smile that set her teeth on edge and, to her utter mortification, Rothley glanced over his shoulder, then turned and executed a bow. Somehow, that bow seemed to convey amused irony even though Rothley was entirely straight-faced. Olivia swallowed, thrust her nose in the air and snapped her attention back to Lady Charnwood, who had finally plumped for pistachio.

While they waited for their ice cream to be served, Olivia made every effort to take her part in the conversation and ignore the fact that Hugo and Rothley stood not twenty feet away. Although she had earlier been impatient to see him again after their kiss, now that he was there, in front of her, large as life and twice as handsome as in her memory, she found herself in the throes of an unaccustomed and most unwelcome nervousness. It was not long, however, before movement caught her eye and a sidelong glance revealed Lady Todmorden being handed from the carriage by Rothley. Lady Rothley then descended and the whole party—together with the two small children Olivia had seen in church—then strolled towards the barouche.

Olivia's face flamed and her skin prickled as she sensed Hugo's eyes upon her. The Alastairs halted by the barouche and Lady Charnwood, suddenly aware of their presence, straightened.

'Lucy, my dear,' she said. 'What a happy coincidence. Are these the grandchildren you were telling me about the other night?'

'They are,' said Hugo's mother. 'We brought them here to sample Mr Gunter's famous ices as a treat. This is Toby—' the young boy bowed solemnly '—and this is Emily.'

The little girl clutched her dress in two chubby hands and bent forward from the waist in a bobbing movement.

'Emily, that's not right.' Toby wagged his finger at his sister. 'You're a girl. You have to curtsy.'

Emily's face crumpled. Before either of the Rothleys could react, however, Hugo swept her up into his arms, saying, 'Well, *I* happen to be an expert on ladies' curtsies, Emily, and *I* thought it was perfect.' He bussed her on the cheek, making a rude noise with his lips. Emily squirmed, erupting into giggles, and Olivia's heart flipped at seeing this different side of him. The cynical, world-weary man of the town had disappeared to reveal a younger-seeming, fun-loving uncle. 'And you, young man,' he added, ruffling Toby's hair, 'showed Lady Charnwood a perfectly splendid bow.'

Toby's mutinous expression dissolved into a cheeky grin. 'Chase me, Uncle Hugo.' He grabbed Hugo's hand and tugged. 'Come on.'

'Toby.' Lady Rothley spoke softly with a faint accent that Olivia could not quite place. 'Remember what we told you. You are not at home now and you must mind your manners, or we shall have to leave you at Grandmama's house.'

Toby released Hugo's hand immediately. 'Yes, Mama.'

Lady Rothley smiled, her blue eyes twinkling on either side of her tip-tilted, freckled nose. 'Good afternoon, ladies. Please allow me to apologise for my son's enthusiasm.'

This was Olivia's first chance to see her ladyship close to and she thought she looked friendly and fun.

'That is perfectly understandable, my dear Lady Rothley,' said Lady Charnwood.

Hugo's brother bowed as he bestowed a charming smile upon Lady Charnwood. 'It is good to see you again, Sally. Thank you again for extending the invitation to your ball to include Mary and me.'

'You are most welcome, Rothley. It is good to see you again after all these years. Now, I know you were all introduced to my daughter, Sophie, the other night, but are you acquainted with Lady Olivia Beauchamp and Lady Helena Caldicot? Girls…' Lady Charnwood smiled at Olivia and Nell '…this is Lord and Lady Rothley, who have just arrived in town…'

Lady Rothley smiled a general greeting, but Lord Rothley's gaze—his ebony eyes the image of Hugo's—travelled without haste over the three girls and Olivia fancied that, as they reached her, his lips compressed as though he suppressed a smile. Her temper stirred as she imagined Hugo confiding their secret kiss to his brother. Rothley bowed again, elegant and assured.

'Delighted, ladies.'

'And this is Lord Hugo Alastair, Lady Todmorden's younger son.'

Olivia, her hackles raised after that lazy appraisal from Rothley, nodded in her most imperious manner and was incensed to see Hugo's lips twitch in amusement as one dark brow rose.

'Enchanted to make your acquaintance, ladies.'

Their gazes fused and—although it might seem fanciful to think such a thing—the very air between them appeared to crackle with tension. Her cheeks heated and she forced herself to break eye contact, knowing she must do everything to avoid raising any speculation that they had already met. As she looked away, however, Olivia found the bright, inquisitive gaze of Lady Todmorden upon her. Immediately upon meeting Olivia's eye Hugo's mother diverted her attention to her grandson, leaving Olivia feeling on edge and vowing to be more careful to mask her reactions in future. She knew only too well that in their world it was imperative for a young lady's actions to be above criticism. What she might say or do in private was very different to how she behaved in public and overfamiliar interaction with a man of Hugo's ilk would do her reputation no good at all.

'Your children are enchanting, Lady Rothley,' said Nell. 'Lady Charnwood? Would you object to me leaving the carriage to speak to them?'

'Of course not, my dear. You may all stroll in the square if you wish, while Lady Todmorden and I talk, but be sure to keep an eye open for your ice cream being served—you would not like it to melt.'

'Olivia? Sophie? Do you care to you join me?' Nell sent a mischievous smile in Olivia's direction and then flicked a glance in Hugo's direction.

Nell stood up and Hugo—nearest to the carriage door—handed out first Nell and then Olivia, Sophie having chosen to remain with her mother. As Hugo's strong fingers closed around Olivia's, tingles chased up her arm and through her body. She glanced up at him, through her lashes, and read the glint of amusement in those dark, half-hooded eyes. She snapped her attention away from him.

Wretch! Making fun of me when I cannot retaliate.

She thanked him briskly, avoiding further eye contact, and then quickly moved away, joining the other ladies and the children. She was relieved that Hugo remained by the carriage, talking to Lady Charnwood. She was not sure her nerves could withstand stilted, polite conversation in a group that included him.

'Of course, Rothley is not Toby and Emily's natural father,' Lady Todmorden was saying, as Nell crouched beside Emily, trying to coax her to talk, 'but he loves them every bit as much as if he were.'

Toby was busily vying for Nell's attention. 'I am six. I can say lots of words. *Much* more than Emily.'

'You're a big boy for six,' said Olivia, to distract him. 'I thought you must be seven years old at the very least. I know a little girl, Susie, who is seven, and you are as tall as she is.'

Toby puffed out his chest. 'Does Susie have her own pony? *I* have my own pony and I can ride him, but it was too far for him to come with us.'

'His little legs would have worn into stumps if you rode him all this way, Toby.'

Olivia's pulse stuttered. Hugo had materialised by her side and now he grasped Toby's hands and swung him around and on to his back, where he clung like a small monkey, giggling. Hugo put his arms behind his back to support Toby, causing his coat to swing open. Without volition, Olivia's gaze travelled downwards from his broad chest to linger on powerfully muscled thighs that a pair of well-cut breeches did nothing to disguise.

She swallowed and averted her gaze, her corset all of a sudden restricting her breathing.

'The waiter is on his way with our ice creams,' said Rothley, for he, too, had joined them. He raised his hat. 'It was a pleasure to meet you, ladies.'

Nell rose to her feet. She and Olivia, still battling to regain her composure, dipped curtsies.

'Say goodbye, Toby,' said Hugo.

'Goodbye! I'm lifting your hat, Uncle Hugo, so you can say it was a pleasure, like Papa.' Toby grabbed Hugo's hat and waved it in the air.

Hugo laughed. 'So you are, Toby. Thank you, for my hands are rather full of small boy at the moment. Good day, ladies. It was indeed a pleasure.'

He nodded, but he did not look at Olivia and she carefully avoided looking directly at him even though every nerve in her body was afire with awareness of him. Instead she focused her attention on Lady Rothley.

'I am pleased to have made your acquaintance, Lady Rothley. I hope we shall meet again very soon.'

She was rewarded with a warm smile. 'I hope so, too. This is my first ever visit to London and it would be pleasant to get to know a few ladies more my own age.'

'Perhaps you might care to bring the children to visit Susie, the child I mentioned to Toby?' Olivia explained about Susie, who was a recent addition to the Beauchamp household—a runaway girl who Papa and Rosalind had rescued way back in February and then decided to bring up as their own child. 'Susie would love to meet some other children, I'm sure.'

'Thank you, Lady Olivia. That is most kind.'

The farewells completed, each party returned to their own carriage and enjoyed their tasty ices.

Later, after Olivia and Nell had returned to Beauchamp House and spent a pleasant half-hour examining Nell's purchases, Nell suddenly fell quiet as she chewed her bottom lip.

'What is wrong, Nell?'

Nell took Olivia's hand. 'I am sorry. I should not have teased you. Please, Livvy…do take care.'

Olivia frowned, genuinely puzzled. 'Tease me? When?'

'Today, in the carriage. I should never have asked if we could go and talk to the children. It was wrong of me. I thought it would be a bit of fun, to tease you after I noticed how you avoided looking at Lord Hugo. But now… I feel…oh, I don't know. I feel a bit as though I have put you at risk.'

'At risk? I am not at risk.'

Nell gathered Olivia's hand to her chest. 'Take care, Livvy. He is dangerous.'

'*Dangerous?* What nonsense!'

Never had she felt in danger when she was with Hugo. Nell did not know what she was talking about. He had never made her feel anything other than safe in his company.

'I think perhaps I did not express myself very well. What I meant is not that he is dangerous *per se*, but he *is* a danger to you. When you look at one another…oh, Livvy.' She shook her head. '*Please* be careful. A man such as he…with his reputation…he knows how to entice women. You've heard the tales of the Infamous Alastairs… but I've also heard them called the *Irresistible* Alastairs. And now I understand why.'

Chapter Eleven

'Well. I thought he would never leave.'

It was the following day, in the early afternoon when Olivia and Nell were at home to their callers, and Lord Clevedon had called, complete with a bouquet of flowers for Olivia, and sat with her, Nell and Lady Glenlochrie for a full half-hour.

'Do not be so ungracious, young lady,' said Lady Glenlochrie. 'You should be honoured such a fine-looking gentleman is showing an interest in you. He is an earl and has a fine estate in Derbyshire and he is old enough now to be thinking of setting up his nursery. Yes, I think your father and your aunt will both be quite content to learn of his attentions when they return from Worcestershire.'

'Well, I am not content with his attentions,' said Olivia, rising to her feet and shaking out her skirt, 'and I have no wish to encourage them.'

Her conscience stirred as she blocked Lady

Glenlochrie's *'Ungrateful gel'* from her ears. She *had* been guilty of encouraging his lordship a little—but only because he was Hugo's friend and she was desperate to prove that an older, more sophisticated gentleman such as Lord Clevedon could find her attractive and interesting. The few times she had seen Hugo since that kiss she had noticed the best way to attract his attention was through Lord Clevedon and she was willing to try anything.

She crossed the drawing room to gaze out of the window, but the garden held no interest for her. Restless energy surged through her. She wanted to be *doing* something, not sitting at home pursuing ladylike occupations such as playing the pianoforte and embroidering and waiting meekly for gentlemen to deign to call upon her. It was hugely frustrating to have to constantly wait. She wanted… Hugo's face, complete with that infuriating, knowing smile of his, materialised in her thoughts. She huffed impatiently and spun round to face the interior of the room again.

Lady Glenlochrie was in the process of levering herself to her feet while Nell hovered by her side with her walking stick at the ready.

'Help me upstairs to my bedchamber, will you, Nell, dear? I hope that if I rest now I shall be recovered sufficiently for the ball tonight. You young things are quite exhausting.'

Guilt swept aside Olivia's restless yearnings.

Poor Lady G. She had travelled from her home in Scotland and taken on the task of launching Nell into society even though she found the hustle and bustle of London exhausting. And then she had broken her ankle, which had resulted in Rosalind coming to London to help. And probably that was good, because then Papa and Rosalind had fallen in love and Rosalind, Nell and Freddie had all come to live at Beauchamp House. But Lady G. was still not sufficiently recovered to face the return journey to Scotland and so she, too, had moved into Beauchamp House. And now, with Papa, Rosalind, Uncle Vernon and Aunt Cecily all absent suddenly, the role of chaperon for not only Nell but also Olivia had landed squarely back on Lady G.'s shoulders. And Olivia knew—because she did not hide her faults from herself—that was no easy task.

She crossed the room to open the door as Nell assisted her aunt into the hall and then they both helped the elderly lady across the hall to the stairs. Lady Glenlochrie bestowed a smile upon Olivia.

'Thank you, my dear. Nell will manage from here—I shall feel safer if I can hold the banister as I climb the stairs. Nell?'

'Yes, Aunt?'

'Will you read to me until I fall asleep?'

'Of course, Aunt.' Nell caught Olivia's eye. 'I shall go to see Susie afterwards, if you care to join us?' She sighed. 'We see so little of her these

days, since Rosalind appointed Miss Pyecroft as
her governess. It would be pleasant to take her for
a walk in the Park later, but if Alex is not home
there will be nobody to escort us.'

Olivia watched Nell and Lady Glenlochrie
slowly ascend the staircase until her attention
was diverted by the murmur of male voices. She
followed the sound. If Alex was in, perhaps she
could persuade him to accompany them to the
Park after all. The voices were coming from the
library. The door was open and Olivia put one
eye to the sliver of light showing between the
door and the jamb to see who was inside. Then
she stiffened as she recognised the classic profile
of the one person visible—Lord Hugo Alastair.

What is he *doing here?*

'Would you care for a glass of wine?'

That was Freddie's voice. Olivia frowned.
Why was Hugo calling on *Freddie*? She noted
he had not sent his card in to Lady Glenlochrie—no doubt scared she would deny him—but
it was still…discouraging…that he had not made
even the slightest attempt to call upon Olivia even
though Papa and Aunt Cecily were out of town.
She cast a surreptitious glance around the hallway.
There were no servants in sight at the moment,
but how long would that last? A misspent childhood of listening to adult conversations she was
not meant to be a party to had left Olivia with no
qualms about eavesdropping on Hugo and Fred-

die who, after all, was in Papa's employ so surely she had a *duty* to know what they were discussing.

A chink of glass alerted her that Freddie was pouring his visitor a glass of Madeira from the decanter kept on a table in the corner. Olivia thought quickly. Not far from the door was a high-backed chair that faced the opposite end of the room. If she could creep unnoticed into the room and curl up in that, they would never know she was there. And, if they did happen to see her...well, this was *her* house. She had every right to go into the library and educate her mind by reading. But she did not think they would see her—the door stood open and would conceal her from Hugo, and Freddie would be concentrating on not spilling the drink as he carried it to Hugo. She could see that Hugo's attention was on Freddie and so she took her chance, hugging the wall until she was as near the leather-upholstered chair as possible, then stepping across the gap and sitting down. No challenge came from the men and she curled her legs under and ensured her arms were tucked in before directing her attention to what was being said at the other end of the room.

'I am sorry the task of watching out for Alex is taking longer than either of us envisioned,' said Freddie. A creak of leather signified he had taken the chair on the opposite side of the empty grate to Hugo. 'I genuinely expected his Grace to be home before now.'

'I do not blame you, Allen; nobody could have foreseen Beauchamp donning leg shackles so suddenly.'

His deep, soothing voice sent waves of longing through Olivia. She crossed her arms over her chest and cupped her shoulders, remembering the way he had held her. Her throat ached even as she reminded herself of his rakish reputation—the opposite of the sort of man she could rely upon. Except…she frowned. His actions… hadn't they almost proved the opposite? Weren't she and Freddie both putting their trust in him? And had he let them down?

Freddie laughed. 'Leg shackles! That is what Vernon always called it. Or parson's mousetrap. And always with a theatrical shudder. Reckoned he wasn't the marrying kind.'

He was right, Olivia thought. Uncle Vernon always swore he'd never get trapped but now, suddenly, he was leaving the family behind and forging a new path. Her throat ached with suppressed emotion. Why did changes have to happen?

Hugo was speaking again and she switched her focus to his words.

'Well, he's well and truly caught now, so it seems. It was the same story with my brother, Rothley. Once he met Mary, he knew. He told me love hit him like a thunderbolt and I've never seen him so happy. Rather them than me, that's all I can say. I'm not convinced by all this love-at-first-sight nonsense.'

'Six months ago I'd have agreed with you,' said Freddie. 'But I lived through the effects of such a meeting when my sister first met the Duke and let us say I am no longer as sceptical as I was.'

Hugo huffed a mocking laugh and Olivia found each breath she dragged into her lungs more painful than the last. Love at first sight… She had always scoffed at the idea but she, too, had watched Papa and Rosalind. And now, it felt very much as though she was experiencing it herself, which was all very well, but what if only one person fell in love? What then?

'Now, back to Alex,' said Hugo, briskly. 'I've done as we agreed and kept an eye on him. He's played cards with Tadlow a few times, but so far he's always come out even. I've joined in a few of the games and noticed nothing shady—they've been in different places, but at normal card parties or in legitimate gentlemen's clubs. Tadlow's not a fool; he won't risk cheating against Alex in such places.'

Olivia clamped her hand across her mouth to stifle her gasp. Sir Peter Tadlow was Nell's uncle—a nasty beast who had planned to force his niece to marry Lord Bulbridge in order to pay off his own gambling debts. Luckily, Papa had put paid to Tadlow's evil scheme earlier that year.

'But I have no doubts he is working to gain

Alex's trust, ready to fleece him, just as Clevedon told me,' Hugo went on. 'I've made enquiries. Tadlow's got links with a gaming club and brothel called Diablo's. It's got a dubious reputation; it's members only—and it's not an easy club to join—and there's some secrecy over who is behind the place. The manager is a ruffian called Wood, but he's just a front man. I've learned Tadlow's introduced more than one green lad to the place and they soon find themselves in trouble. I suspect his plan is to entice Alex into a game there before long.'

'I've tried to warn Alex again about Tadlow, but he's in no mood to listen to me.'

Olivia could hear the dejection and concern in Freddie's voice.

'I am fond of him,' he continued, 'and I should hate for him to get into further hot water with his father, especially when he has been trying so hard to keep out of trouble. He disappeared without trace for days on end the last time he found himself deep in debt and unable to pay his dues. That inadvertently resulted in my being offered this job with the Duke and I should hate for another such an episode to result in my losing it, selfish as that may sound.'

'All I can do is to watch out for him as much as I can—as long as I can find out where he is going in the first place. That is not always easy, let me tell you.'

'Well, I can help you out there, Alastair. Before she left, Lady Cecily tasked Alex with escorting the girls and Lady G. to their evening entertainments and, to give him his due, he has done so. Tonight they attend the Denbys' ball, tomorrow is, of course, Almack's and on Thursday they go to the Pendletons' soirée, so at least you know where Alex will be at the start of each evening. By Friday, surely, his Grace will be home and you can relinquish the charge you have so manfully shouldered.'

'I shall speak to Lady Denby about tonight. She is an old…acquaintance, shall we say.' Olivia's teeth ground together at the amused warmth in Hugo's voice. 'I am sure she will be happy to extend an invitation to me, even at this late hour. I can watch for Alex leaving Almack's tomorrow and Mama can, I am certain, ensure my attendance at the Pendletons'.'

The sound of movement behind her had Olivia shrinking into the chair in an attempt to make herself as small as possible. She was elated at the news that Hugo would attend the Denbys' ball tonight and her wayward imagination immediately envisioned him requesting her hand for a dance. She could not wait—she would tell Hetty to lay out her favourite pale blue silk evening gown.

After the door had closed behind the two men, however, Olivia's thoughts turned to Alex and Sir Peter Tadlow, and what she had learned and anger simmered deep inside. She would *never* let her beloved brother fall foul of such a wicked plan and vowed that she, too, would watch over him as much as she could until Papa came home. She could not bear his disappointment if he were to be denied Foxbourne after all his efforts to stay out of trouble.

Later, Olivia told Nell about Sir Peter's scheme to cheat money from Alex and, ultimately, Papa. There was no one else in whom she could confide and no one they could ask for help. Freddie already knew what was going on and neither girl could see any benefit in alerting him to the fact that they knew what Sir Peter was up to, and Lady Glenlochrie was an old lady. *She* could do nothing to help or protect Alex. Olivia couldn't wait for Papa and Aunt Cecily, or even Dominic, to come home. *They* would know what to do and she would not feel so alone and so...*responsible*. She had always worried about Alex and tried to protect him from the worst of his self-destructive ways but the rest of the family had always been there, too. Now, there was only her and she had not realised until now how heavy the burden of ultimate responsibility must weigh upon her papa.

The Denbys' ball was the customary squeeze and, after Lady Glenlochrie settled down at one end of the spacious drawing room on the first floor, ready and eager for a gossip with the other chaperons, Olivia and Nell—their dance cards filling nicely—waited with a group of friends for the dancing to begin. Alex had made his way straight to the card room on the ground floor, telling Olivia to send for him if he was needed. She tried to persuade him to stay upstairs and to dance with some of the young ladies, but he had merely cast her a scathing look and stalked off.

'Livvy.' Nell leaned in to speak. 'I have just seen my Uncle Tadlow. He was headed for the stairs and, presumably, the card room, but I have yet to see Lord Hugo. I thought he told Freddie he would be here to watch over Alex.'

The two girls moved apart from their friends, keeping their voices low.

'Tadlow won't cheat here, Nell. He would not take the risk of getting caught in Lord Denby's house. He would be ruined. No, he will do his worst at some shady gambling club like that Diablo's that Hugo told Freddie about.'

'You are probably right.' Nell did not look convinced. 'And I hope, too, you are right to put so much trust in Lord Hugo. I cannot help but worry—'

'Hugo knows here is not really where he is needed,' interrupted Olivia. She had heard enough of Nell's doubts and warnings about Hugo over the past few days. She knew her friend was only concerned about her, but there was a limit. 'It's after Alex has taken us home that Hugo will be needed to keep watch. *I* am perfectly capable of keeping Alex out of trouble while we're here. All *you* need do is make my excuses if I disappear. You may tell anyone I'm promised to dance with that I have developed the headache and suggest they dance with one of the girls without a partner.'

Olivia scanned the room as she spoke. For all her brave words, she hoped Hugo would arrive soon. The music began and her first partner came to claim her hand. For the time being Alex must look after himself. She smiled at Lord Sudbury and set her mind to making polite conversation with him.

Three dances later, Hugo still had not arrived. As Olivia's partner led her from the floor, she manoeuvred him over to where Nell stood with her next dance partner.

'Excuse my interruption,' said Olivia, as soon as her own partner was out of earshot. 'I have the headache, Nell, so can you please make my excuses to…' she consulted her dance card '… Mr Beaton?'

'I am sorry you are unwell,' said Nell. 'Is there anything I can do to assist?'

'Thank you but, no. I am certain a few moments of peace and quiet away from the music will prove beneficial.'

'I shall make sure to tell Mr Beaton, Livvy. I do hope you feel better soon.'

Nell sent her a speaking look before turning again to her partner and Olivia made her escape, running lightly down the stairs to the entrance hall.

The card room was set up with several tables spread around the room and it took no time at all for Olivia to spot Alex, at a table in the corner with three other men, including Tadlow. Her breath caught as she recognised Mr Randall—that disgusting man who had made advances to her that night at Vauxhall Gardens—and Lord Bulbridge. She only knew the latter because of poor Nell's lucky escape from marriage to the brute.

She breathed a little easier as she recognised the other occupants of the card room—respectable members of the *ton*, most of whom she knew. She was confident Tadlow would not dare to cheat here, but it would not hurt him to know that Alex's sister was keeping an eye on him. Resolutely, she crossed the room and stood by Alex's shoulder. The three other men rose to their feet as Alex twisted his neck to peer up at her. He stared blearily for a moment or two, then struggled to his feet, where he swayed. His eyes appeared unnaturally dark and his eyelids kept drooping, almost as though he were on the verge of sleep. Olivia frowned, foreboding knotting her stomach as he propped both hands on the table as though to support himself. He reminded her of Lady Glenlochrie when she had overdone the laudanum in a bid to ease the pain of her broken ankle.

'Wh-wh-what are you doin' here, Sis?'

'Lady Glenlochrie wishes to speak with you, Alex. Will you come with me?'

'Here, Beauchamp, you can't leave the game in the middle of play, man,' said Tadlow, flicking a disdainful glance at Olivia. 'Let her ladyship wait.'

Olivia raised her chin. '*Thank* you for your contribution to our private discussion, sir. I shall, of course, be happy to wait until the hand is complete.'

Olivia glanced at the various piles of money in front of the four players. Alex's was the smallest of the four, but there was no clear winner and it appeared the stakes were within reason.

'I have seen men emasculated by their wives before, but never by their *younger* sisters,' drawled Tadlow. 'Let us finish this hand in order that Beauchamp can obey Lady Olivia's summons without further delay.'

He smirked as Alex subsided on to his chair and reached for the glass before him with a hand that visibly trembled.

'Allow me to fetch you a chair, Lady Olivia,' said Mr Randall.

She shuddered, recalling his slimy behaviour at Vauxhall Gardens, and barely nodded her thanks as he collected a chair and placed it between his chair and Alex's. Then he bowed.

'We have not been introduced, but…will you do the honours, Beauchamp?'

'No, I won't,' said Alex ungraciously. 'M'sister ain't staying and she d-d-don't need an acquaintance with *you* fellows.

Olivia's face flamed at Alex's rudeness. Not that she had any wish to be introduced to any of these scoundrels, but whatever was the matter with Alex? He was abrupt and disrespectful at home at times, but—like her—he knew enough to watch his manners when out in polite society. This was unlike him. Surely he hadn't had the time to get so drunk since their arrival and even he would not drink to excess at a ball such as this. What he did afterwards, when he was out and about with his pals, was a different matter. Her heart crawled up into her throat and she looked anxiously at the rest of the occupants of the room, but everybody was busy concentrating on their own games, taking no notice of anything else going on. The two footmen on duty to supply the players with drinks stood like sentries near the door, their gazes firmly fixed on the opposite wall.

Olivia lowered her voice and put her hand on her brother's arm. '*Please*, Alex. Come with me. You can play cards again later.'

Alex jerked his arm, dislodging her hand as Tadlow sniggered.

'Yes, go on, Alex. Do as your little sister bids you.'

Alex turned to Olivia. 'Go back…d-dance. I 'shcorted you, di'n't I? What m-m-more ish a man to do?' His words were a disjointed mumble and his hand, as he pushed at her, missed her entirely and flopped to swing by his side for a moment before he heaved it back up to the table and fumbled to pick up his cards.

There was nothing she could do without making a huge fuss, which Alex would hate and which would only make him dig in his heels more stubbornly. She rose from the table, glared at the three other men and stalked to the door. Inside, her nerves churned until she felt quite sick. Something was wrong with Alex. He was not just foxed… she had seen him enough times in that state to recognise the signs. By this time of the evening he should be the life and soul of the party…alcohol seemed to sharpen his wits, not dull them as she had just witnessed. She headed back to the ballroom, crushed, desperate and feeling very alone. Why did this have to happen now, when Papa was away? She had always prided herself on her resourcefulness, but how could she cope with this on her own? How she missed the security of knowing her family were around her, ready to support her.

She hesitated at the door of the ballroom, scanning the men present. Was there anyone she could confide in? Beg for help? But to do that would be to expose Alex's folly to someone outside her family. Perhaps Neville Wolfe? She'd seen him earlier. He was a loyal friend to Alex and would not spread gossip, but he was young himself, and a bit of a fool at times, as young men often are.

No. Neville would be no match for those men with Alex. She would wait a bit longer, until Hugo arrived. *He* would know what to do. He already knew the danger Tadlow posed to Alex and had proved he could be discreet.

He had promised Freddie he would watch over Alex, so where was he?

Chapter Twelve

Hugo strolled into the Denby ball and halted, adjusting his cuffs as he took stock of the dancers and those watching them: the chaperons, seated together, gossiping behind their fans; the hunters, prowling the perimeter of the ballroom as they surveyed their prey—the young ladies with generous dowries and influential family connections; the wallflowers, clustered together, their heads defiantly high.

He had stayed away as long as he could, delaying the moment when he would see Olivia—beautiful, desirable Olivia who kissed like a dream. He knew tonight he would face a battle to avoid her—that damned kiss had opened a door within his soul that, no matter how he tried, he could not quite shut again. He swallowed down a self-deprecating snort—he was well on the way to behaving in the same way as all the other lovelorn fools who constantly surrounded her.

He hadn't suspected he could feel such a long-ing to simply *dance* with a woman and now, since Lady Charnwood's introduction, there was not a single thing to stop him asking her. And it wasn't only the desire to dance with her that had caught him entirely unawares. *He* wanted to be the man to escort her to supper. He wanted to talk openly with her and make her laugh…see her smile at him…and only him.

Knowing he ought not to do any of those things gnawed at him. She haunted his thoughts every waking moment and danced through his dreams every night. Hence his tardy arrival. The less time he spent resisting all that temptation, the better.

His roving gaze found her soon enough. She was on the opposite side of the ballroom, stand-ing among a cluster of friends—including, he was irritated to see, Clevedon—looking as though she hadn't a care in the world. Which, of course, she hadn't—she was wealthy, well born and beauti-ful. Her pale blue gown clung to her, outlining her willowy elegance, and her dark hair was piled on her head, with soft waved tendrils left loose to frame her face. Hugo took his time, enjoying the simple pleasure of just watching her from afar. But gradually he realised she was putting on an act. The people around her were talking, but Olivia only joined in when addressed directly—the rest of the time her gaze darted around the ballroom as she bit into her bottom lip.

And then she saw him and her expression lit up, a smile widening those luscious pink lips. Hugo's body responded to her clear joy at seeing him even as he cautioned himself to take care—her unguarded expression would surely cause any observer to suspect an existing intimacy between them and her reputation would suffer. She was young and naïve and had not yet learned to conceal her true emotions, but she must learn to do so if they were to escape detection in future.

He frowned. There could be no future. He was only interested in women for one purpose and she was too innocent and too highly connected for him to even *think* of her in those terms. She deserved a young swain, not a world-weary cynic like him. Or Clevedon. Hugo had seen the Earl arrive at Beauchamp House earlier, clutching a bouquet, and Hugo—on his way to confer with Freddie Allen—had been forced to hang around outside until Clevedon had left again. He did not want Clevedon to know he was looking out for Alex in case he passed that information on to Tadlow. Hugo prayed Olivia was too clever to fall for Clevedon's courtship. He could not bear to see her joy in life battered and squashed by marriage to a man who could never be a proper husband to her.

He tried to keep his attention on the dancers, but he could not resist sneaking another look at Olivia. Her expression was no longer full of joy, but…she looked desperate. And, as their gazes

clashed again across the room, he thought back
and realised that her earlier joy had been liberally
mixed with relief.

Bloody conceited fool!

He had assumed her glow of happiness when
she first saw him was purely down to her pleasure
at his arrival. But there was clearly something
else troubling her and his heart clenched just with
the knowing that she was upset. So, despite his
misgivings, he stood his ground as Olivia began
to make her way to him, keeping his gaze on the
couples forming the next set.

Was it Clevedon? Had he done something else
to try to compromise Olivia when he had called
on her? He noted the bastard tracking Olivia's
progress around the room, but then forgot all
about him as Olivia paused next to him, her arm
brushing against his sleeve. The hair on the back
of his neck rose as the smell of violets awakened
his senses. Olivia kept her attention on the dancing couples and her voice low. He had to strain
to catch her words.

'Alex is playing cards with Tadlow. I tried to
persuade him to leave, but he would not listen.'
There was a pause. 'He looks strange, almost as
though he is drugged.'

'Stay here. I'll go and check on him.'

Hugo headed downstairs to the card room.
And just in time, by the look of it as Tadlow and
Bulbridge, with a slumping Alex between them,

emerged from the card room. A footman pointed towards the rear of the house and, as Hugo drew closer, he heard the man say, 'Through that door, follow the passage and the door to the back yard is the one at the end, sir. There's a gate through to the mews from there.'

'Thank you, my man,' said Tadlow. 'We cannot have our inebriated friend here kicking up a rumpus. It is far better to remove him discreetly through the back than risk offending your master's guests.'

Some instinct made Hugo glance over his shoulder. Olivia, her troubled gaze fixed on Alex, was hurrying towards him. Hugo waved her back. She kept coming until she was by his side.

'Stay out of this,' he growled.

'He is *my* brother,' she hissed through gritted teeth.

'Stay back. You cannot help. Please. Trust me to look after him.'

He didn't have time to see if she obeyed him. If he didn't act quickly, the men would be gone. They were already heading off towards the door the footman had pointed out, Alex's arms slung over the shoulders of the other men as he stumbled in an effort to keep up with them.

'Tadlow!'

The man's head swivelled to peer back at Hugo. He scowled.

'What is it, Alastair? As you can see, we have our hands rather full here.'

'I am come to relieve you of your burden,' said Hugo. 'Beauchamp's carriage is at the front door.'

'This way is more discreet. My carriage is waiting out this way.'

Hugo lengthened his stride and overtook the trio. He faced them. They kept coming and he found himself walking backwards. Olivia, he was relieved to see, had stayed back and was watching, wide-eyed.

'What is a gentleman's carriage doing at the back entrance, Tadlow? Did you plan to leave this way?'

'Keep your nose out of my affairs,' snarled Tadlow. 'Beauchamp owes me. We have unfinished business.'

One bonus of Hugo's misspent past was that men such as Tadlow assumed he was as indifferent now as he ever was. And that assumption made men indiscreet as they revealed things they might otherwise hide, not realising that the man they knew from before was not the same man today. Hugo could at least now hold his head up that he had begun that process of change, even if it had taken him longer than most young men to come to his senses. If only he could imbue some of that sense into young Beauchamp.

'Beauchamp.' Alex did not respond, his head drooping listlessly although he was taking some of his weight on his legs. 'Alexander!' His head snapped up at that. His wavering gaze fixed on Hugo's face, then he grinned. 'Thought you were m'father for a minute.'

The entire time Tadlow and Bulbridge had continued to advance, and now Hugo found himself with his back against the door at the end of the passageway.

He stepped forward, shoving Tadlow aside to grab Alex's arm. 'Come with me, Beauchamp. You don't want to go with these two, do you?'

'Go? Go?' Alex's head swivelled. 'Where we goin'? Diablo's? Don' wanna go there. *Told* you… it's crooked.'

'You heard the man, Tadlow,' said Hugo. 'I don't want to cause a scandal here in Denby's house, but you'd best leave Beauchamp be. He's going nowhere.'

'Brave talk for one man against two. Now, get out of our way.' It was Bulbridge who spoke this time, a squat, coarse-featured, unmannerly man. 'I don't know what's got into you, Alastair—interfering in things that are none of your business. Although…' and he glanced behind him before fixing Hugo with a leer on his face '…I can see which part of your anatomy is leading you. You've no chance there, you fool. Stand aside.'

Tadlow pushed between Hugo and Alex. About to grapple with him, Hugo paused. Olivia was still watching and, beyond her, people were still moving to and from the card room. He should take this argument outside rather than risk a scandal in here, in front of witnesses—Olivia in particular. He stood aside, opening the door for the three men as, behind them, Olivia started forward. Hugo waved her back again, more urgently this time. What was likely to happen was not for a lady's eyes. To his astonishment, she obeyed, spinning on her heel before hurrying back towards the main staircase.

Hugo followed the three men into a short passageway, dimly lit by a single candle in a wall sconce. There was a door at the far end and a narrow flight of stairs led down to the right, presumably to the kitchen and other service areas in the basement. They soon reached the door at the end and, as they manoeuvred Alex through and into the yard, Hugo saw Alex revive a touch and start to resist the men who were manhandling him. His head lifted, his legs straightened, and he began to struggle. 'No...back... Livvy...'

Hugo overtook the men again, blocking their way to the gate set into the surrounding wall.

'You heard him. He wants to go back. For the last time, leave him with me and we'll say no more about this.'

Tadlow released Alex, shoving him towards Bulbridge, who swung him round and backed him sharply against the wall. Tadlow came towards Hugo, his hands balled into fists.

'And I say it for the last time, too, Alastair—get out of our way.'

Tadlow did not trouble to keep his voice down and every sinew in Hugo's body hardened as the implication of that—coupled with the sound of the gate behind him creaking open—registered. Even as he began to turn, raising his own fists, a blow to the side of his head sent him staggering back. He kept his feet as Douglas Randall—Bulbridge's cousin—stalked towards him. Hugo feinted with his left and then, as Randall blocked him, he jabbed hard straight at the other man's nose. His fist connected with a satisfying crunch and Randall reeled away. This was no time for gentlemanly conduct. With three against one Hugo could not allow the man time to recover and he followed him up, grabbing his shoulder and swinging him around as he let fly with a roundhouse punch to the side of his face and followed that immediately with a solid punch to the gut that floored him. Then he spun to face Tadlow, but hesitated as Olivia burst through the door into the yard and slammed to a halt by Tadlow's side, her mouth a perfect O of horror.

Tadlow wrapped his arms around Olivia, entrapping both her arms and lifting her so her feet flailed helplessly off the ground. With a roar of rage, Hugo charged at Tadlow, but Bulbridge then thrust Alex away and barged Hugo aside. They grappled and, even as they swayed together, each attempting to loosen the other's hold, Hugo saw Randall attempting to get to his feet and his heart sank.

'Liv!' Suddenly, Alex was on Tadlow's back, his arm around the man's neck as he throttled him. 'Let my sister go, you bastard,' he snarled and Hugo saw him sink his teeth into Tadlow's ear.

That gave Hugo renewed strength and he heaved again at Bulbridge, breaking his hold. He stepped back smartly and jabbed once, twice, three times at the man before he could recover his balance. Blood spurted from Bulbridge's nose and mouth, but still he came at Hugo. The swiftest of glances showed Alex with Olivia, pushing her behind him as he—swaying slightly and with a scowl of pure concentration on his face—stood between her and Tadlow and then all his attention was on Bulbridge as they fought. He must disable the man quickly, for Alex was no match for even Tadlow—the weakest of the three men—in his current state and if Randall recovered enough to get involved, all would be lost.

At least, he thought grimly, *Alex will never again trust Tadlow after this.*

Then the door back into the house opened and Clevedon stepped through into the yard. Everyone seemed to freeze, for the briefest of seconds, as the Earl took in the scene. Then he caught Hugo's eye, nodded and strode across to haul Randall to his feet. He dragged him to the gate and shoved him through before returning to Tadlow. Bulbridge backed away from Hugo, but he followed, jabbing relentlessly until the Viscount's back hit the wall. The man looked almost done and Hugo grasped his collar and hauled him to the gate.

'Don't you dare let me see your ugly face near the Beauchamps again,' he growled before throwing Bulbridge to the cobbled ground of the mews beyond. He was then almost knocked aside as Tadlow rushed past him and grabbed Bulbridge, tugging him to his feet. Hugo started after the men, intending to make sure they did actually leave, but Clevedon gripped his shoulder.

'Allow me to escort these gentlemen off the premises.'

He did not wait for a response but strode off, following the three men hobbling in the direction of the road.

The breath whooshed from Olivia's lungs as Hugo returned to the yard. She rushed to him and framed his face with her hands, peering closely in the dimming twilight. His breathing sounded harsh in the sudden quiet. His hand—large, warm, comforting—slid around her waist, pulling her close.

'Are you hurt?' His deep voice curled around her and through her, heating her blood, making her own breath hitch.

No,' she whispered. 'Hugo. I—'

Her heart clenched as she spied a dark line trickling from the corner of his mouth. She stripped off her evening glove and touched his mouth with trembling fingertips. The indrawn hiss of breath told her all she needed to know. She moved closer, sliding her fingers through his hair, relishing the solid strength of his hard body against hers as his scent filled her. He'd been in danger and she needed to know he was safe.

'It is you who is hurt. I am so sorry.' She brushed her lips across his cheek. Saw his lids close. Felt the swell of his chest as he drew in a long, deep breath.

'You have no reason to apologise.' He bent his head, his forehead touching hers as his warm breath feathered her skin. 'This is not your fault.' His fingers stroked featherlight along her jaw. 'I am so sorry you had to witness that.' He heaved in another breath. 'Oh, God!' His voice cracked. 'When he grabbed you… I felt… I wanted to—'

A groan filled the air and Hugo stiffened, releasing Olivia as he stepped back.

'As I said—' he swept a hand through his hair '—it was not your fault. You can blame your reprobate brother for that.'

He jerked his head towards Alex, who groaned again. Hugo's tone was now matter-of-fact, as though that tender moment had never happened. Hurt and confused by his sudden withdrawal,

Olivia went to Alex—who was sitting on the ground, back propped against the wall, knees bent, head buried in both hands—and crouched beside him.

'Alex? Alex? Are you all right?'

'He must be very drunk to be in such a state.'

'My head. Wanna sleep.'

He groaned again and Olivia glanced round at Hugo. 'I know my brother. He can hold his liquor better than this and, for all his careless ways, he would never drink himself into this state when he was responsible for escorting me and Nell.'

'Ahem!'

The cough came from close behind her and Olivia sprang to her feet. Lord Clevedon had returned and now stood by her side, staring down at Alex—and how had she forgotten about him? What if he had come back when she was in Hugo's arms?

'My lord, I trust you are not injured, too? Thank you *so* much for coming to our aid.' She glanced at Hugo, who was scowling at his friend. He really did seem to object to her even talking to Clevedon. Was it because they were friends? Or was it because he viewed Clevedon as a more worthy rival than the younger men who courted her? Whatever the reason, she took heart from it. Perhaps Hugo was not as indifferent to her as he pretended to be.

'I sent a message to Lord Clevedon with a footman, Lord Hugo. He is your friend and he was the only person I could think of who might help us.'

'It was my pleasure, my lady, and I am uninjured, thankfully.'

Hugo joined them. 'You have my thanks, too, Clevedon. Now, we must decide what to do about young Beauchamp here. He can hardly go back inside as he is.'

He bent and grasped Alex's chin, tilting it up. Alex's eyes were screwed tight and he groaned again. 'Earlier, I thought he had the look of a man who had taken opiates.'

'He would never—' Olivia began indignantly, but Clevedon interrupted her.

'It wouldn't surprise me if those three didn't slip him something in his drink,' he said. 'I've heard of such a thing happening and they were pretty determined to get what they thought they were owed.'

'Is Alex in debt to those men?' Olivia clutched Clevedon's sleeve. 'Tell me, please. I must know.'

'This is hardly an appropriate subject for discussion.'

There was a note of warning in Hugo's voice, but Olivia ignored it. She knew exactly what he meant—it was because she was a female and they deemed this men's business. She bridled at yet again being pushed aside as irrelevant.

'How can I protect him if I do not know the worst? Please, Lord Clevedon. Tell me why they were taking Alex to that place. Diablo's, was it Alex said? What is Diablo's? It does not sound very respectable.'

'Alastair is right, Lady Olivia, and you should forget you ever heard of Diablo's.'

And just like that, the men dismissed her. She was unimportant and didn't need to know the facts. She balled her fists in frustration. She wanted to know. Alex was her brother. It was her responsibility to see he came to no harm. Was he already in debt or had they prevented the worst from happening?

'You cannot go back inside looking like you've been in a brawl, Alastair, so why do you not wait here with Beauchamp? I shall escort Lady Olivia back to her friends and then I shall arrange for the Beauchamp carriage to come round and take Beauchamp home.'

Hugo stepped close to Clevedon, his stance challenging. 'Mind you are discreet. We would not want the lady's reputation to suffer, would we?'

Olivia puzzled over the menacing undercurrent in his voice as he spoke to his friend. Clevedon, however, appeared not to notice.

'But of course, my dear Alastair. Soul of discretion, you have my word. And I shall personally accompany Lady Olivia and her companions home, as their escort is indisposed.'

'Very well.'

Hugo sounded most grudging, but Olivia was grateful to Clevedon for his forethought. Lady Glenlochrie was so old-fashioned she would be horrified at the thought of driving home without a gentleman to escort them.

'Thank you for looking after Alex, Lord Hugo.'

She smiled at him, wishing she could say more...wishing she could touch him. She yearned to feel his strong arms around her but she knew that was not possible and so she must be content with the brief smile he gave her in return. She bent over Alex and kissed the top of his head.

'I'll see you in the morning, Alex, dear,' she whispered and then straightened and walked through the back door and into the short passageway that led to the door into the main part of the house.

Clevedon followed her and then led the way to the inner door and opened it to peer into the house beyond. Fear gripped Olivia as she belatedly understood Hugo's warning to his friend—the consequences of her and Clevedon being seen were too horrible to think about.

'The coast is clear,' Clevedon whispered. 'Follow me.'

They reached the vicinity of the door into the card room without being seen and that awful tension that had gripped Olivia melted away.

'Please promise you will not tell anyone about this.' Relief made her garrulous and the words tumbled from her as Clevedon crooked his arm and Olivia tucked her hand into his elbow. They walked towards the staircase for all the world as though the Earl was merely escorting her from the card room back to the ballroom. 'If Papa should hear about what happened, then he won't let Alex have Foxbourne and then—'

Conscious she was gabbling, she fell silent.

'Foxbourne?'

'I shouldn't have mentioned it. I am sorry.'

'You can trust me, my dear.' Clevedon patted her hand. 'You have my word I shall not breathe a word of any of this to anyone. Foxbourne… now… is that not the name of Rockbeare's place?'

Olivia explained, in the briefest of terms, about Foxbourne and Alex.

They had reached the top of the stairs. In a few moments there would be no more time. 'Tell me, sir, please—is Alex in debt to those men?'

'You really do care about your brother, don't you?'

'Of course I do. I would do anything to help him. Anything. Which is why I must know about Diablo's.'

'He is a fortunate man, to have such a fiercely protective sister, but you may rest assured that after this evening your brother will never trust those scoundrels again.'

Clevedon would be drawn no further and Olivia had to be content with that. The remainder of the ball passed without incident. Hugo did not return and Clevedon escorted Olivia, Nell and Lady Glenlochrie back to Beauchamp House as promised.

Chapter Thirteen

The following morning a somewhat battered and bruised Hugo called upon Freddie Allen to acquaint him with the happenings of the previous evening. He had formulated a plan of sorts to try to keep young Beauchamp out of trouble and away from the gaming tables, and Freddie had been enthusiastic about Hugo's suggestion for winning Alex over. Hugo was very aware that it would take much diplomacy on his part to get Alex to agree to his proposal—a young man's pride, as Hugo well remembered, was a prickly subject. Freddie sent a request to Alex to join them in the library and, after a suitable length of time, the door opened to reveal the younger of the Duke's sons. Hugo watched Alex through narrowed eyes as the young man slouched across the library and flung himself into a leather-upholstered wing chair next to the empty grate. Hugo flicked a glance at Freddie—

who was already seated in the matching chair—
and read the concern in the furrows of his brow.

Freddie pushed himself to his feet. 'Can I get
you a glass of Madeira, Alex?'

Freddie and Hugo already had drinks.

Alex shrugged. 'If you like.'

Sullen. Resentful. Disengaged.

Hugo remembered those traits very well.

Without warning, Lucas's words came back
to him.

*'You always were a deep one...hiding your true
feelings...wary of letting anyone close...afraid
you'll turn out like our old man...'*

Hugo rolled his shoulders as though to rid himself of a sudden weight.

Lucas was wrong. He'd shed that protective
shield of sullenness at a younger age than Alex—
by the age of twenty he had already moved on to
the pleasures of life. Just because he didn't wear
his heart on his sleeve didn't mean he was *hiding* his feelings. A man needed *some* privacy, for
God's sake. Besides, didn't he have some excuse,
growing up with that brute for a father?

Hugo thrust down the memory of his father as
Freddie crossed to a side table and poured a glass
of Madeira. He forced himself to stay seated and
not to go and help the other man, instinctively
knowing he would resent the implication he could
not manage. Hugo hadn't liked to ask the cause

of Freddie's lameness and Freddie hadn't offered the information.

Freddie hobbled back, leaning on the crutch he used to help himself get around. He passed the glass to Alex, who accepted it with a muttered 'Thanks', and he sat down again.

Alex looked from Hugo to Freddie and back again. 'I suppose this is where you rip up at me for what happened last night? Are you going to tell my father?'

Hugo sipped his drink. 'That all depends.'

'On what?'

'What you intend to do about avoiding men like Tadlow in the future. Do you accept they were out to fleece you?'

Alex's lips set in a mutinous line. 'S'pose so.'

'And?'

'What d'you want me to say?'

'That you'll avoid them in future?'

Alex surged to his feet and paced around the room. 'I'm not a bloody fool, Alastair. Of course I'll avoid them. Although what business it is of yours I fail to understand. What are you doing here anyway? And how come you got involved last night? Nobody asked for your help. I can look after myself.'

'You were out of your mind, you damn fool.'

'I didn't drink that much. I reckon they slipped me somethin' in my drink.'

'You were *supposed* to be escorting your sister

and Lady Helena, but you were more concerned with your own selfish pleasures than with their welfare. What if something had happened to either of them?'

'Oh, so that's it, is it, Alastair?' Alex bent over, thrusting his face close to Hugo, who battled to keep his hands on his lap and not retaliate. 'You're sniffing around her again, are—?'

'Alex!'

Alex snapped upright and stared at Freddie in astonishment.

'If you wish to apportion blame, then place it on my shoulders,' he said. '*I* asked Alastair to keep an eye out for you until your father comes home. You would not heed Alastair's warning the night you took Olivia to Vauxhall Gardens and our only concern is to make sure you do not lose Foxbourne. I have no ulterior motive and neither, believe it or not, does Lord Hugo.'

'Still don't see why he's here now.'

He's so ready to believe the worst of everyone, he'll lose Foxbourne through sheer bloody-mindedness if he's not careful.

'Freddie told me of your skill with horses and about the prospect of running Foxbourne Manor for your father. It sounds like an ideal opportunity. I wish I'd been given such a purpose to life when I was your age.'

Alex's brows met across the bridge of his nose as he glowered into his drink. Hugo waited. When

Alex raised his gaze to Hugo it was with a mix of caution and enthusiasm, almost as though he were holding himself back with the fear of being disappointed.

'Father has promised he will sign the place over to me.'

'*If* you prove yourself,' Freddie interjected.

Alex scowled again. 'He knows I'm good with horses. He won't find anyone better to be in charge.'

'And that is in part why I wished to speak with you,' said Hugo. 'I have a favour to ask of you.'

He sipped his own Madeira. Alert for any nuances of expression from the younger man, he recognised the flash of intrigue in his expression.

'My stepfather, Sir Horace Todmorden, has bought this mare…she's a prime piece of horseflesh, but she has turned nasty, biting and kicking until none of the grooms will go in the stall with her, let alone ride her.'

Alex straightened in his chair, leaning forward as Hugo spoke.

'Where did he buy her?'

'At auction. He suspects she was doped—she was docile enough during the sale and while being led home.'

'Doped and docile, eh?' A sudden grin flashed across Alex's face. 'Bit like me last night—I couldn't summon even a spark of energy to resist Tadlow, even though I didn't want to go any-where near bloody Diablo's.'

'Well, believe it or not, she is even wilder than you now the drugs have worn off,' said Hugo, with an answering grin. 'Would you be willing to take a look at her? The alternative is to have her shot, but her conformation is superb and Sir Horace is keen to breed from her. Not at the price of injured men, though.'

'Of course. Although town isn't the best place to sort out a horse's problems. 'Tain't a natural way to live, see? I like to work with them in a small paddock. They're less likely to feel threat-ened if they have the delusion of freedom.'

Hugo found himself nodding in agreement. He'd never really thought about it, but what Alex said made sense.

'Sir Horace is an ex-cavalryman and he has plenty of contacts still at the Horse Guards. I'm sure they can find you a safe area to work with her. Although we'd have to get her there safely first.'

'We'll find a way,' Alex said with confidence. He drained his glass. 'When can I go and look her over?'

'Now, if you'd like to.'

'I'll go and change my clothes, then. Give me ten minutes.' Alex leapt to his feet and strode from the room, a completely different man from the one who had entered.

Freddie also rose. 'If you'll excuse me, I must get on. I don't want to give the Duke any reason to complain about my slacking off work when he comes home.'

'When do you expect him?'

'Either tomorrow or Friday.' Freddie rammed his crutch into his armpit and hobbled towards the door. He turned before he left and smiled. 'I've no doubt you will be the most relieved of us all when he returns.'

Hugo smiled, but after Freddie left he stared into the empty grate, lost in thought, his treacherous mind bringing back the slide of his hand around Olivia's waist, the delicious scent of violets, her gentle hands cradling his face and reliving that near-irresistible urge to seize her, to kiss her, to *take*, despite—or maybe because of—everything that had happened. His rakish instincts had clamoured at him—what did it matter that she was too young, too beautiful, too *innocent*? They had roared their demands, their need for satisfaction. Only Alex's groan had jerked him back to reality and he had, thank God, come to his senses before Clevedon returned. And he must continue to keep those urges on a tight leash and, more importantly, he must learn to keep those unwanted emotions—the yearning, the tenderness, the need to *protect*—safely locked away. Olivia was only on his mind now because he happened to be in her home. Once he had fulfilled his obligation towards her brother, he would soon forget her. There were plenty of warm, willing women out there who knew how to play the game.

'Oh!'

The feminine gasp jerked him from his musings. He looked around into her wide silver eyes and his heart twitched with longing. He set his jaw, battening down that unnerving need to be wanted, to find somewhere to belong.

'You should not be in here, alone with me.' His voice emerged as a growl.

'I did not know you were here.' Her pert nose was in the air as she rounded the sofa and sat by his side. Her scent—not only that hint of violets, but the scent of *her*...of a delicious, delectable, desirable female—filled him.

With longing. With desire. With...

It took time to identify that feeling, but she filled him with hope.

'You should go.'

The words came almost without thought. That same feeling of protectiveness arose within him, quashing any lustful urges. It was up to him to protect her from her own innocence...she surely had no idea... He surveyed her expression and caught the glint of determination in those striking silvery eyes of hers, the irises ringed with dark grey—and he wondered. Was it innocence? Or was she a risk-taker? A tease? Out to entice and then to refuse. He had watched her with her coterie of admirers. She was not innocent of the effect she had on *them*. What she might not realise was the difference between toying with those green lads and playing with a man of his experience— an older man less easily manipulated. There were too many wolves out there, prowling around the young innocents, eager to taste young flesh. *He* might feel compelled to protect her from herself, but others would not be so gentlemanlike.

'That is not what you said last night. You were happy to see me then, happy to accept my help.'

'That was different. An emergency. Olivia… you know you should not be in here with me. Your brother—'

'Liv!'

The roar made them both start. Hugo stood and faced Alex, who strode across the room, a dark scowl on his face…directed firmly at his sister and not at Hugo for a change. Alex grabbed Olivia by the arm and dragged her to her feet, shaking her. Hugo clamped his jaw against a protest and stepped back so he would not act upon his sudden urge to punch Alex on his nose.

'I *told* you Alastair was waiting in here and that you weren't to come in. Why must you persist in being such a bloo—blasted nuisance?' He pushed her in the direction of the door. 'Go on. Out! And *please* have a bit more care for your reputation in future.'

Hugo bit back a smile at the absurdity of Alex

lecturing Olivia on correct behaviour. Olivia stuck her nose in the air.

'Without me,' she announced, 'you, Alexander Beauchamp, would be much poorer and, probably, still drunk or drugged, lying insensible in some squalid room somewhere with a dirty, diseased—'

'Silence!' Alex strode towards Olivia and she skipped towards the door, keeping beyond his reach.

'I deserve *some* credit for helping you last night. It was *me* who had the nous to send for Lord Clevedon to help you. Otherwise Lord Hugo would have been overpowered because you, brother dear, could barely stand.'

Alex wagged his head at her, waving his hand as if shooing a dog away. 'Have you got irritating little sisters, Alastair?'

Hugo shook his head. 'I have no sisters, irritating or otherwise. But—although I agree your sister should not have come in here *knowing*...' and he captured Olivia's gaze, raising a brow at her, prompting pink to flush her cheekbones '... that I was in here alone—I am happy to have this opportunity of thanking her for her cool head and her prompt action last night. Without her, as she rightly says, the outcome could have been very different.'

Her beaming smile made him feel a hero.

Alex scowled. 'I suppose you have a point,' he grumbled. 'But, now that's done, let's go. We have important business, Sis. Run along and attend to your sewing or your flowers or whatever other crucial activities await you.'

Sympathy swelled inside Hugo, but he realised that to voice such would not only reignite the squabble between brother and sister, but also encourage Olivia. The *tendre* she had developed for him could lead nowhere. *She* would not see the risk in pursuing it. *He* knew only too well what the result might be if she did not take care.

He bowed. 'Good day to you, Lady Olivia.'

She held his gaze boldly and, a split second before he broke the contact, she bobbed a curtsy.

'And good day to *you*, Lord Hugo.'

'You are in a lively mood, Livvy,' said Nell, as they left Lord and Lady Postbridge's garden party the following afternoon. 'You have left at least three young men nurturing high hopes that they might win your hand before the end of the Season.'

They had attended the garden party with their friend, Lizzie Tubthorpe, and her mother, who had taken Lady Glenlochrie's place as chaperon. Lady Tubthorpe and Lizzie had walked on ahead, giving Nell and Olivia an opportunity to exchange views not only on the party and the other attendees' gowns, but also on the beaux who had clustered around them like bees around nectar.

Olivia was satisfied that she had hidden her

low mood successfully. She thought entirely too often about Lord Hugo Alastair even though her common sense *knew* he was totally unsuitable for her. There were plenty of other men just as handsome as and far more acceptable than that rogue, but they simply failed to interest her in the way Hugo did.

'Who is your preferred beau?' Nell continued teasingly.

Olivia waved her hand in the air. 'Those boys? Not one of them. Besides, I am not like you, Nell. I did not come to London with the purpose of finding myself a husband. I mean to spend a year or two enjoying myself before settling down.'

'I might have come here with the original intention of marrying well,' said Nell in an unusually acerbic tone, 'but our circumstances have changed since then, as you well know. Now your papa is my guardian I am no longer in danger from my Uncle Tadlow's scheming and so I am no longer in any rush to wed.'

Olivia slipped her arm through Nell's and hugged it close to her body. 'I am pleased to hear it, my dear step-aunt, for it means we shall continue to have fun together as we coax as many young men as possible to fall hopelessly in love with us and then watch at a distance as they enjoy the agony of their broken hearts.'

Even as she spoke such words, an image of Hugo arose in her mind's eye and her heart ached for him. Was this love? Well, if it was, it was not much fun.

'I did wonder...' Nell fell silent.

They were nearing the carriage now and, as one, their steps slowed.

'What did you wonder?'

'Well. I...now, do not fly up into the boughs, Livvy, but... Lord Hugo...there is something there. Between you.'

Olivia bit back a gasp. Could Nell read her mind?

'I do not know if it is because of what happened at Vauxhall Gardens, but I saw the looks you exchanged last night.' Nell's violet eyes were huge with concern. 'You are both constantly aware of where the other is, even if you are on opposite sides of the room. And I know that you think about him...no, do not deny it, for I know it. You bring his name up in conversation. Your eyes light up when he is present. And when, such as today, he is not there...your gaiety seems almost *too* gay, if that makes sense?'

She would die rather than admit to Nell how her heart yearned for Hugo.

'It does not matter what I think of him. He is a penniless rake and I am...well, I am my father's daughter. I am expected to marry well.'

'He is the son of a marquis. He is almost as high born as you are.'

'My father would not countenance him.'

Olivia's throat ached with suppressed pain. It didn't seem to matter how strong her feelings were, neither Hugo nor Papa would take note of her wishes. It had been the same her entire life—Mama had only noticed her when she misbehaved and her brothers only when she did something outrageous or nagged them. Otherwise they mostly ignored her. She was nothing but an unwanted irritant in their lives. And now Hugo... It seemed the only times he took notice of her was when she annoyed him. Well, if that was what it took to get his attention, that was what she must do.

'Anyway, this conversation is stupid,' she said airily. 'I have no wish to marry. Now, let us hurry. Lady Tubthorpe is beckoning us.'

The carriage deposited them at Beauchamp House and they went inside to an ecstatic welcome from Hector and a skipping Susie, who sang at the top of her voice, 'Dom-in-*ic*. Dom-in-*ic*. Dom-in-*ic*.'

Olivia and Nell exchanged a look.

'Susie!' Olivia caught hold of the little girl. 'Are Dominic and Aunt Cecily home?'

She had missed the calm good sense of her aunt more than she liked to admit. Even though Olivia could not confide what had happened to her aunt, she knew that, somehow, she would feel better with her back home.

'Dom-in-*ic*!' shouted Susie.

The governess, Miss Pyecroft, came hurrying from the back of the house.

'Oh, my goodness, ladies, I am so sorry. We were downstairs and when the news came that Lord Avon had returned, Susie rushed up here before I could stop her. We were making jam tarts together and my hands... I had to wash them. Although I see—' and she grabbed hold of Susie by the wrists '—little Miss Susie had no such compunction. Susie, really...come with me now. You must have left sticky hand marks everywhere.'

As she disappeared into the nether regions of the house, she called over her shoulder, 'Lord Avon is in the drawing room, if you wish to see him.'

Olivia exchanged a look with Nell. 'I wonder if Aunt Cecily is travelling home with Papa and Rosalind.'

They went to the drawing room, where Dominic was chatting to Alex and Freddie. He looked up and smiled as they entered.

'Just in time to save me from telling the tale twice,' he said.

'Did Aunt Cecily not travel back with you?'

Dominic's lips firmed, 'No. She formed a desire to visit Great-Aunt Drusilla, so I dropped her off at Leyton Grange on my way back to London.'

'Great-Aunt *Drusilla*?' Alex grimaced. 'But none of 'em can stand the old battle-axe. What's she gone there for? And how long before she comes home?'

Dominic shrugged. 'I do not know. She and Father—I do not know. But she won't be back for a few weeks at least. Father and Rosalind should arrive home tomorrow, though, and Uncle Vernon and Aunt Thea—for that is what she likes to be called, not Dorothea—will come here in a few weeks' time after their honeymoon trip to the Lakes.'

Dominic soon left the drawing room to go upstairs and change out of his travel-stained clothes. Olivia followed him.

'What were you going to say about Papa and Aunt Cecily, Dom?'

'Nothing,' he said as he took the stairs two at a time.

Olivia hurried after him, lifting her skirts clear of her feet. She caught up with him just before he disappeared into his bedchamber.

'Tell me. Please. Did they argue?'

For that is what it sounded like he had been about to say—even though Papa and Aunt Cecily never argued. Not like Uncle Vernon and Aunt Cecily. Dominic paused, his expression softening as he looked down at Olivia. Her heart quailed, her stomach churning at that look. Dominic was only ever kind to her when he felt she was in need of his big brotherly protection; otherwise he was as bad as Uncle Vernon with his teasing.

'They *did* argue, Dominic. I can tell, so please do not lie to me. When will Aunt Cecily be coming home?'

'Livvy.' He put his hand on her shoulder and squeezed gently. 'It is nothing to worry about. It was only the slightest of disagreements.'

'But why? Why would they quarrel?' To her horror, Olivia felt tears burn behind her eyes. 'They *never* argue. She *will* come home, won't she?'

'Of course she will.'

But something in his eyes as they flicked away from hers...in the uncertain way in which he said those four words...warned Olivia that it was by no means certain.

'Did she send me a message?'

Dominic gave a rueful smile, then pulled her into a hug. 'Sorry, brat, but, no. She was a little...preoccupied.' He pulled back then and smiled down at her. 'But don't fret. You still have Father and me and Alex. We are still a family.'

Except Papa now has Rosalind. He won't have time for me. And if...

Olivia swallowed, her throat aching. If they had children, where would that leave her? Her world seemed to be turning upside down. She could see herself in the future, becoming less and less important to her family as they busied themselves with their new lives.

'Besides, you will probably get married your-self very soon.'

She stared at her brother, shock making her stomach clench as the implication of his words hit her. 'Is Aunt Cecily getting married?'

Surely not…her father, uncle and aunt, all in one year? How could life change so very drasti-cally in such a short time?

'This is strictly between us, brat,' said Domi-nic, 'but she *may* do. Lord Kilburn's estates border Leyton Grange—she refused an offer from him earlier this year but it appears she is having sec-ond thoughts.' He patted her cheek. 'Don't worry, Livvy. It may never happen.'

Dominic disappeared into his room and closed the door, leaving Olivia standing alone in the up-stairs corridor, fighting tears as she wondered what was happening to her precious family. How *could* Aunt Cecily abandon her like this? She was the only mother she'd known since she was five years old. Her own mother had rejected her, but Aunt Cecily had always been there. Now, though…she had turned her back on Olivia with-out a thought. Was she really so unimportant? So…*unlovable*?

Angrily, Olivia swiped at the tears that now wet her cheeks.

I do not care. I'll show them I don't care.

Chapter Fourteen

Olivia stared at her brothers suspiciously. Since Dominic's return they had been uncommonly protective towards her and that only served to worry her more. That Alex was privy to more information about what went on at Uncle Vernon's wedding was clear. And she hadn't heard her brothers argue once—and that was unheard of. She'd bet they'd argue if she told Dominic what Alex had been up to while he'd been away—but then she remembered that much of that was her fault in the first place, so she did not risk opening that particular topic of conversation.

'You *both* intend to escort us?' she said. 'Why?'

It was the evening of Dominic's return to London, and she had come downstairs, dressed and ready for the Pendletons' soirée. The Pendletons' twin daughters—Lynette and Louisa—had made their debut this year and were friends of both Olivia and Nell. Now here were Dominic and

Alex, dressed in their evening finery, waiting in the drawing room for her, Nell and Lady Glenlochrie to be ready to leave.

'You should be grateful to have two such handsome, elegant gentlemen as your escorts,' said Alex, with a swagger and a smirk. 'I promised Aunt Cecily I would escort you while she's out of town and that's what I'm doin'.'

'And I am at a loose end,' said Dominic, 'so I may as well go there as anywhere.'

Olivia eyed him gloomily. 'You do know that whenever you show your face at any of these society events I suddenly become *much* more popular with all the simpering young misses, Dominic?'

He smiled. 'Can I help it if I am irresistible?'

'Hmmph. The question is, Brother dear—is it you who is irresistible, or the prospect of being a future duchess?'

She had been hoping Hugo would be at the soirée to watch over Alex as Papa was still not home; she had hoped she might snatch a quiet word with him—she intended to pay him some of what she owed him—and she had also fantasised that he might, finally, dance with her. There were bound to be a few informal dances for the younger set tonight, while the seniors played cards and gossiped. Those hopes were much less likely to come to fruition with Dominic there. He could be so stuffy at times and she just knew he would object to her even speaking to Hugo.

* * *

When Hugo appeared in the doorway, flanked by Lords Clevedon and Sudbury, Olivia's heart seemed to perform a somersault in her chest, leaving her temporarily gasping for breath. He was so handsome. So sophisticated. His dark gaze swept the room—where much of the furniture had been removed to provide space for dancing—and came to rest upon Olivia. His expression seemed to harden and he looked away. Exactly as he had reacted to her when he first caught sight of her at the Denby ball, she realised with a sinking heart.

It was so difficult to understand what he truly thought or felt. He seemed determined to hide any genuine feelings behind a barrier of alternating disapproval and boredom and yet…she couldn't be so wrong about that kiss. Could she? And then, in those few, unguarded moments after the fight… his anguish…that tender moment…*that* was not her imagination. But now, yet again, he seemed as remote as ever and she felt as confused as ever.

Why do you fool yourself that a worldly sophisticated man like Hugo would be interested in a silly little girl like you? Even your own family don't think you important enough to be told the truth of why your aunt hasn't come home.

Then Lord Clevedon caught Olivia's eye, smiled and said something to Hugo and Lord Sudbury before leaving them in the doorway, clearly making his way towards Olivia. On the brink of returning to the safety of Lady Glenlochrie's side, she hesitated. She could not risk annoying his lordship after his help at the Denby ball. So she waited, trying to fathom Hugo's expression as he tracked Clevedon's progress around the room. His features seemed to have hardened, his lips set, his dark brows lowered. Then he glanced at Olivia and immediately his expression blanked and he directed his attention to Lord Sudbury.

That he was annoyed with his friend was clear, but why? Was it...could it be that he did not want Clevedon to dance with her? Was he jealous, if only a tiny bit? That thought buoyed her hopes, but also stirred her indignation. If he did not want to speak with her or dance with her, that was up to him. But he had no right to object if another man chose to do so.

Then Lord Clevedon was before her, bowing.

'Might I have the pleasure of this dance, Lady Olivia?'

She smiled at him, bobbing a curtsy, then placed her gloved hand in his. She'd show Lord Arrogant Alastair she wasn't about to stand around like a wallflower waiting for him to ask her to dance.

Who does he think he is, anyway? Nothing but a rake, with no title of his own and no land or any-thing. I can look far higher than Hugo Alastair...

She ignored the inner voice that whispered that she did not want to look higher than him. It was him, and only him, that she wanted, but his casual dismissal of her both hurt and infuriated her.

'Avon has returned, I see,' Clevedon remarked as they circled and met and parted again through the steps of the country dance. 'Does that mean the Duke will soon be home as well?'

Olivia was shaken from her brooding by his question. 'Yes. I believe so. My stepmother's grandfather is travelling with Papa and the Duchess, so they travel at a slower pace than Avon.'

She flicked a glance at the doorway. Hugo was still there, his dark gaze on her, so she smiled up at Clevedon. If flirting and dancing with his friend was the only way to command Hugo's attention, then that was what she would do.

'You present a most charming picture this evening, my lady,' said Clevedon, bowing at the end of the dance. 'It is warm tonight, but you manage to maintain your cool poise when all about you are wilting in the heat.'

Olivia laughed. 'Appearances, my lord, are deceptive in that case. Inside, I am melting.'

He appeared somewhat taken aback and she regretted her choice of words, for that phrase conjured up how she had felt inside when Hugo kissed her. Just the memory of his lips on hers... his tongue in her mouth...heat flushed her chest and neck and crept inexorably to her cheeks.

'Might I procure you a glass of lemonade?'

Clevedon beckoned a footman stationed near

the door. Hugo was still watching them, his eyes narrowed, and she tilted her chin. Good. He would see it was not only *young* men who found her of interest. She could attract a sophisticated gentleman like Clevedon, who must be thirty if he was a day, and it was a bonus that he happened to be Hugo's friend.

'Thank you, sir. I am rather thirsty.'

Besides, she was conscious that Clevedon knew enough to cause a scandal for her and for Alex if he chose to talk of what happened at the Denby ball. They were in full view at a ball—how could there be any danger? It would not hurt her to be pleasant to him.

'Would you care to stand over there by the window and catch the breeze, if there is any to be had?'

'Thank you; that would be a relief.'

Clevedon instructed the footman to bring two glasses of lemonade to them in the window embrasure and then steered Olivia towards the window, which was partly shielded from the room by a large urn of flowers. The fresher air admitted by the raised sash was most welcome and Olivia was confident in her ability to manage any unwelcome behaviour by the Earl.

She sipped gratefully at the cool lemonade, savouring the sharp tang of the lemons.

'That is better.' Clevedon leant against the wall of the alcove and eyed her as he drank. 'And we have the advantage that those flowers deflect some of the noise from the room. Tell me, how are you enjoying your first Season?'

'It is everything I hoped it would be,' said Olivia promptly.

He chuckled. 'I hear a "but" in there somewhere.' When she did not respond, he went on, 'You have surely achieved everything every young girl dreams of when coming to town for the first time: you have taken society by storm and, despite what happened at the Denby ball, I have not heard a breath of criticism attached to your name.'

Her gaze flew to his. He smiled reassuringly.

'Your secret is safe, my lady. Never fear.'

He moved closer and Olivia tensed, gripping her glass in two hands and raising it to chest level to prevent him getting too close. His gaze flicked down to that protective manoeuvre and his eyes crinkled as they lifted again to hers. He leaned even closer, his lips close to her ear.

'It is a challenge for a man to snatch a private word with such a popular young lady, not to mention one with two very protective brothers. But I have always relished a challenge. Tell me…can you name one single man who hasn't fallen immediately under your spell? I'll wager you cannot and, if you can, then I denounce that man as a fool.'

An image of Hugo arose in her mind's eye.

Did one kiss count as him falling under her spell? Her heart sank. No. For it was she who had kissed him. He had merely responded, as any red-blooded male might, to what she had offered. She eyed Clevedon again and swallowed, suddenly uncertain of allowing him to manoeuvre her into this semi-private spot.

There was no advantage to encouraging Clevedon if Hugo could not see them—she'd only thought to make him a little jealous. Her rambling thoughts froze. Dominic always called her a *manipulative little madam* when she tried to get her own way. And that's exactly what she was doing now…using Clevedon in an attempt to—what was it he had said?—in an attempt to have Hugo *fall under her spell.*

She got that squirming, shameful feeling in her stomach that she often experienced when she knew she was in the wrong.

Clevedon brushed the back of his fingers across her collarbone and she straightened, looking him firmly in the eye.

'Thank you for the lemonade, sir. I am quite refreshed and it is time I returned to my chaperon.'

'As you wish, Lady Olivia. You are right to be cautious. Reputation is everything for a young lady, is it not? You may rely on me not to set tongues wagging.'

His words sent a shiver dancing down her spine. Was that a veiled warning? No. Surely not. Her imagination really did run away with her at times.

Clevedon bowed and stood aside. As she passed him, she felt the brush of his hand on the nape of her neck and down her back. She could do nothing but ignore it. She could not challenge him over his inappropriate caress when she had willingly put herself in a situation where he could take advantage. Aunt Cecily had warned her often enough about *never* going off alone with any man—even into a semi-public situation like that window embrasure.

If you do, your actions are bound to be misconstrued. Never give any man a chance to get you alone.

Those words echoed through her head and her spirits—already low—plummeted further. When would she come home? Olivia *needed* her. Papa and Rosalind were all very well, but it was Aunt Cecily to whom she had always turned. Her calm good sense always helped Olivia make the right decision.

'Might I beg a second dance, my lady?'

She wanted to refuse, but she found herself agreeing to Clevedon's request, wary of provoking him when he knew so much about Alex. His smile told her she'd made the right decision, but she consoled herself that he could pay court to her all he liked, she would never marry him. On that thought, she scanned the room. Hugo was nowhere to be seen and neither was Alex, although Dominic was dancing with Louisa Pendleton and Nell was dancing with Lord Silverdale, one of Uncle Vernon's friends. How she hoped Alex had not been lured into another disastrous card game.

They reached Lady Glenlochrie, and Clevedon scribbled his name against a dance later that evening, bowed, and walked away. Olivia sank into a vacant chair and Lady Glenlochrie leaned towards her, raising her open fan in front of her face to keep her words private.

'That is most encouraging, my dear. You did quite right, not lingering for too long by the window. I kept my eye on his lordship, you may be sure of that, and there was nothing untoward that I could see. Your papa *will* be pleased when he returns tomorrow.'

Olivia battened down her irritation. 'Lady Glenlochrie, I know you mean well, but I have no wish to encourage Lord Clevedon or anyone else for that matter. I do not wish to marry yet.'

'Nonsense! If a man such as Clevedon should offer for you, your papa will bite his hand off, gel, make no mistake. He is a splendid catch. And, as behoves an obedient daughter, I make no doubt you will conform to your father's wishes on the subject of your marriage.'

Olivia only just managed to prevent her eyes rolling at that.

Lady G. is so old-fashioned—she belongs in

the last century. Papa would never force me to marry someone I do not care for.

That thought sparked another, however. A less welcome thought. Papa might never force her to marry someone she objected to, but would he be amenable to her marrying the man of her choice if he disapproved of him? She suspected she knew the answer to that and it was not the answer she wanted.

She thrust aside all thought of Hugo and marriage—*not that he is interested in me. He is merely a convenient example, that is all*—and turned to Lady Glenlochrie. There was little point in arguing with her so Olivia simply smiled, collected her reticule from where she had left it while she danced and stood up.

'I need to visit the retiring room, ma'am.'

Lady Glenlochrie inclined her head, then returned her attention to her neighbour and their gossip and Olivia made her escape. She exited the room and stood irresolute on the landing before heading for the card room, situated towards the rear of the house. In the doorway, she almost bumped into Hugo, on his way out of the room. Every nerve ending tingled and her breath grew aggravatingly short. She really wished she could prevent these unwanted reactions to the man. She tightened her grip on her reticule.

'Have you seen Alex?' she asked.

'He's in there.' Hugo flicked his thumb at the

card room. 'He's playing with Charnwood and a couple of other decent men. There's no need for you to concern yourself; I'm keeping an eye on him.'

'May I see?'

Olivia stood on tiptoes to try to peer over his shoulder and Hugo's dark eyes crinkled at the corners as he stepped aside to allow her an uninterrupted view of Alex, who looked relaxed and happy.

'Do you not trust my word, my lady?'

Olivia elevated her nose. 'I do not believe you always tell the whole truth, no. And I need to be certain Alex is not gambling with unsavoury characters.'

'I can assure you that Alex has seen the error of his ways and is not likely to get embroiled with men like Tadlow again.'

Then his lips firmed. Olivia found it hard to tear her gaze from his mouth; found herself longing to kiss him again. Was that very shocking? Of course it was, but she could not help how she felt. And as long as *he* did not realise it, her pride would remain intact and she could hold her high.

'I wish I could say the same about you,' Hugo then muttered.

Startled, Olivia looked up. *'Me?'*

'Yes, you. Look. We cannot talk here, it will be remarked upon. Follow me, but at a distance. And for God's sake, be discreet.'

He stalked away without waiting for an answer and took the stairs to the second floor. Olivia followed—reluctance slowing her pace. She knew that tone of voice—although she did not know what gave Lord Hugo Alastair the right to think he could dictate to her about *anything* she might choose to do. On the landing, she looked around in time to see Hugo disappear behind a pair of floor-length curtains. She followed.

They were in a deep embrasure where the window overlooked the street. A gas lamp outside cast a pale illumination over Hugo's grim expression. She cast her mind wide for words that might lighten his mood…anything to avert the lecture she felt sure he was bursting to deliver.

'I prefer my choice of venue for an illicit *rendezvous*.'

No sooner were the words out than the memory of their encounter in Sophie Wray's bedchamber exploded into her brain, complete with every detail of that kiss. Heat erupted and, without volition, she moved closer, placing one hand on his chest as she tilted her face to his. His chest expanded as he drew in a fractured breath, his eyes dark fathomless pools in his pale face. Then he covered her hand with his and slid it up to rest on his shoulder. His fingers feathered over her collarbone and neck and up to her cheek. She leaned into his touch and stepped even closer, sliding her other arm inside his coat and around him, stroking his back, breathing in his spicy, masculine scent. Their breath mingled as their gazes fused, and then her eyes drifted shut as that delicious, melting sensation gathered deep inside her, pooling between her thighs.

Lips brushed her skin with the most delicate of touches—dancing along her jaw and the sensitive skin at the side of her neck. She swallowed her moan and tilted her head back as he traced her collarbone and teased along her neckline with lips and tongue, leaving her tingling and craving more. Then his arm snaked around her waist and hauled her close as he seized her lips. She pressed into him, soothing her tight, aching breasts against the solid wall of his chest. She opened her mouth, meeting the thrust of his tongue with her own, matching his every move.

His jaw rasped her fingertips as she stroked and explored his face and her other hand dipped lower, skimming the silk of his waistcoat, tracing his spine as it curved into his waist and then the hard swell of his buttocks—rounded and firm. She felt the shift of his muscles as she squeezed and a low groan rumbled in his throat. He stilled. She didn't want him to pause. Didn't want to give him time to think…to have second thoughts. She thrust her fingers through his hair and cupped the back of his head, holding him still as she angled her head and deepened their kiss. She was rewarded by him gathering her closer still, half-lifting her until her entire body fitted to his and she could feel a hard ridge pressing against the softness of her belly.

And then he stopped.

He straightened, his hands at her waist as he pushed her away. He put his fingers to her lips and his lips to her ear. 'Shhh.'

Jolted back to reality and the outside world, Olivia became aware of voices on the landing, just the other side of the curtain. Nerves jangled as she feared discovery, but then she relaxed as she realised, from their conversation, that the voices belonged to two maids and that they were moving away.

She gathered her wits, leaning her forehead against Hugo's chest as he held her. She felt… content and yet, at the same time, on edge. She had dreamed and fantasised about that second kiss, but her imagination had been nowhere near equal to the reality. She'd lost herself—she'd had no concept of where she ended and he began. They were one. And there was more wonder, more pleasure to discover. She knew it as readily as she knew her own name.

As the maids' voices faded, Hugo moved away from her, his hands dropping to his sides. She immediately felt his loss and wrapped her arms around her own waist in comfort.

'I came here with the intention of talking to

you, not to carry on from where we left off the other day.'

He didn't sound angry. Or regretful. But he did sound like one of her brothers might, when they were about to take her to task and not one bit like a man who was captivated by her kisses. She recalled his words, the first evening they met. *I prefer my ladies willing. And experienced.* Her spirits plummeted. Of course he did—he was an experienced rake and although she had proved the first to him he clearly was not impressed by her skill, even though she couldn't help that she wasn't as experienced as other women he might have kissed. Ruthlessly, though, she quashed any hint of sadness. She was with him now—she would not spoil their time together with misery or, even worse, tears. Growing up with her brothers had instilled in her the knowledge that men *hated* females who cried.

She gathered her courage.

'Talk *to* me? Not with me?' It took effort to tease him, but anything was better than turning into a watering pot, as Alex would scornfully call it. 'That sounds suspiciously like a lecture to me, Lord Hugo.'

Chapter Fifteen

Hugo chuckled. She surprised him at every turn. For a fleeting second misery had swum in those expressive eyes of hers and her pain had tugged at his conscience and stirred—deep within him— the urge to soothe it away and to put a smile on her face and a laugh in her voice. Then there was no misery, just a teasing light, and the transition had been so swift, so smooth, that he could not be sure he had not imagined the entire change of mood.

'Not quite a lecture, more a warning. About Clevedon.'

A frown tugged at her brows. 'What of him?'

'I saw you—dancing with him. And after-wards, in that alcove.' And he had wanted to tear the bastard apart with his bare hands. He nudged her chin up, trying to instil in her how serious he was. 'Do not think to use him, my sweet. You are playing a dangerous game.'

'I do not know what you mean. I am playing no games.'

But she was. He knew it. He had seen the glances she sent his way. He knew women. He knew when someone was trying to get his attention. If only she realised the effort it cost him to ignore her—but he must be strong, for her sake.

'If you say so.'

'You don't believe me?'

'You play with fire if you are encouraging him to no purpose. Unless, of course, you have a burning desire to be Countess of Clevedon?'

She thumped his chest. 'I do not want a husband. Not yet, anyway.'

Through her indignation, however, he heard embarrassment quiver and he sought to soothe her. Her pride and her self-belief were just two of the things he admired in her.

'All I mean is that you should take care. Leading on a man like him—an older man who is on the lookout for a wealthy wife—is very different to games of flirtation with the young bucks who surround you and who profess to be dying of love for you.' He was envious of those young men, who could court her with impunity. 'But you ought not to encourage Clevedon, or any man of his ilk. Goad a man like that too far and who knows what trouble you might let loose.'

He had trusted that her experience at Vauxhall Gardens would keep her wary of Clevedon, but had his actions at the Denby ball changed her opinion of him? Hugo could not possibly admit the real truth about why Clevedon was so unsuitable. All he could do was try to set her straight, and encourage her to think of the consequences of her actions.

She pouted at his words, then peeked up at him through her lashes.

'Do I goad *you*, my lord?'

That look rocketed through him, heating his blood. She chased every sensible thought from his head. Did she realise the effect she had on men? On him? No, of course she did not. She was an innocent. And yet...

He did not doubt she was an innocent in fact, but she was one of those females instinctively aware of her own sexuality...her own allure. And she knew exactly how to use it. And if he ever saw her use that look on Clevedon...his hands clenched again into fists.

No.

He calmed himself. For all her attempts to attract Hugo's attention, he had not once seen her use that kind of lure with Clevedon.

Or with any other man.

Only him.

A knowing smile flirted around those full lips, swollen from his kiss, as her gaze dropped to his hands. He quickly unclenched them as she reached for one and caressed it between both of hers. It was all he could do not to haul her into his arms, kiss her senseless and introduce her there and then to the delights of seduction…show her the pleasures that awaited her…the sensations a skilled lover might coax from a woman's body.

Let Clevedon try to entice her away from *that*.

But that would be unfair. Not to mention immoral. And when had he turned into such a stuffy, strait-laced prig? He resorted to the only response he could to try to get her to see sense.

He laughed.

He gazed down at her, half-hooding his eyes and allowed his top lip to lift in a slight sneer.

'Sweetheart,' he drawled. 'I am merely claiming my reward for acting as nursemaid to you and that brother of yours. This—' he curved one hand around her skull and tilted her head up, taking her lips again in a ruthless assault '—is merely a taster to put me in the mood for later tonight, when you are tucked up in your bed with your innocent dreams.'

She pushed him away and wiped the back of her hand across her mouth, shooting icy shards at him from those extraordinary eyes of hers.

'How *dare* you kiss me like that, without my permission!' Her brows were elevated in haughty disdain, as though she were a queen addressing a subject. Far from angering him, he admired her spirit. 'Until now, Lord Hugo, you have proved useful in enabling me to gain a little experience

in the art, but I suggest you do not try again unless *expressly* invited.'

She opened her reticule and withdrew a small
but bulging pouch which she then thrust at him.
'This is part of what I owe you, sir. Once I pay
the remainder, there will be no need for further
contact between us. Good evening.'

She flung aside the curtain—apparently heed-
less of anyone who might see her—and stalked
away. As luck would have it, there was no one
else on the landing.

Hugo permitted himself no regrets. This was
for her own good. Better that she hate him than
continue to harbour that hope that shone so clearly
every time she looked at him. Better, too, that he
slam the door on his own feelings and that point-
less, raw eagerness to see her, even from afar, to
talk to her, to ask her dance.

He simply could not see how this…this…what-
ever it was blossoming between them—he could
not see how it could end well for either of them.
When her father returned to London he would
for certain show an interest—and not in a good
way—were he to become aware that a man of
Hugo's ilk was paying *any* kind of attention to
his daughter.

Hugo would still protect her from Clevedon,
but only by dint of staying close to his erstwhile
friend rather than to Olivia. *Someone* needed to

protect her—from her own impetuosity as well as from the prowling wolves of the *ton*.

Wolves like Clevedon. And himself.

He made two vows.

He would try to warn her father about Clevedon, even though the Duke would be highly unlikely to listen to anything Hugo had to say.

And he would avoid any future contact with her.

It took him all of one day to break that second vow. It seemed he couldn't help himself. He was walking around Grosvenor Square, on his way to his mother's house, when a squeal of laughter and a series of frenzied barks from the garden in the centre of the square caught his attention. And the mere sight of her—her jet-black hair gleaming in the sunshine as she chased a giggling child, who trailed a chip straw bonnet from one hand—thumped him in the heart and he found himself gasping for breath.

And instead of obeying his inner common sense that commanded him to walk on by—to leave her angry—he found he could not bear for her to think so very badly of him and so he changed direction and strolled into the garden, the gate nearest to Beauchamp House having been left unlocked. A footman standing just inside the gate stared at him, but the recognition was mutual—it was the same man who had admitted him to

Beauchamp House when he called on Freddie—
and although he kept his eye on Hugo, the man
made no attempt to stop him.

That gigantic hound that belonged to the Duchess was gambolling at Olivia's heels and he was
the first to notice Hugo. He charged up to him
and Hugo—even though he knew the dog to be
friendly—still had to steel himself not to flinch
in the face of the sheer size of him. Hector's dis-
appearance from their game captured Olivia's attention and she slowed, glancing after the dog.
Then she slammed to a halt, her mouth a perfect
O of surprise. Her cheeks glowed pink and, without her hat, her hair had worked loose from the
controlling hair pins.

This is how she would look after a night of
bed sport.

Hugo felt his body respond to that wayward
thought as he walked up to her and he cursed his
newly discovered streak of morality—the voice
of conscience that urged him to protect her rather
than to seduce. Seduction was his speciality—he
knew exactly how to please and satisfy a woman
with his body and there were many, many women
in the *ton* who could testify to his skill. How much
easier it would be, and more agreeable, to follow
his male instincts to take and be damned to the
consequences. But knowing the consequences for
Olivia would far outweigh the consequences for

him meant he could not—for the first time in his adult life—pursue his own desires.

Which had left him floundering in, for him, unfamiliar territory.

'Good afternoon, Lady Olivia.' He tipped his hat.

Olivia dipped a curtsy, but the tip of her chin and the martial light in those temptress eyes of hers suggested she had not forgiven him for his behaviour the night before. And he could not blame her. He had behaved exactly like the rake she believed him to be. Except she had no idea of the restraint he had exercised and he could not tell her.

'Good afternoon, my lord.'

Her voice was decidedly frosty, but the effect was wasted when the fact she was panting ever so slightly put him even more in mind of pleasurable romps and beds and—

He swiped those thoughts away. He was not here to rekindle her feelings for him—was he?— but to...his thoughts lurched to a halt. He did not know quite why he was here. Or, indeed, why he had chosen to walk to Mama's house via Grosvenor Square when there were several other routes he might have taken. But he was here now...

He smiled. 'Would you care to introduce me to your friend?'

Olivia elevated her chin, but she beckoned to the child, who eyed Hugo shyly as she came forward. Olivia held out her hand for her bonnet and put it on—tucking the loose tresses away—before introducing the child as Susie, her father and stepmother's adopted daughter. Susie stuck her thumb in her mouth and mumbled around it.

'She is still a little worried by men in tall hats.' Olivia, arms folded, watched Susie rather than looking at Hugo. 'She was raised by her foster parents on an isolated farm and I don't believe she had ever seen a fashionable gentleman until she met Papa.'

'She does not appear to be intimidated by that great brute, however,' said Hugo, as Susie, losing interest in the adults, ran after Hector to fling her arms around his neck. 'He is almost as tall as her, but she shows no fear.'

'That is because she trusts Hector. She knows *he* would never hurt her.'

He supposed he deserved that subtle dig.

'How did she end up with your family?'

'Her foster parents were cruel and she ran away from them.'

'She is fortunate to be taken in by your father. Speaking of whom, can you tell me when you expect him back in town?'

'Some time—' Olivia's jaw snapped shut and her eyes widened as her attention latched on to something beyond Hugo's left shoulder '—today,' she finished.

Hugo spun on his heel. Sure enough, a travel-soiled carriage with the Duke's crest emblazoned on the door had pulled up in front of Beauchamp House.

'We must go.' She did deign to flick a glance at him then. 'Please wait until we are indoors before you leave the garden.'

It was a demand rather than a plea. She certainly had spirit; not by a flicker did she betray any embarrassment over what had happened between them in that window embrasure.

'You are asking me to skulk in the bushes?' He hardly knew whether to be amused or offended.

'I have no wish for Papa to know we are acquainted. I will not risk him finding out about Vauxhall because he will blame Alex and then—'

'Yes. Very well. I get the gist—you will do anything to protect that scapegrace brother of yours, will you not?'

She gave a slight shrug of her shoulders. 'Of course. Do not think I am ungrateful for your assistance but...yes. I will. At least you no longer need concern yourself with my family. You have proved useful, but you may return to your carefree life without guilt.

'Now, come, Susie. Let us go and welcome Papa home.'

Olivia left the garden without a backward glance and Hugo followed her progress across the road to the carriage. Had he got her completely wrong? Had she just been playing with him, the same as he had accused her of doing with Clevedon? If she had, the reason why was clear enough—she had needed his help to watch out for Alex.

Although that still did not explain why she had kissed him so enthusiastically.

The Lady Olivia who had—almost carelessly—dismissed him just now was not the Lady Olivia who had clung to him and sighed in his arms last night, before he had intentionally infuriated her. But...*could* he have been wrong? An old saying came to mind—while the cat's away, the mice will play. Quite apart from the need to protect her brother, had Olivia merely made the most of the Duke's absence to experience a bit more of life? Had he allowed himself to be reeled in with the rest of her admirers—believing she had feelings for him when in reality she was simply enjoying herself and gaining experience? Was he just another damned gullible fool?

He had never felt so wrong-footed by a woman. Who was she really? The naïve girl or the scheming woman?

Anger tore at his gut, but he forced himself to remain out of sight until the Beauchamps disappeared inside the house. He would do that much for her. Then he strode from the garden, nodding to the footman to relock the gate as he passed. As he neared his mother's house, though, his steps slowed. No matter what Olivia's purpose had been in kissing him—in enticing him to feel more for her than he had ever felt for another woman— the fact remained that he did care for her. And— amazingly for a man who had mostly only ever considered his own pleasures—the compulsion to protect her still hummed in his blood.

She was so busy watching over Alex—but who was watching over her? Hugo would do one last thing for her—he would warn the Duke to keep a closer eye on her. Hell, if she was in Hugo's care, he would have her under permanent lock and key because that was the only way he could ever be certain she was not up to mischief.

The problem now was—how, precisely, did he warn the Duke without landing both Olivia and Alex in trouble?

And *that* particular dilemma was resolved as early as the next day, when he walked into the morning room at White's and there, by the fire, sat the Duke of Cheriton. Hugo gave himself no time for second thoughts. He crossed the room and cleared his throat. The Duke glanced up and his expression changed from one of polite enquiry to recognition and then to curiosity. He folded his newspaper with a rustle and placed it on the table by his side.

'Alastair.' He nodded as his silvery-grey eyes— so like his daughter's—narrowed. 'To what do I owe this privilege?'

'Mind if I join you?'

'Please do.' Politeness rather than warmth coloured the Duke's tone.

Hugo sat in a nearby chair and signalled to a footman to bring him a drink. Now that the moment had arrived, he felt somewhat awkward. It was one thing, vowing to do the right thing, quite another to do it when faced with Olivia's powerful father.

After several silent minutes, Cheriton enquired: 'And what might I do for you?'

Hugo's gaze jumped from the glass of brandy he had been contemplating to the Duke's face. This was more difficult than he had anticipated. He could not see how Cheriton would fail to wonder at Hugo's sudden interest in his family.

'It is more a case of what I might do for you,' he said at last. 'Something I overheard and thought you should know, that's all.'

'Well?'

'It concerns your daughter—Lady Olivia.'

Cheriton's eyes turned icy. 'What about her?'

'Best keep an eye on her, that's all. There are some unsavoury types sniffing around her.'

Hugo started to rise, but Cheriton reached out and caught his wrist in a steely grip.

'Explain yourself,' he growled.

Hugo stilled. He looked down at the hand gripping his arm, then raised his eyes to the Duke's and raised his brows.

Cheriton held his gaze for a fraught number of seconds, then released his grip and leaned back in his chair.

'What do you know?' he asked in a more conciliatory tone.

Hugo hesitated. It went against his code of honour to name Clevedon but…his need to protect Olivia was stronger. He had no choice.

'Clevedon.'

Cheriton's brows shot up. 'Clevedon? Unsavoury?'

He looked Hugo up and down, and he didn't need to add—*who are you to call the Earl of Clevedon unsavoury?* His opinion of Hugo was clear in that disdainful look.

Hugo gritted his teeth. 'He's in love with someone else—' He could not bring himself to admit it was Lord Sudbury. Who knew if Cheriton could be trusted with such sensitive information? 'He needs a wealthy wife and he's set his sights on your daughter. He'll break her heart.'

The Duke's eyes narrowed and he studied Hugo, who battled to keep his expression blank. When he spoke again, his voice was very quiet, sending a shiver down Hugo's spine.

'And why, I ask myself, are you concerning yourself with my *eighteen-year-old* daughter's welfare, Alastair?'

Hugo stood. 'I don't approve of naïve little chits

being used as pawns, that's all. Just watch out for her.'

As he strode away he heard the Duke say, 'Oh, I shall do, Alastair. You may be sure of that.'

Chapter Sixteen

'You wished to speak to me, Papa?'

Her father stood up as Olivia entered his study. 'I do. Thank you, Freddie. That will be all for now.'

Olivia waited until Freddie had gathered up his papers and limped from the room, trepidation coiling inside her. What had Papa found out? Did he know about Alex? But, no. Or he would be speaking to her brother, not to her. So why had he sent for her?

Hugo.

Her insides somersaulted as his name popped into her head. As they always did. Even though she tried very, very hard to never think of him, somehow he was always there. At the edge of her consciousness, just waiting to catch her unawares…waiting until she forgot to brace herself and forcibly keep his memory at bay. And then the memories would erupt, right into the centre of her thoughts, and the black cloud would descend, reminding her of her splintered heart and her shattered dreams.

He had returned her kiss at the Pendletons' soirée. He had *groaned*. She had been sure he had felt something. But then, afterwards, he had reverted to that same cool, detached, arrogant way of his and taken no notice of her *whatsoever*. It was no longer a matter of him not asking her to dance, or taking her to supper. He did not even *look* at her. Not once. He had kissed her and then dismissed her. And she had vowed to do the same with him. And she had been proud of her effort in the Square yesterday. She had been as cool as cool could be. And *she* had dismissed *him* this time. Take *that*, Lord Arrogant Alastair.

But that did not stop him invading her thoughts whenever she was unwise enough to allow her guard to drop. Well, she would keep—

'Livvy?'

The gentle enquiry jerked her from her thoughts. Papa was holding a chair for her, waiting for her to sit down. She plastered an airy smile on to her face.

'I am sorry, Papa. I was debating which gown to wear to the opera this evening.'

Papa raised a single brow. Olivia wished she could master the art—she had spent hours in front of a mirror trying to mimic that look, but to no avail. Pity—it was a very effective expression, suggesting just the right degree of cynicism. She'd love to be able to quell Lord Arrogant Alastair with just one such look—she thrust him from her thoughts and sat down. Papa pulled another chair close and took her hand.

Olivia's heart plummeted as fear rocketed through her.

'Is it Aunt Cecily? Has something happened?'

A frown darkened Papa's expression. 'No, nothing has happened and it does not concern your aunt. Why should you think that?'

She could not confess that deep panicky feeling she always experienced whenever the thought of losing one of her family came into her head. That was *her* secret and Papa had enough to worry about.

'No one will tell me why you have squabbled.'

Papa sighed. 'Livvy. We have not squabbled. We are rational adults—we do not have squabbles.'

Olivia put her nose in the air. No one *ever* told her anything, just because she was the youngest. And female. And then they wondered why she had become adept at winkling out secrets!

'Now, I wish to ask you about somebody, but I need to trust you not to reveal this to anyone else. Can you be discreet?'

Her curiosity aroused, Olivia nodded eagerly. From thinking that no one ever told her anything, it seemed Papa was about to confide in her. She preened at the thought he was treating her as an adult—someone to be consulted, rather than a child to be tolerated or ordered about.

'Who is it, Papa?'

'Lord Clevedon.'

'Clevedon?'

Sick dread crowded her throat. *Had* Papa found out? Had he already sent Alex away?

'Yes,' Papa went on. 'I have already spoken to Lady Glenlochrie and she told me that his lordship has called upon you and that you often dance with him.'

The air left her lungs in a relieved whoosh. 'Yes, that is true…' A horrible thought occurred to her. 'Papa? Lord Clevedon has not offered for me, has he? Because if he has, despite what Lady G. says, I do *not* wish to marry him. You will not make me, will you?'

Relief flashed across Papa's face as he gathered her other hand in his. 'No, no, I have not even seen Clevedon. And you must know I would never force you to wed against your wishes, Livvy.'

'Thank you, Papa.'

'That is all I wished to ask you.'

Olivia stood to go. 'Papa?'

'Yes?' He was already halfway around his desk, his attention on a stack of correspondence.

'What made you ask Lady G. about Lord Clevedon?'

'Oh…' Papa stared at her, a distracted frown on his face. 'It was…someone warned me to watch out for his lordship, that is all. You have good birth and a large dowry. There will be fortune hunters among your suitors—you know the ways of our world and I know your aunt has warned you of such men. They can be charming and declare their undying love, until they have their hands on your dowry. Such marriages, where one spouse cares more than the other, can be…lonely.' The fleeting sorrow that crossed Papa's face told Olivia that he was remembering her mother and his first marriage. 'I have been warned Clevedon is one such man.' He shrugged. 'Who knows if it is true, but as you do not care for him it is, I am pleased to say, immaterial.'

'Yes, but who would tell you such a thing, Papa? Do I have a guardian angel?'

He barked a laugh. *'Angel?* He is no angel, sweetheart, believe me. And it's best you do not know his identity. I don't know why he chose to warn me, but I shall be keeping my eye on him as well as on Clevedon, you may be sure of that.' He stared at Olivia and the harsh planes of his face softened. He rounded the desk in long strides and pulled her into a fierce hug. 'No one will harm you, sweetheart. Not while there is breath in my body.'

Olivia left the study, her thoughts in a whirl. It had to be Hugo. Who did he think he was, kissing her one minute and then lecturing her about Lord Clevedon the next and even warning Papa against him? It seemed *he* did not want her—unless it was to kiss her in dark corners—but he did not want anyone else to show an interest in her either.

That was called being a dog in a manger.

Unless, of course...hope sprang to life again, deep in her heart.

Unless he did want her for himself.

The following few weeks soon disabused her of *that* notion.

Following Papa's return, it proved nigh on impossible for Olivia to contrive a private encounter with Hugo—Papa and Rosalind were more mobile than Lady Glenlochrie and it was hard to give them the slip. And then Aunt Cecily came home as well—well, Papa had stormed off to Oxfordshire to fetch her and there was definitely something wrong, but no one would tell Olivia what had happened. Aunt Cecily was tight-lipped and unhappy as she tried to pretend everything was normal and whenever Olivia tried to talk to Papa about it, he just chucked her under the chin and told her it was nothing to worry about. Why could they not understand that telling her that made everything worse? Caused her to worry all the more?

And so now there were three of them to watch her. It was so frustrating. Dominic and Alex never had this trouble. Anxiety was her constant companion, her insides winding tighter and tighter with every day that passed, until she felt ready to explode. Why did everyone treat her as though she was a child not to be trusted with the truth?

And trying to accept that Hugo simply didn't care a jot for her made her feel infinitely worse, particularly when she couldn't fully bring herself to believe that either. With his brother and sister-in-law in town, Hugo now attended many of the same events as Olivia, but he avoided her; he never asked her to dance or engaged her in conversation or asked to escort her to supper. And none of that really surprised her, but it still hurt. If they did happen to meet face to face, he bowed and greeted her politely, but he sent her no secret signals to encourage her to still hope.

And yet…and yet…there were times—many times—when she caught him watching her as she talked and laughed and danced with other gentlemen. He would quickly avert his eyes when she saw him, but those times kept alive a tiny flicker hope in her heart.

'Dominic?' Olivia ignored her brother's blatant exasperation as he looked up from the book he was reading. 'I desperately want to go for a ride in the Park, but there is no one to accompany me. *Please*, Dominic. Say you will go with me.'

'Ask Alex. I'm in no mood and, besides, it is starting to rain.'

Olivia peered out of the library window. The

sky was grey and it was true that one or two drops had spattered on to the glass.

'Alex is out.'

'Are you certain? I heard him not ten minutes ago.'

'Yes, I'm sure.'

She'd watched him leave, after overhearing him tell Freddie he was riding in the Park with Hugo—something about one of Hugo's stepfather's horses that Alex had been helping him with. She needed to go the Park and see Hugo and, hopefully, talk to him. She missed him.

'Please, Dom. I am bored and I want to *do* something. Please take me. Stepmama and Aunt Cecily are too busy with the preparations for tonight.'

Papa had managed to persuade the renowned opera singer, Angelica Catalani, to sing at Beauchamp House that evening, but that had meant a mountain of last-minute preparations, even though the guest list had been kept short and very select—*intimate* and *exclusive*, according to Aunt Cecily. It seemed everywhere Olivia went, she was beneath somebody's feet.

Dominic's attention was fixed once again on the book in his hands.

'Ask Lady G. to take you in the carriage,' he said without looking up. 'You'll keep dry that way.'

'But you aren't busy and I want to ride. You

have no idea how frustrating it is, not to be able to go anywhere or do anything on my own. You are so lucky. Ple-e-ease, Dominic, my darling, my most favourite brother.'

He looked up again at that, but only to purse his lips and shake his head at her. She felt like stamping her foot, but she refrained. If she fell out with him, he'd never agree to escort her.

'Papa says I have too much energy and I shall be expected to sit still tonight when Signora Catalani performs, and no one will allow me to help them. *Please*, Dominic.' Olivia eyed her handsome brother as he turned a page and reached for the glass of wine by his side. 'Surely you are not afraid of a few spots of rain? What would your harem of admirers make of that, I wonder? The bold Marquess of Avon afraid of getting his hair wet.'

That caught his attention.

'Firstly, I am not afraid of getting wet and, secondly, my hair would be protected by my hat, as you well know.' He put a mark in his page and laid the book aside with a sigh. 'You are not going to give up until I agree, are you?'

Olivia hid her triumphant smile as he unfolded his tall frame from the chair.

'Come along then.' He looked her up and down. 'You are already changed, I see. I'll tell Grantham to send word for the horses to be brought round.'

Olivia let her grin spread at that. 'No need,'

she flung over her shoulder as she exited the library ahead of him. 'I already did that. The horses should be ready and waiting for us outside.'

'You little—!'

Olivia laughed and skipped quickly out of her brother's reach as he swatted at her backside.

Olivia soon spotted Hugo and Alex, together with four other riders, who were grouped together in a quiet corner of the Park. Alex was riding a beautiful black horse in a large circle while the others watched.

'Why is Alex doing that?' she asked Dominic, turning her own horse's head in their direction. 'Is that the horse that belongs to Hugo's stepfather? What is wrong with it—it looks like Alex is schooling it.'

'He is.' Dominic reached across and grasped Olivia's rein, halting her mare. 'Hugo?'

Blast.

Dominic frowned at her. 'Hugo?' he repeated.

Olivia shrugged. 'Slip of the tongue. I heard Alex call him that. I meant Lord Hugo, of course.'

'You are not to go over there and disturb them,' said Dominic, releasing her rein. 'The horse is a bit wild from what Alex told me. It's taken him several days to persuade her to trust him. This is the first time he's ridden her out.'

'Well, I had no intention of riding up to *Alex*. I

just wanted to go a little closer to watch. You *know* how I love to watch him working the horses.'

Olivia nudged Sprite with her heels and simultaneously tickled the flank of Dominic's horse with her whip. The horses ambled forward. Dominic, his attention on Olivia, did not halt them again.

'Since when?'

'Since…well, since Papa has promised him Foxbourne, that's since when, clever-boots. It's important to me to see Alex settled and happy. Isn't it important to you?'

'Of course it is. But we do not need to mix with Alastair's sort to do that.'

'*Alastair's* sort? Why, whatever do you mean?' They were now close enough to the group watching Alex for Olivia to recognise the men who were with Hugo. 'Do you refer to Lord Clevedon? Or perhaps it's Sir Horace himself that you object to. Or the Marquis of Rothley?' The fourth man was a stranger, but from his clothing she guessed him to be a groom. 'Really, Dominic. You can be obnoxiously top-lofty at times.'

'And you are a manipulative minx,' grumbled Dominic. 'Do not think I haven't noticed what you are up to—and don't think I don't realise that Clevedon has been paying you court of late. Although why such a sensible chap should be interested in a little menace like you, I quite fail to understand.'

Olivia elevated her nose. 'I always did think

you somewhat slow on the uptake, Brother,' she said, safe in the knowledge that they were now too close to the others for Dominic to clip her around the ear as he used to when they were younger. 'I, in case you have failed to notice it, have been declared Catch of the Season. *That* is why Lord Clevedon is interested in me.'

'I'd be doing him a favour if I set him straight,' Dominic muttered as they drew even closer to the group of men. 'No one deserves a lifetime with you, you little madam.'

Olivia huffed, but could not reply as they were now within hearing distance.

Maybe she *was* manipulative, but it had been seven days since that kiss and she had not once had an opportunity to even speak to Hugo. It was up to her to make sure they met and had the opportunity to speak, or how would he ever realise…?

Her thoughts stuttered to a halt. Realise what?

That we are made for each other.

She swallowed. She was a scandal waiting to happen. She knew it. And yet…she simply could not help herself. Her restlessness grew by the day as the end of the Season approached. Her family was changing and she felt as though she did not quite belong anywhere any more. Quiet dread churned constantly, low in her stomach, and she simply could not meekly sit and wait for things to happen—she was compelled to get out there and move them along. She brushed aside her doubts, buried her fears. There would be time to nurse her wounded pride later, if Hugo continued to ignore her. For now, she owed it to herself to do all that she could to get him to notice her. Besides, she still owed him the final instalment of the money she owed him. That thought buoyed her. It was the perfect excuse.

The men acknowledged their arrival with nods and smiles.

'Good afternoon, sirs,' said Olivia, smiling straight at Hugo.

He simply looked bored and her hopes—so high a few minutes ago—were dashed.

Clevedon reined his horse around to line it up on the opposite side of Olivia to Dominic. 'Well met, Lady Olivia. Have you come to watch your brother work his magic?'

She had little interest in talking to the Earl, but Hugo was now speaking in a quiet voice to his brother and taking no notice whatsoever of Olivia. *Hmmph.* What did she have to do to get his attention? It was ironic that she was surrounded much of the time by admirers, but the one man whose attention she craved seemed totally uninterested.

'Indeed,' she said in a bright voice. 'Alex is *such* a marvel with horses. I simply adore watching him at work.'

Attuned to Hugo and his every move, she noticed the swift sideways glance in her direction. Good. He wasn't completely unaware of her then.

'What made you come along today, my lord?'

'Oh, I was merely passing and stopped to watch. Quite fascinating. I never suspected your brother possessed such skill. Sir Horace has been telling me about the trouble they've had with that mare since he bought her and how Alex has changed her. I understand from Sir Horace that your father has purchased Rockbeare's place in Buckinghamshire with the intention that Alex will run it on his behalf?'

'But I—' Just in time, she stopped herself from reminding him that she had told him about Foxbourne after that fight at the Denby ball. Conscious of Dominic listening on her other side, she continued, 'that is… I thought no one was to know about that yet?' She glanced at Dominic for confirmation.

He shrugged. 'If Alex wishes to risk people knowing all about it when the entire deal might still fall apart, that's up to him. He always treads his own path, you know that, Sis.'

He then rode his horse over to join Sir Horace, leaving Olivia with Clevedon and thus affording them the opportunity to talk without being overheard. Not that she wished for such a thing. She bit back her *humph* of disgust. Trust Dominic! She'd wager a whole month's allowance he wouldn't have left her alone like this with Hugo.

'Alex is a fortunate man,' said Clevedon. 'Many fathers would have withdrawn his allowance after some of the trouble he's caused, let alone rewarded him with an estate and a thriving business. Let us hope he manages to keep his nose clean long enough for the deal to be finalised.'

'Oh, he will.' Olivia put her nose in the air. 'I shall do everything in my power to keep him out of trouble for the next few weeks. In fact—' she indicated Dominic with a flick of her head '—we both will. We stick together in our family.'

'That is what family is for, is it not?' he said. 'Now, if you will excuse me, my lady, I spy Sudbury over yonder and I have a message for him. Until we meet again.' He raised his hat and nodded before setting off at a trot.

Olivia could not believe her good fortune. Here was the perfect opportunity and she rode over to Hugo and Rothley, her brain working furiously to think of an excuse for joining them. Hugo's expression blanked as she halted Sprite facing them, but Rothley smiled and raised his hat again. Undaunted—well, a touch daunted, maybe, but she did not have the time to nurse bruised sensibilities when with each day that passed the end of the Season drew closer—she pressed ahead, a last-minute idea occurring to her just in time.

'Excuse my interruption, gentlemen, but I wonder if you have heard about our musical soirée this evening? It is all rather last minute, but my father managed to prevail upon Signora Catalani to sing at Beauchamp House tonight.'

'Catalani?'

Good. At least Rothley sounds suitably impressed.

Hugo, however, merely regarded her, one supercilious brow raised as if to say *I see right through you.*

'It is years since I heard her perform,' Rothley continued. 'Is her voice as good as it was?'

'Better, I should say,' said Hugo.

'I am persuaded Lady Rothley would love to hear her sing and I therefore invite you all to join us this evening.' Surely it would not matter if the event was a little bigger than the gathering Rosalind and Aunt Cecily had planned? Surely they wouldn't begrudge one or two additional guests?

Hugo's lips compressed and she saw his chest expand as he drew in a long breath. 'You should accept, Luke. Mary will love it.'

Rothley's dark gaze flitted between Olivia and Hugo, and she swore she saw him bite back a smile before he said, 'The invitation is for you, too, Brother. It would not be the same experience without you there, is that not correct, Lady Olivia?'

'Indeed, sir.'

'And Mama will be thrilled to have us both there together. You know how she always puffed us off in society, even when we were the biggest rogues out there.'

Hugo laughed at that. 'Dearest Mama. Always ready to defend her sons, no matter what.'

'What's that about your mother, boys?'

Sir Horace and Dominic had joined them. Olivia's heart sank. Would Dominic see through her ploy? She'd committed herself too far now to retreat and so she told Sir Horace all about Signora Catalani and repeated her invitation to Beauchamp House that evening.

'Oh, that is most kind. Lady Todmorden is exceedingly partial to a spot of opera. I do wonder, though…such an invitation, proffered without your parents' knowledge…?' Sir Horace raised his grey, bristly brows at Dominic.

Dominic, to give him credit, did not hesitate. 'In my father's stead, please allow me to confirm my sister's invitation to you and your family, Sir Horace.'

'Much appreciated, Avon. I accept on behalf of us all.'

Pure delight spread through Olivia at the thought of the entire evening with Hugo in her own home. Now she must work out how she might speak privately with him without her family noticing. She had the perfect excuse—she had borrowed and scraped together enough money to pay the remainder of what she owed him.

She knew she must take extra-special care to

hide any interest in Hugo from her family this evening. The constant effort required to hide her aching heart behind a smiling face had proved exhausting and she suspected she was no more skilled than Aunt Cecily at disguising her unhappiness. She would be utterly mortified if any of her family were to guess it was Hugo who was the cause of her low moods.

But Hugo would be there…tonight…in the same room as her. She hugged that little nugget close to her heart as anticipation swirled deep inside her. Her behaviour *was* outrageous, she knew, but the Season would soon end and then she would not see him again until next year. That thought wrenched at her heart. She could not bear the thought of not even seeing him, even though it was increasingly clear that he did not feel the same compulsion to see her.

Chapter Seventeen

You're a damned fool.

He knew it and yet still he would go tonight.
And he would go because—ridiculous, lovelorn
idiot that he was—he had missed her. Hugo stared
unseeingly at his reflection in the mirror as his
valet brushed off his black tailcoat in readiness
for the musicale that evening. The past week had
dragged unbearably, but he had consoled himself
that it was for the best if he gave her a wide berth.
Now at least he had the satisfaction of knowing
that *that* decision had been wise—look at what
had happened this afternoon when they had met
quite unexpectedly in the Park. Her face was an
open book and Lucas's earlier suspicions of a mutual attraction had been confirmed as fact, but
Mama, it seemed, had *already* noticed…

They had arrived back in Bruton Street and Sir
Horace had been full of that unexpected invitation to Beauchamp House.

'A small and most exclusive gathering, my dear Lucy, and we are *all* invited.'

'Catalani!' Mama clasped her hands at her breast. 'Oh, how wonderful. But…what on earth prompted Lord Avon to invite us?'

'Oh, it wasn't Avon, my love. At least—it was not he who originally invited us. It was Lady Olivia. Very sweet of her—she thought of Mary, you see, and how much she would enjoy hearing Catalani sing.

'But I have never attended an opera in my life,' said Mary. 'I do not know why Lady Olivia should think of me.'

'I suspect,' Mama had then said, her eyes sparkling as she smiled at Hugo, 'that Lady Olivia had *quite* another purpose in inviting our family.'

And now, thanks to his incorrigible mother, the entire family were aware that there was…*something*. A growl vibrated in his throat but, out of respect for his valet as he helped Hugo into his form-fitting tailcoat, he swallowed it back. He only hoped Mama would be discreet around the Duke.

Safety in numbers. He repeated the mantra as he trod down the staircase of the house in which his chambers were situated and again as he waited for the rest of his family to collect him in the carriage. And he repeated it again as he followed Lucas and Mary and Mama and Sir Horace up the magnificent marble staircase of Beauchamp

House. As long as they were within sight of others, he knew Olivia would not directly approach him.

It was a *most* select gathering, he saw, when they were shown into the salon. A space at one end had been cleared for the musicians and the singer, and chairs—Hugo counted twenty-one in all—had been spaced throughout the remainder of the room to accommodate the guests. It was quite some coup for Cheriton to persuade the oft-times capricious Catalani to perform at a private musical soirée. The London theatres—Catalani was the resident soprano at the King's Theatre in Haymarket—would now close until the winter and it was her habit to tour a few of the provincial towns during the summer.

She had not yet arrived, it seemed. The musicians were in place, playing quietly as the guests mingled and chatted. A footman offered a glass of wine from a tray, which Hugo accepted and then cast his gaze around the company. He stilled when he saw her. She was stunning, sheathed in a gown that clung to her slender form and set off her pale skin and black hair to perfection. She stole his breath…he wished—

A nudge dragged him back to a sense of his surroundings.

'Close your mouth, Brother. You look like you're catching flies.'

He snapped his jaw shut and glared at Lucas,

who shrugged. 'She is gorgeous, I grant you. But you need to decide if she's worth the hassle you'll get from her father if he gets wind you're interested.'

'I am *not* interested.'

Lucas raised a brow.

'Not in the way *you* mean,' Hugo growled.

'With a lady like her, Little Brother, there *is* no other way to be interested, if you get my meaning.'

Freddie limped towards them then, a welcoming smile on his face. Hugo introduced him to Lucas.

'I hear Alex is doing a grand job with Sir Horace's mare,' said Freddie and Hugo gratefully followed his lead into a general conversation about horseflesh.

He was relieved when Angelica Catalani finally swept into the room and he selected a chair towards the rear of the salon, after watching Olivia sit near to the front. The trills and swells of Angelica's remarkable voice washed through him almost unnoticed as he spent the entire time watching Olivia. At a break in the entertainment drinks were again served and Hugo snatched a glass of wine and headed for the terrace outside before anyone could engage him in conversation. He could not trust himself to discuss the singing that he had barely heard. He would be hard pressed to name one piece Catalani had sung. He crossed the narrow terrace and stared out across the darkening garden, as rigid as one of the dimly seen statues dotted below. Eventually, he released his pent-up breath with a whoosh, raised his glass, tipped back his head and drained it with one gulp.

'*Here* you are.'

He stiffened, and carefully set his wineglass on to the stone balustrade before he turned. They were a mere ten feet from the open window and the room beyond.

'What are you doing? Your entire family is in there.' He jerked his chin towards the salon.

'We are quite safe. Papa is discussing politics with Lord Castlereagh. Once they get started, they will not stop until Signora Catalani is ready to sing again. And my aunt and stepmother are talking to your brother and his wife.'

'That is not what I call safe,' he growled.

Frustration sent his blood surging around his body. He wished he might claim his frustration was due to anger at her risk-taking, but the tightening of his trousers suggested it was a different sort of frustration altogether. She looked so...*edible*...standing there, her silvery eyes glowing as she looked into his.

'Nell is keeping watch. If anyone looks like they might venture outside, she will come out quickly and join us.'

He scanned the windows. Sure enough, he

could see Lady Helena, her back to the window as she faced the room.

'It is still an unnecessary risk. Why did you follow me out here?'

'Why?' Her voice rose. 'Because I—' She stopped and he saw her bring herself back under control. His heart ached for her, but he would do nothing to foster false hope in her. When she spoke again her words were measured, the only sign of agitation a crease between her dark brows. 'I wanted to see you. I *needed* to see you.'

Hugo rubbed his hand across his jaw. She appeared to believe herself equal to anything. How on earth could he get through to her that she must take better care of her reputation?

'That is no reason. You know the ways of our world—it is scandalous for us to meet unchaperoned and you would be ruined if we were discovered. You cannot always have what you want, Olivia. You are old enough to understand that.'

'But why not? You are the son of a marquis. I am the daughter of a duke. We are very nearly equal and I assure you I do not aspire to be a duchess.'

'*Even* if I wanted you, it is not a case of our respective births, as you well know.' He swept a hand through his hair in utter frustration. 'My past is sufficient to send any respectable father rushing to barricade his daughter behind locked doors. You must have heard the renewed stories about Rothley and me.'

Lucas's reappearance in society had resurrected all the old tales of wild and scandalous behaviour.

'Those are ancient history.'

'Hey!' He laughed, swatting gently at her. 'Less of the ancient, if you please.'

She laughed back and he battled the urge to sweep her into his arms and to kiss her.

She needs to be protected. From me and from herself.

'I did not mean *you* are ancient, simply that those stories are the past. You are only eight years older than me. It is not so much. Papa is *ten* years older than my new stepmother.'

'And, as your papa would no doubt point out very quickly, I have no prospects.' He would not tell her about Sir Horace's offer of Helmstone—that was way off in the future and would only feed her hope when he must starve it. 'And I am in constant debt—my allowance is paltry. It would be barely enough to keep you in hats, my sweet.'

'I do not care about hats. Or about m-money.'

Only because you have never had to go without either of those things.

He hardened his heart and turned to pace along the terrace and then back to her. 'Besides, you need to understand this—I have no desire for matrimony, not to you or to anyone. I have an enviable life—I answer to no one.'

There was a pause. 'That does not sound enviable to me.' She sounded thoughtful. 'And neither is it true.'

She's right. And it's not true.

But they were words he could not say. He cocked a haughty brow in reply, but she merely shook her head at him.

'If you answer to no one, it implies you have no one to care about you and no one that you care for. And yet you have your mother and your stepfather. And your brother and his wife. And me.'

And if only that *were true.*

He waved his arm. 'Unnecessary emotional baggage. And unwanted.'

'I do not believe you.' She placed her hand on his chest and his heart twitched at the gentle pressure. 'You have changed. The man in those stories…that is not who you are now.'

Why would she not listen? What she wanted… what she asked…it was impossible.

'What is it you want from me?' The words burst from him. He swung around and braced his hands on the balustrade, leaning his weight on them as his chest heaved with each tortured breath. He swung round to face her. 'Should I take you to my bed? Is *that* what you want? Because that is where we are heading if you do not stop this. There is only so much I can take, only so many times I can resist you and what you offer.'

His fury subsided as he took in her stricken expression…the pale hand that rose to splay across her chest…the movement of her slender throat as she visibly swallowed. He steeled himself against the longing to haul her close—to hold her and soothe away her pain—as he glared down into her silver-grey eyes.

'You *must* stop this for both our sakes.' She visibly flinched at his harsh words. 'The only future acceptable for a lady of your breeding is marriage and I am *not* the marrying kind.' He could resist touching her no longer and reached for her hands as he gentled his voice. 'If you continue to contrive such clandestine meetings it can only be a matter of time before we are caught. You will bring shame on your family and ruin upon yourself and all for nothing. You *know* your father would never, ever countenance a match between us and *I* know you would accept nothing less than marriage, despite appearances to the contrary.'

She bent her head at that, staring down at their joined hands. Then a single teardrop splashed on his skin.

'But I cannot help myself,' she whispered. 'I long to spend time with you and you will barely even acknowledge me when anyone else is around. What am I supposed to do?'

'You are *supposed* to remember your upbringing and what is expected of you as the daughter of a duke. You are *supposed* to conform to society's edicts. You are *supposed* to be the perfect young lady and to marry appropriately when the time comes.'

'So I am expected to wait patiently and never even *try* to follow my heart simply because I was born a woman? It's not fair.'

'Life *isn't* fair.'

The truth of that ripped at him, leaving him raw and vulnerable as the memory of his father and his violent childhood loomed large.

A sob tore from her. 'But I love you. And do not tell me that I am too young to know what love is.' She tilted her face to his, tears spilling. 'I am *not* too young to know how I feel and I am woman enough to recognise how you feel about me. I might lack certain experience, but I am wise enough to know that if you did not care for me, you would have tried to bed me long ago. But you did not. Instead, you have done your utmost to protect me—not only from the folly of my own actions, but also from *yourself.*'

He stiffened, then stepped back, flinging her hands from his as he hardened his heart, knowing he must, once and for all, make her *believe* he did not care.

'You have no experience in what goes on between a man and a woman,' he said through clenched teeth. 'You are a beautiful and desirable young lady and I respond to you as a man would to *any* such woman. You are too young and too inexperienced to distinguish between lust and love and your naivety will lead you into trouble if you do not grow up very quickly. *Stay away from me.*'

He fought to maintain his forbidding frown as she touched his mouth, the pad of her thumb drifting across his lips. She lowered her hand and stepped back and he suffered the bleak reality of loss.

She stood tall.

Proud.

Every inch the daughter of a duke.

'Very well. You have made your position clear. It is time to accept I cannot always have what I want and I must stop making this impossible for us both.' The sadness in her eyes tore at his heart. She removed a small drawstring bag that had dangled from her left wrist and thrust it at him. 'This is the last of the money I owe you.'

She turned away and walked to the salon window where she paused for a minute and raised her gloved hands to her face, patting at her cheeks. Then, back straight, she disappeared into the salon, as the opening strains of an aria from *The Magic Flute* drifted out of the open windows into the night.

It was the outcome he had planned, so why then did he feel so wretched? It wasn't just her tears—although they had tugged at his heartstrings. How he felt now was not even about Olivia, as such. It was about him. His feelings weren't the result of guilt or shame that he had upset her. This tearing, heart-wrenching desolation was for himself. It was pure misery. It was the knowledge that he had just sent away the woman he loved with his whole heart and being, and it was the deep gut-wrenching knowledge that he could do not one damn thing about it. He would have to continue his life without her.

He waited ten minutes before following her inside and resuming his seat at the back of the room. The only person who noticed him slip back into his chair was his mother and his heart sank as her beady gaze wandered from him to Olivia, who had regained her seat at the front of the audience. His mother might believe she was being discreet, but he knew her only too well and she had clearly taken note of both Olivia's and his absence and would be, without a doubt, drawing her own conclusions.

After the final song Catalani finished to huge applause, with the audience on their feet. She lapped up the adulation as her due, bowing and smiling graciously.

Hugo kept an eye on Olivia as the guests again mingled while waiting for supper to be served. Although she conversed with others easily enough she was clearly unhappy, earning her worried looks from both her father and her aunt. He set his jaw. There was no more he could do. Olivia would get over her infatuation with him eventually.

As for what he felt for her…his feelings were so muddled he could no longer think straight. If he had ever thought in the past about permanence…marriage…it had been a thought speedily dismissed. The memories of his father had ensured that. He wanted none of that misery. And he—like Lucas, until he had fallen in love with his Mary—had vowed never to wed.

And now? If he could stand aside and counsel himself, his advice would be to stay well away from Olivia, despite—if he were brutally honest—suspecting that what he was suffering from was not unrequited lust but something much, much more profound.

Love.

The word crept into his thoughts. Swelled his heart. Made his pulse pound and sweat prickle his back. Could it be? For either of them? For despite what Olivia had said, he could not believe she knew what love was. Hell, *he* did not know what love was and he was eight years older than her.

He sat with his family to eat supper and Olivia sat with hers. After ascertaining her whereabouts he did not look in that direction again, but mindlessly ate his food as the conversation washed over him. Then a shadow fell across him and the talk at the table ceased. He looked up, straight into the silvery gaze of the Duke.

'Might I have a word, Alastair?'

'Of course.'

Hugo pushed back his chair and stood, wondering what on earth Cheriton wanted with him. He followed him out on to the terrace.

'I wanted to thank you for what you have done for Alexander.'

The breath left his lungs in a silent gust of relief. He'd steeled himself against an accusation about Olivia, certain someone had seen them earlier and told her father. He silently reiterated his vow to keep his distance. This man standing before him—a hugely powerful man used to commanding his world—would want more for his beloved daughter than a cynical, world-weary rake of a second son with only his stepfather's goodwill, which could be withdrawn at any time, to secure his future.

Hell, of course she deserves better than me. All that youth, beauty and innocence...she deserves the very best in the land.

'How did you know?'

'Sir Horace has been regaling me with tales of the wonders Alex has wrought with that mare. He told me it was your idea and, again, I thank you for thinking of it.'

He thrust out his hand and Hugo shook it. Then he took a huge breath. He owed Olivia this much. He would avoid her, for both their sakes, but someone needed to continue to watch over her.

'That matter we spoke of once before,' he said.

The Duke frowned. 'Clevedon? I have spoken to my daughter. She has shown no interest in the man so you do not need to concern yourself further, Alastair.'

'But Clevedon still has an interest. You sh—'

He fell silent as Cheriton lifted his hand, palm facing Hugo.

'It is a family matter, Alastair. My sister is home now and, between us, you may rest assured my daughter has all the protection she needs.'

The Duke nodded, swung around and strode back to the house, leaving Hugo frustrated that he had not put his case more clearly.

Olivia waited until she was alone in her bed that night. Until then, she went through the motions and behaved as though there was nothing amiss, shrugging aside Nell's anxious enquiry about what she had said to Hugo. And what he had said to her. Nell, at least, would be relieved. She would no longer be asked to cover for Olivia while she pursued her silly childish daydream of an all-time love with Lord Hugo Alastair.

Once alone in her bed, however, she relived that final interview and, though her heart felt as though it was being shredded with the sharpest of claws, she knew she must grow up and accept that Hugo simply did not want her—not in the way she had dreamt of, anyway. That had been a fantasy of her own making. And she would not be his lover—she could never follow that path, not even for him.

So she lay in her bed and she did not allow herself to shrink from facing up to her stupid juvenile behaviour. It was the least she could do. She must accept that she could not have what she wanted simply by force of will. Real life wasn't like that. Other people, such as Hugo, had opinions and desires and needs and expectations, just as she did. And she must respect all those things, even though they differed from hers.

She had asked him once, teasingly, if she goaded him. Now she knew the answer.

She heard again the helpless fury in his outburst. *What is it you want from me?* She pictured again his haunted eyes in haggard features. She had pushed him too far. Did she never learn? She had always done the same with her brothers... badgered them until, finally, they lost their tempers. Or gave in.

And then, as she had struggled to control the emotions that threatened to choke her, his anger had receded, revealing a glimpse of tenderness as he had taken her hands. But it had been an implacable tenderness. He had been resolute and—she now realised—she respected him more for that inner strength. The same solid aching lump filled her throat now as then.

She must move on from believing that, if only she persisted, Hugo would come to realise the depth of his feelings for her and find some way for them to be together. She could not force him to feel more for her than he did and, besides, a miracle would be needed for her father to consider a man like Hugo as a suitable son-in-law. Dominic was right—she must stop trying to manipulate everyone in the hope they would eventually give in and see things her way. She must stand back and allow others to do as they wish.

She could not blame Hugo for her ridiculous fantasies—it was not his fault she had somehow elevated him to the status of a hero, merely because he had saved her from a horrible situation entirely of her own making.

It was time to face reality and time for her to behave as a woman, not as a girl with foolish daydreams.

Chapter Eighteen

Two days later, Olivia sat on the sofa in the morning room, picking disconsolately at the stitches she had only just set. They were all wrong, just like her life. She sighed.

'Livvy?'

'Yes?' She glanced at Nell, who was sitting on a chair nearby, also sewing. She saw the concern in her friend's violet eyes and her throat thickened. Which made her cross, because it was stupid, blatant self-pity. She bent her head again to concentrate on the handkerchief she was hemming.

'Will you not tell me what is wrong?'

'I am tired.'

Silence reigned. Olivia sighed again. 'I am sorry. I did not mean to snap at you.'

'I do not believe you are simply tired, Liv,' said Nell. 'And I hate to see you so unhappy. Please talk to me. Is it Lord Hugo? What happened the other night? You did not…he did not…?'

Olivia shifted impatiently. 'No. Of course we did not. I am not that foolish.' She bent her head to the handkerchief again and stabbed her needle through the fine lawn. 'Oh, blast it!' She sucked at her finger and cast the handkerchief aside. 'Now I shall have to stop sewing or I shall get blood all over everything.'

Nell reached across for her hand and examined her fingertip. 'It is a mere pinprick. It will soon stop bleeding.'

Unlike my heart.

Her vision blurred.

'Livvy...' Nell rose from her chair and sat next to Olivia, putting her arm around her. 'Is Lord Hugo really worth all this risk?'

The pain in her chest spiked, radiating out. 'I thought he was.'

She hadn't confessed the truth of their conversation at the musical soirée. She had allowed Nell to assume it had been as before—with snatched kisses and murmured endearments. Not that Hugo had ever murmured endearments to her except in her dreams, but she had felt compelled to embellish their meetings somewhat. To make them sound more romantic and less... She scowled down at her lap. If she honestly, truthfully sorted fact from fiction in her head, he had only ever taken what she had offered. Yes, he had resisted taking more than kisses, but not once had he ever uttered words to encourage her instinct that he cared for her on some deep, elemental level. Was she really guilty of allowing her own desires and daydreams to colour reality? The answer, she knew, was yes. Her heart, already bruised and tender, squeezed tight and she bit back a gasp at the pain as tears blurred her vision.

'Olivia?'

The burden of keeping her anguish to herself grew too heavy and she told her friend, in halting terms, the truth of what had happened that night.

'He told me I must stay away from him.' Her tears spilled over. 'Oh, Nell! How can I have been so stupid? I thought I could win him over. I th-th-thought he cared for me, but he does not. Or at least, not enough…not in the same way I care for him. And now…and now…oh, Nell, I cannot face him again.'

'You have no choice, Livvy. You are bound to see him, but you shall ignore him. You are a Beauchamp. You are the Catch of the Season. You shall not even glance in his direction…your orbit flies high above the likes of a disreputable second son.'

Olivia blurted out a sound halfway between a laugh and a sob. 'Oh, Nell. You sound so fierce.'

Nell put her arm around Olivia. 'Whatever you do, do not let him suspect for one moment that you still care. You have more spirit than to let one thoughtless, heartless rake defeat you. Yes, you will see him. But there will be other gentlemen there, too, and you will put on a brave face and you will show Lord Hugo Alastair exactly how popular you are.'

'He already knows. And he does not care.'

This time, Hugo stuck to his promise to himself. He continued to avoid Olivia, declining invitations to events where she was likely to be present. It proved harder than he expected to stay away from her. He could not stop thinking about her, and his mother—as discreet as an elephant in a herd of cows—was not helping.

'Why do you not think of settling down, Hugo?'

'Look how happy and content Lucas is with Mary and the children.'

'I thought maybe there was a hint of something between you and Lady Olivia, son?'

'Now you have Cedar Lodge there is nothing to stop you. It is a perfect place to raise a family.'

'Sir Horace and I would adore having our grandchildren living closer to us. I know it's impossible for Lucas's family, but...'

And she would eye Hugo with her head on one side and those bright eyes of hers until he was almost ready to pack in the whole idea of Cedar Lodge and helping Sir Horace run the Helmstone estates. He did not know how he would stand the entire summer at Helmstone if this was how she kept on. Mama was adamant that Hugo should stay at Helmstone itself and not live on his own out at the Lodge while Lucas and his family were there.

One place he was certain to run into neither his mother nor Olivia was White's. And it was while he was there that Alex slouched across to join him one day.

'Don't often see you in here, Beauchamp,' said Hugo, signalling to a waiter for another glass and a bottle of claret.

'Need a bit of peace to think. Too noisy at home…some crisis or other.'

Hugo stilled. 'Is your sister all right?'

Alex stared. 'Liv? 'Course she's all right. Some ruckus concerning my aunt and—well! That's family business. Not for outsiders.'

Hugo lost interest.

'Why would you think it's about Liv? Have you two fallen out? Not so long ago, you were always skulking around corners together.'

'That,' said Hugo, with as much hauteur as he could muster, 'was when we were desperate to keep you away from Diablo's.'

Alex barked a laugh. 'I don't need telling twice. No fear I'll fall for that again.'

They drank in companionable silence for a while.

'We went over to Foxbourne yesterday,' said Alex. 'My father said that if I stay out of trouble and debt, I can take it on. The house needs a bit of modernisation and I'll move there in September.'

'You've just got to stay away from trouble until then?'

Alex nodded. 'I should thank you for not letting on about that Vauxhall business.'

Hugo shrugged. 'It was nothing. I've been dodging trouble most of my life, so I know what it's like. Although…' He hesitated, but then realised that maybe his experiences might help Alex to realise he wasn't the only one with baggage from the past. 'I've been given a chance at a future now, as well.' He told Alex about Cedar Lodge and Helmstone. 'I sometimes find myself wondering how different I would have been had Sir Horace been my father instead of that…bastard.'

'What was he like, your old man?'

'Evil. A drunkard. Violent. Unpredictable.'

'Is that why you and your brother were so wild?'

Hugo shrugged. 'Yes, I suppose so. But it doesn't work, you know.'

'What doesn't?'

'Wild living. Drink, drugs, gambling, women—they will never fully chase the shadows from your soul. I should know. I tried it long enough.'

And now, the one thing that would finally banish his demons—Olivia—was the one thing he could not have. Hell, if he were her father, he would never let her within half a mile of a creature like him! But only now could he fully admit he loved her; only now, when it was safe to do so because he rarely saw her and never spoke to her.

'Take my advice, Beauchamp. Don't leave it as long as I have to get wise. You love to work with horses, so concentrate all your efforts on making a success of running Foxbourne.'

Alex huffed an uneasy laugh. 'Well, at least I'm trying now to stay away from those vices, though it's deadly dull at times.' Then he brightened. 'That's what I came across to tell you. Sir Horace has invited me to Helmstone for a few weeks, until the Brighton races. Wants me to look at some of his racehorses.'

About to take another mouthful of claret, Hugo slowly lowered his glass and stared at Alex.

'How would you feel about staying with me at Cedar Lodge instead of at Helmstone?'

Mama couldn't possibly quibble with that.

Alex grinned. 'Perfect.'

Olivia watched the grey streets of London slip away as the carriage bowled along the road to Brighton. With each mile her heart grew more leaden. Hugo was back there, in London, and she would not see him again until the spring. No matter how she tried to convince herself that what she felt was an infatuation that would fade, she could not truly believe that.

All she had seen of him since the musical soirée had been fleeting, distant glimpses. It had been painfully obvious he was avoiding her—probably afraid she would force him to kiss her again or some such—and she knew it was for the best, but… She sighed and diverted her thoughts to other matters. She had become quite adept at distracting herself and there had been more than enough happening just within her own family to keep her thoughts from drifting to Hugo more than a dozen or so times a day. So she hardly thought of him at all, really.

The cause of Aunt Cecily's unhappiness had shown up in London in the shape of Zachary Graystoke, the half-Romany son of an earl with whom Cecily had fallen deeply in love. *Their* story had ended happily, with their wedding two days ago. Their marriage, however, meant that Aunt Cecily would no longer be a permanent fixture in Olivia's life and neither would Uncle Vernon. He had returned from his honeymoon with his new wife, Aunt Thea—who was actually lovely, and great fun, even though Olivia had been prepared to thoroughly dislike her for stealing her uncle's heart—but they already had plans to make their home together at Woodbeare, Uncle Vernon's estate in Devonshire—a full fifteen miles from Cheriton Abbey. At least *they* would join the rest of the family in Brighton next week, but now Aunt Cecily and Uncle Zach were away on *their* honeymoon.

Despite Olivia's determination not to be selfish—she truly *was* pleased that both her uncle and her aunt had found such happiness—she still could not help but feel that everyone she loved abandoned her.

Misery squeezed her heart. Mama had found her only daughter boring and now Aunt Cecily was gone. Dominic and Alex—neither of whom were coming to Brighton, preferring instead to visit friends' estates rather than be with their family—found her irritating and of no consequence whatsoever in their lives and her father and her uncle now both had new wives to occupy their time.

She felt like her whole world was crumbling from beneath her feet. Had it all been an illusion? Ever since Mama died, her father, aunt and uncle had been there…her rocks, always on her side, constantly supporting her. But now that solid foundation had shifted and she felt…shaky…vulnerable. She had never before questioned their love for her, but these rapid changes had stirred up doubt. Mama made no secret of her indifference to her only daughter. Were the rest of them simply more adept at hiding their true feelings? Was she as unimportant to them as to her mother?

They would all probably be delighted once she was wed and off their hands, then they could pass all responsibility for her on to her husband and forget all about her.

But that wouldn't be Hugo. Not the man she really, truly wanted with all her heart. Because even *he* dismissed the way she felt as of no importance, setting her aside without a thought… he did not even care enough for her to *try* to persuade Papa…

She swallowed past a hard ball of despair. She had promised herself she would stop hankering after the unattainable, but it was hard. It was heartbreaking. And it was lonely. She battened down that sense that everyone ended up rejecting her, chiding herself for her self-pity. She had so much; she was very fortunate; she should not be so ungrateful.

None of that helped.

She sighed again.

'What is it, Livvy?' Rosalind was watching her with a worried expression from the opposite seat. 'Is the motion of the carriage making you unwell?'

Olivia forced a smile. 'I am quite well, thank you, Stepmama. I am just tired.'

'It has been a long, eventful Season for us all,' said Rosalind. She sighed, a faraway look in her eyes, as though she were reminiscing. '*Most* eventful.' Her attention snapped back to Olivia and Nell. 'I confess I am looking forward to going to Brighton. A daily walk breathing in that bracing sea air will be just the thing—London is growing far too warm and stuffy for my liking.'

'I doubt London will ever fully meet your approval, Ros,' Nell teased. 'Other than that it is the place where you met the love of your life.'

A light blush settled over Rosalind's cheeks and she flashed a warning look at Nell.

'I am sorry if that was inappropriate,' said Nell, 'but you are still my sister, even if you are also Livvy's stepmama. I cannot censor every word that I say.'

'No. I understand that. It is just…it is a difficult adjustment for me, having three stepchildren who are similar ages to my brothers and sister,' said Rosalind with another sigh. 'I feel more like an older sister than a stepmother. Livvy, my dear… I know I cannot take Cecily's place—she has been a mother to you all these years—but I hope you know that I am always here for you, just as I am for Nell.'

'Thank you, Stepmama.' Olivia forced a smile, swallowing down an upwelling of self-pity. Rosalind was kind, but she could never take Aunt Cecily's place. 'The change of scenery in Brighton will probably do us all good. Papa said there are some splendid rides over the South Downs— it will be a pleasant change to be able to gallop Sprite again.'

'Indeed.' Rosalind's face lit with her smile. 'It will be lovely to give Kamal his head again after our sedate outings in the Park.'

Papa had sent their riding horses—including Rosalind's beautiful Arabian gelding, Kamal, and Olivia's Sprite—down to Brighton with the

grooms a few days ago. Olivia felt her spirits lift
a little. There would be plenty to occupy her in
Brighton—far too many new experiences to give
her time to grieve over Hugo.

*Maybe out of sight will mean out of mind. I
must forget him.*

Papa had leased a house on Marine Parade and,
had it not been for her despair at the prospect of
not seeing Hugo again for several months, Olivia
would be completely enchanted by the position of
their short-term home overlooking the beach and
the ocean. The Brighton Season was in full swing,
enlivened by the presence of the Prince of Wales
and his set—not that Olivia had any great desire
to mingle with *them*, because they were, for the
most part, even older than Papa and therefore of
little interest to her even if he *was* the Prince Re-
gent and just about the most important man in
the land. But still they had balls and routs, soi-
rées and theatre outings to attend, the library and
shops to visit, sea bathing to experience for the
first time—to shrieks of delight—and the enjoy-
ment of riding across the Downs that stretched
for miles behind the town.

More than enough to keep any young lady
happy and occupied.

Many of the young gentlemen who had paid
both Olivia and Nell such marked attentions in

London had also repaired to Brighton and so their social commitments were as hectic as ever. Olivia buried her despair beneath a desperate outward gaiety as she tried to pretend—especially to herself—that everything was all right. But, hidden from sight, her insides continued to wind tighter with each day that passed until she felt ready to explode.

She found herself counting the days until they could return home to Cheriton Abbey—at least there she could find some solitude and not feel obliged to paint on a constant happy smile, even though life at home would be very different with no Aunt Cecily and no Uncle Vernon. But it was Hugo she missed most of all. It was not even as though they'd spent that much time together, but in Brighton there was no thrill when she woke up in the morning, wondering if she would see him later. She knew she would not see him. There was nothing to look forward to.

The week after their arrival in Brighton, however, Olivia's bruised heart suddenly somersaulted in her chest at the sight of Hugo, strolling nonchalantly into the ballroom of the assembly rooms at the Castle Tavern. Her blood sang through her veins and her breath stalled. She raised her fan to her face, plying it gently to help hide her reaction and the sudden flush that heated her skin.

He's followed me! He missed me! He's changed his mind!

There were people all around and too many watchful eyes, so she strove to remain casual. She had her pride after all. Not even Nell must know how her hopes flared from nothing to a roaring blaze within a few seconds of that first sighting. He had entered alone and now he prowled the room, bowing and exchanging a word here and there, but never lingering. He was searching.

For her?

Her heart beat a hectic tattoo as she touched Nell on the elbow to gain her attention. She put her lips to Nell's ear.

'Cover for me, Nell. Please.'

Before she had moved two paces, Nell caught her hand. 'Livvy? Where are you going? Please, let me come with you. Do not take any more risks.'

Olivia clutched Nell's hand between both of hers. 'No. Stay here, please. You have my word I will not leave the building. There is someone I need to speak to, but I will not take any risks, I promise.'

She gave that reassurance without a qualm—she knew beyond any doubt that Hugo would not harm her and there was therefore no risk at all.

'Very well. But for fifteen minutes only. After that, I shall find your papa and tell him you have disappeared. And I am certain you do not wish me to do that.'

'Thank you, Nell. You are the best friend ever.'

Chapter Nineteen

Olivia squeezed Nell's hand before releasing it, then she strolled around the room until she could see Hugo again and could be sure he had seen her. But she would remember her vow and let him take the lead. No longer would she pursue her dream unless she was certain it was his dream as well. And so she waited as he crossed to her side, her pulse racing with pure delight at the sight of him—tall, dark and slightly dangerous-looking in his black evening clothes. She carefully concealed that delight as she bobbed her head in greeting.

'Good evening, Lord Hugo. I am surprised to see you here. I was not aware you had plans to visit Brighton this summer.'

He bowed, then passed a hand around the back of his neck as though he were uneasy. He did not even smile at her, but merely looked bored. Her joyous optimism dimmed somewhat.

'I had no intention of coming into town, but Alex told me that Clevedon is here.'

It was true that Lord Clevedon was in town, but...

'Alex?' Olivia frowned. 'But he is not in Brighton.'

'He comes in from time to time. He is staying with me, at my house on Sir Horace's estate. It is on the western outskirts of town.'

So the friend Alex was staying with was *Hugo*? Her thoughts whirled as she processed these new facts. These *secrets*. She had known Sir Horace had an estate in Sussex, but she'd had no idea it was so close to Brighton. And she'd no idea Hugo had his own house. Or that he would be in the area during the summer.

Her happiness dipped even lower.

'Alex has been advising my stepfather about his racehorses,' he continued. 'They have become quite close.'

'But...he has not visited us. I thought...well, I did not think he was so close to Brighton. He did not tell me.'

And neither did you. The suspicion she was an utter fool began to take hold of her. *You knew I was coming to Brighton and yet you never mentioned you would be nearby.*

'He is keeping a low profile as far as your father is concerned and he's trying hard to stay away from temptation. After they went to Foxbourne a couple of weeks ago, Alex was left in no doubt that if he gets into any more trouble or debt your father will put a manager in there.' Hugo scratched his jaw, frowning. 'I did not come here to talk about your brother. Come, let us walk as we talk. It will be less likely to be remarked upon.'

Without waiting for her reply, he began to stroll. He did not even proffer his arm. Resentment began to simmer, deep down inside, as she sensed his purpose in seeking her out was not for the pleasure of her company but to—yet again— lecture her.

'Alex has been into town a time or two to meet up with Neville Wolfe, which is when he saw Clevedon.'

Olivia put her nose in the air. 'I fail to see why Lord Clevedon should concern you, sir.'

As it happened, her time had been so fully occupied she had barely noticed Clevedon's presence in Brighton, but the sea would freeze over before she admitted as much to Hugo. She might not have spoken for all the notice he took.

'You should beware of him. He is not what he seems.'

'That he is a friend of *yours* is warning enough, I assure you.'

Again, she may as well not have spoken.

'You must not encourage him. He has only followed you here because he is desperate.'

'Desperate enough to want me? I see.' Olivia

dipped a small curtsy. 'Thank you for revealing your true opinion of me, sir.'

His voice deepened. 'Olivia. You know that is not what I meant.'

Her entire being responded to that deepened tone with a quiver, enraging her all the more. She raised her chin.

'It is *Lady* Olivia to you, sir. And I shall speak to whomever I choose, whether or not that might be construed as encouragement by a random casual observer such as yourself. In fact, if I choose to flirt outrageously with his lordship, I shall do so with no compunction whatsoever and certainly without consideration as to *your* opinion in the matter.'

Hugo thrust a hand through his hair. 'Please. Take care. Talk to him by all means—you will come to no harm as long as you conduct yourself as the proper young lady you were raised to be. But be on your guard. I have told you before, you must take care around men of his ilk. You are too innocent to know what could happen when such men are driven to desperation.'

'How dare you!' Olivia kept her voice low, but she was utterly furious. By what right did he lecture her? Far from encouraging her to be careful, his lecture goaded her into throwing caution to the wind and be damned. 'Your opinion, sir, is nothing to me. You are not a member of my family and you have no right to even *comment* upon how I conduct myself.'

She felt tears of rage scald behind her eyes, but she gritted her teeth. She would never reveal the utter agony erupting inside her, nor the fury—this time with herself—for having allowed hope to blossom yet again.

He doesn't want me, but he doesn't want anyone else to have me either.

Either that, whispered a snide voice in her head, or he thinks you aren't good enough for his friend.

'You, sir, are despicable. You denounce a friend behind his back. You steal kisses when it suits you and then you have the gall to lecture *me* about proper conduct? I never, ever wish to speak to you again.'

Olivia whirled on her heel and stalked away, heading for the ladies' retiring room where she might regain her composure. As she walked, she became aware—from the curious looks she attracted—that she was scowling and that her teeth and her hands were all clenched tight. She hauled in a deep breath and forced herself to relax. She slowed her pace and again made use of her fan to mask her expression and to waft cooling air across her hot face.

'It is a wonder you did not snap your fan, my lady, your grip was so intense.' The amused drawl in her ear brought her to a halt. Lord Clevedon bowed, his smile sympathetic. 'And that would have been a shame…it is a very pretty fan.'

Olivia halted, mortified that anyone, let alone Clevedon, should have witnessed her fury. Behind him, she glimpsed Lord Sudbury strolling away.

'What has put you in such a rage? I am always willing to provide a sympathetic ear…perhaps you would care to join me in the tea room for refreshment?'

I'll show Hugo how little his warnings signify!

'Thank you, sir. That would be most pleasant.'

She hoped devoutly that Hugo was watching as Clevedon settled her at a table and signalled to a waiter to bring tea.

'Would you care to share your concerns? Is your brother in trouble again? Really…' He hesitated, and Olivia raised her brows. 'This,' he went on, 'is not a subject I would normally mention to a lady but I know how you have tried so hard to keep Alex out of debt and I know you must be desperately worried to think he will now lose Foxbourne Manor. He is so very much looking forward to it, is he not? I am sure it will break his heart when your father carries out his threat to put in a manager instead.'

The shock knocked all thoughts of Hugo and his duplicity from Olivia's mind.

'What…? I fail to understand, sir. Are you telling me that Alex has run up more gambling debts?'

Dear God, Papa will be furious, especially after Alex promised him so faithfully.

The very thought of the consequences brought sour, scorching bile into her throat.

This will tear our family apart even more.

'I am so sorry, my lady.' Clevedon looked contrite. 'I saw you with Alastair just now and I assumed he had apprised you of Alex's latest troubles and that was the cause of your anger. I see now I was mistaken. Please forgive me.'

So Hugo knows Alex is in debt again and he did not see fit to warn me?

Anger and resentment swelled. He was as bad as the rest of her family—assuming that she was too young and too delicate to handle the stark truth.

Clevedon sipped his tea, casting his gaze around the room. 'I am pleased to have this opportunity for a quiet chat, my dear. You are so very popular, it is difficult to snatch a few moments of your time. Tell me, how you are enjoying your first visit to Brighton?'

'Very much so, sir.' She recalled Hugo's claim that Clevedon had only come to Brighton in pursuit of her. 'And you, sir? Are you a regular visitor?'

'Oh, indeed. I come every year, for the sea air and for the races.'

So you are wrong, Lord Know-It-All Alastair. But proving him wrong did nothing to quell the deep rage that rumbled inside her and neither did it relieve the ache in her heart. She wrenched her traitorous thoughts away from that untrustworthy rogue.

'Lord Clevedon?'

'Yes, my lady?'

'Will you tell me how much money Alex owes and to whom?'

Clevedon straightened. 'I cannot—'

Olivia held up her hand to silence him. She leaned forward slightly and lowered her voice. '*Please?* I know all about gentlemen not discussing such matters with ladies, but Alex has always confided in me. I want to help him—' *I must help him. I have to keep what's left of my family together* '—but to do that I need to know the worst.'

'And what could you do to help even if I did tell you?'

'I have some of my allowance left.' Not much, after repaying Hugo what she owed, but she did have some. 'Or I could appeal to the gentleman concerned to give Alex more time to pay.'

'I did offer him additional time, but—'

'*You* offered him? You mean to tell me that Alex is in debt to you?'

Clevedon gave her a rueful smile. 'I am more sorry than I can say, my lady. I promise you I tried to dissuade him from continuing to play once he began to lose, but he would not listen to me. The others at the table had no idea of what was at stake, which is why I bought up all his vowels at the end of the night.'

She felt sick. 'How…how much?'

'Close to five thousand guineas, I'm afraid.'

Her head swam and she pressed her fingers to her temple. 'Dear God.' She looked up at Clevedon. 'But…you will give him more time to settle his debt, my lord? I am persuaded you will.'

'Unfortunately, it is a matter of honour for a gentleman to pay his gambling debts immediately and Alex is a proud young man and *most* stubborn. He would accept no longer than two days—until tomorrow at six o'clock. If he is unable to raise the funds, I believe it is his intention to admit the truth to your father.'

'Alex will never find that amount of money in so short a time.'

'Gambling.' Clevedon sighed. 'It is the ruin of so many in our society. It truly is a curse. I feel a sense of shame that I have somehow contributed to your brother's downfall although, as I said, I really did try to discourage him from continuing once he had plunged deep. I wish there was a way I could help that might prove acceptable to Alex. Waiving the debt is not an option, I fear.'

'There must be a way.' Olivia sank into thought. 'I wonder…?'

She looked up.

'You might feel this is a risk after our little… er…encounter at Vauxhall Gardens.'

She gasped, feeling the blood drain from her face. 'But…you did not know that was me.'

'Not at the time or, of course, I should have behaved very differently,' he said. 'But I hope my subsequent action in persuading Alastair to return the necklace to you—and the fact that your little adventure has remained a secret—will persuade you that I am to be trusted?'

Her stomach churned at the knowledge that all the time Clevedon had courted her in London, he was fully aware of what she had done. But he was right. He *had* returned her necklace and he had also kept her secret. She should give him credit for that.

'Go on.'

'I propose a small wager, just between us.'

Olivia's heart quailed. 'I do not wish to play piquet again.'

'No, of course not. Now, let me think. Ah… I believe I have it. Do you have your riding horse here in Brighton?'

'Sprite? Yes. Papa had the horses sent down from London.'

'Perfect. As we are here for the horse races next week, it seems appropriate that we might settle this wager with a race between the two of us. Our horses should be well matched. You have seen my fellow in Hyde Park. He has the longer stride, but I'll warrant your little mare can fly when given her head.'

'She goes like the wind,' said Olivia proudly. She studied Clevedon. 'What wager do you propose?'

He shrugged. 'I am feeling magnanimous. If you win, I shall hand over Alex's vowels.'

'And if I lose?'

He smiled. 'One kiss. That is all.'

It sounded too good to be true. Olivia was completely confident in her riding prowess and in Sprite's ability to outrun Clevedon's lumbering nag. Plus, she would be on horseback—completely safe from any attempt by Clevedon to corner her. It would be lily-livered, surely, to refuse the challenge? Except…

'But I thought *you* were in debt? Such a sum of money…' Her voice trailed into silence as she took in his thundering frown.

'Where did you hear such a slander?'

'I… I… I do not recall. Is it untrue, then?'

'Of course it is. I have no debts other than to a few tradesmen. Certainly nothing to worry over and nothing like that sum.'

Olivia hung her head. 'I am sorry.'

'You are forgiven. What others say is hardly your fault, but you should not believe all you hear. There are any number of people out there who delight in making mischief by embellishing the facts.'

She did not believe Hugo was that sort of man. Although what, truly, did she know about him?

He has always treated you with respect and kindness. Always.

Except he kissed me and then rejected me.

Qualms churned her stomach over what she was about to agree to, but her anger over Hugo's treatment of her and her fear for the future of her family spurred her on.

'Where do we race and when?'

'It will have to be tomorrow, before Alex is driven to admitting his latest folly to your father. Will you be able to get away?'

'I…yes, I believe so.'

They were due to go on a picnic ride tomorrow with Uncle Vernon and Aunt Thea, newly arrived in Brighton. She could feign illness and then, after the others had ridden off, tell the grooms she felt better and would catch up with the party.

'I can be ready just after three o'clock.'

She explained about the picnic ride to Whitehawk Down, where they had planned to ride around the racecourse before the races next week and then go further up on to the Downs to have a gallop and enjoy the spectacular views over the coastline and the sea. Olivia had been looking forward to the outing, but she was willing to sacrifice her pleasure if it saved Alex.

'We should go the other way then. Allow me to think.' Clevedon stared down at his teacup for a few minutes. 'I have it. Have you seen the chalk pit near to St Nicholas's Church?'

'Yes.'

'We shall meet there, at the end of the pit furthest from the town. Our course will head across country, up the hill to the north of the church. There is a windmill up there…do you know it?'

'I do.'

Olivia had noticed that windmill last week when she had ridden past it with her family, on an outing to see the Devil's Dyke—a scenic V-shaped valley popular as an excursion with visitors to Brighton.

'Good. So we race up the hill to the windmill, we ride around it and then head west, towards a stone barn you will see in the distance. We ride straight across the road that leads out to Devil's Dyke and then, when we reach the barn, we ride around it before heading back down to the town along the carriage way that runs past the barn. The first back to the church is the winner.'

Olivia frowned as she committed the course to memory.

Clevedon smirked. 'You need not fear you will get lost—you merely need to follow me.'

'Then it is fortunate that I fear no such thing,' she retorted, 'for *I* shall be in the lead. Sprite and I will be showing you a clean pair of heels, you mark my words.'

'Livvy?'

Olivia twisted around at the sound of her name. She had been so engrossed she'd forgotten the time and Nell, worry furrowing her brow, had clearly been searching for her. She put her lips to Olivia's ear. 'Fifteen minutes! We agreed.'

Olivia stood up. Clevedon was already on his feet. 'Thank you for the tea, sir. I feel greatly refreshed now. I shall remember what you said.'

As she and Nell made their way back to the ballroom, she scanned the surrounding faces for Hugo, but there was no sign of him.

The following day was bright and sunny, with a blustery wind blowing inshore. As the time for the race approached Olivia grew more and more nervous, but her pride—coupled with her concern over Alex and the impact on the family if he were to be denied Foxbourne—would not allow her to back out, or simply fail to turn up. She wondered what Alex was thinking. Was he worried sick about admitting what he had done to Papa? She could only imagine the pressure he must feel watching the clock slowly tick nearer and nearer to six o'clock. Eventually, just before two o'clock, she came to a decision. She dashed off a note to Alex, telling him not to worry because his debts would soon be clear. *That* would set his mind at rest. She even jokingly suggested that he might come to the church to cheer her to the finishing line.

After writing to Alex, Olivia dressed in her riding habit and tucked the letter into her pocket. She would wait until everyone had gone before sending one of the grooms to deliver it. Uncle Vernon and Aunt Thea had arrived by the time she came downstairs, but then Papa announced he was unable to accompany them—kept at home by urgent business requiring his immediate attention—a complication Olivia could have done without. He disappeared into a parlour he had commandeered as an office—along with Freddie and Medland, his man of business, who had posted down from London with important papers—before the grooms brought their horses to the door.

'Ooh!' Olivia bent slightly, holding her stomach as she groaned. 'Argh!'

'Livvy?' Rosalind was by her side in a trice. 'What is wrong? Have you a pain?'

Olivia nodded, then gasped again for good measure.

'Perhaps we should postpone our outing,' said Uncle Vernon. 'With Leo not able to go and now Livvy not well…someone should surely stay with her?'

'No! I shall be all right,' said Livvy hurriedly.

She caught Rosalind's eye and endeavoured to inject special meaning into her look.

'Oh. Yes, of course,' said Rosalind. 'I had not realised…that is…yes, you go and lie down, Livvy. I am sure it will pass soon enough.'

From the corner of her eye, Livvy saw Aunt Thea tug at Uncle Vernon to get his attention.

He bent to her as she whispered into his ear. His cheeks reddened a little and he straightened quickly—women's problems weren't normally even mentioned within a gentleman's hearing, but dear Aunt Thea—not a member of the aristocracy, but a humble glassmaker's daughter—probably didn't realise her faux pas.

Nell was the only one present not to regard her with sympathy. She, instead, sent Olivia a searching look; she knew full well that Olivia's courses were not yet due. But, fortunately, she said nothing and everyone soon left the hall, leaving Olivia behind. She listened for the clatter of hooves as the party rode away—they were accompanied by grooms to care for the horses when they stopped for their afternoon picnic—and some of the indoor servants would follow in a carriage with the food and drink. As soon as she judged it safe, Olivia sped from the house and caught up with Tommy, one of the younger lads, who was leading Sprite back to the stables.

'Wait!'

'Yes, milady?'

'I have changed my mind and I shall go with the others after all. Help me up, will you, Tommy?'

'Do you want me to ride with you, milady? You shouldn't ride alone.'

Olivia waved an airy hand. 'That will not be necessary. It will take me a matter of minutes to catch them up. In the meantime, though, I have an errand for you.' She delved into her pocket and handed him the letter. 'Please deliver this to Lord Alex. He is staying at—' She hesitated as she realised she knew neither the name of Hugo's house nor that of Sir Horace's estate.

'I know where he's staying, milady—Cedar Lodge on the Helmstone estate. It's but a short way out of town. I can be there and back fast enough.'

'Very good, Tommy, and thank you. But make sure you only hand it to my brother. Do you understand?'

She certainly didn't want Hugo getting his hands on it. She wouldn't put it past him to turn up and spoil the race out of some misguided sense of propriety. In fact, she now deeply regretted telling Alex the route of their race. At the time she'd thought only to amuse him with the idea of her beating Clevedon in a contest across country.

Tommy touched the peak of his cap and then linked his hands to boost Olivia on to Sprite's back.

'Are you sure you'll be all right on your own, milady?'

'Of course I shall. This isn't London, after all.'

Chapter Twenty

Olivia rode up a side street, away from Marine Parade—where she might see someone she knew—and then turned along St James's Street. She trotted Sprite briskly across the Steyne and into North Street, which would take her to the chalk pit and St Nicholas's Church. Apart from one or two curious stares—all from strangers and, by their appearance, townsfolk—no one took any notice of her, much to her relief.

Clevedon was waiting for her, as arranged, a smile on his face. Olivia quashed any lingering doubts as she eyed his grey gelding. There was no way that animal could outrun Sprite. He barely looked fit enough to gallop a furlong, let alone a mile or more. They rode side by side until they turned off the road.

'When you are ready, say the word and the race will be on.'

Olivia slid a sideways look at Clevedon and

quashed the uneasy feeling coiling deep inside. There was nothing he could do to her. She could see the windmill up the hill ahead of her and, in the distance, away off to the left, she could see a stone building, flanked by a huge tree.

'Is that the barn you spoke of?'

'It is.'

'Very well then. Are you ready…? Go!'

By the time they reached the windmill, Sprite was pulling ahead of Clevedon's grey, who was puffing hard. Now was the time to build a lead, before the grey could recover his wind. The final, downhill stretch would favour his longer stride— although Sprite was the more nimble animal which would prove an advantage. As she steered Sprite around the windmill, Olivia glanced back over her shoulder. The grey was not as far behind as she would have liked and she urged Sprite on, setting her in a straight line for the barn in the distance. Fortunately the Devil's Dyke road, as they crossed it, was clear of traffic and a quick scan of the surrounding countryside showed it to be devoid of human life.

With any luck, she would get away with this and no one would be any the wiser.

She leaned forward to urge Sprite to greater effort. At this angle, if she lifted her gaze, she could see the sea, the sun creating a lattice of sparkles on the waves whipped up by the wind.

There was no time to sightsee, however. She had a race to win.

Another glance behind. Good. She was now four or five lengths clear of the grey, whose neck and chest were dark with sweat.

The barn ahead was an imposing stone building with a clay-tiled roof, built by the side of a curving carriageway and overhung by that massive tree, an oak. As Sprite drew level with the barn, Olivia steadied her, ready to steer her around the far end and begin the last leg of the race back down to the church.

'Aaaargghhhh!'

Her heart, already racing with exhilaration, leapt into her throat and she flicked another glance behind.

'Oh, no!'

She reined Sprite to a halt and jumped to the ground before running back to the prone figure of the Earl of Clevedon. She slid to a halt and dropped to her knees.

'My lord! Clevedon!' She grabbed his shoulders and shook him. 'Are you all right?'

His eyes flew open and, before Olivia could reassemble her wits, he had grabbed her wrists.

'What?' She tugged and twisted to no avail as she attempted to scramble back, away from him. 'Let go of me!'

He sat up, his hard grip not slackening for a

moment. Then he leapt to his feet, still holding on to her.

'Calm yourself. You might as well accept this—there is no one here to save you and—' he dragged her close and wrapped one arm around her waist '—as you can see, your strength is no match for mine.'

Olivia stopped struggling at his words, knowing he was right. She fought to control her breathing and stiffened her spine. She would not show her fear. 'What is the purpose of this, my lord?' Her voice dripped scorn. 'You realised you could not win and thought to take a kiss anyway?'

He threw his head back and laughed. 'A kiss, my precious, is the least of my intentions. By tomorrow, both you and your arrogant father will be *begging* me to make an honest woman of you. At least you have *some* spirit and you are—' he released her hand to spear his hand through her hair, knocking her hat to the ground '—enticing enough. Let us hope our children will inherit those traits.'

His grip around the back of her skull was like iron, holding her head immobile as he kissed her. His thick tongue invaded her mouth and it was all she could do not to gag. Then his other hand slid low, to cup her bottom, and she felt him pull at her skirt, gathering it, until his hand was on her skin and one finger traced the crease between her cheeks.

He slid his mouth around to her ear. 'Yes,' he whispered. 'Enticing enough. We shall do very well and your dowry will pay off Bulbridge and his blood-sucking leeches.'

Sick dread coiled in her stomach. What he planned...the thought of being...*intimate*...with *him*...

His mouth again covered hers and, as he continued to fondle her bottom, she battled to control her nausea, swallowing repeatedly to keep the contents of her stomach down, fearing the consequence were she to succumb to the urge to vomit.

She listened, hoping against hope to hear a horse or a carriage passing by. Something. Anything. But the only sound was the wind as it whipped through the branches and leaves of that oak tree. Her mind went shooting off at tangents as she silently berated herself for landing in such a stupidly risky position. This was what everyone had warned her of—Papa, Aunt Cecily, Nell. Even Hugo... Her heart shredded at the thought of him and her throat thickened with unshed tears. They had warned her of the consequences of her impetuous behaviour, but she had thought she was up to every trick in the book. She'd thought she could handle everything.

Realising that the fear spiralling through her would effectively paralyse her, she desperately tried to divert her thoughts away from what *might* happen and to concentrate on what was actually happening at this moment. Her thoughts whirled, seeking a way out. If she could keep him talking, maybe she could escape him, but that would only be by cunning for he was right—she was no match for him physically, a fact brought home to her as he began to drag her towards the barn, his arm yet again wrapped tightly around her waist.

Olivia resisted at first but, realising that would get her nowhere, she relaxed, going with him. Surprised, Clevedon paused. He frowned down at her.

'There is something I wish to say.'

Olivia injected as much ice as possible into her words and put her nose in the air, playing the outraged lady for all she was worth. She moved slightly so she was facing more towards him and, as she had hoped, his arm loosened a little, allowing her the freedom to turn more. She couldn't delay until she was in a better position lest he realise her plan, so she angled her right leg back, then swung it forward hard, bending her knee, aiming at his 'wedding tackle', as Alex called a man's private parts.

She was sure she'd succeed but, at the last minute, Clevedon twisted and her knee connected harmlessly with his hip. She could have cried with frustration as he grabbed her by the upper arms, shaking her. But he wasn't angry, he was grinning.

'As I said, I like spirit, my dear.' Almost casually, it seemed, he raised one hand. 'But I cannot allow such defiance to risk spoiling my plans.'

His palm connected with Olivia's cheek and pain exploded through her head as it whipped sideways with the force of the blow. Tears sprang to her eyes and her tongue exploded in agony where she had bitten it. Her ears rang and a sob tore to the surface, rasping up through her throat, as she felt her knees buckle.

'Clevedon!'

The roar shattered the surrounding silence and Olivia's insides tangled and jumbled together until the only cogent thought in her head was *Hugo*.

Rage the like of which he had never known seized Hugo. As he had galloped along the carriageway that led from Helmstone down to the Dyke road he had seen Olivia fail in her attempt to knee Clevedon in the balls. Then, as he wheeled Falcon around the corner of the barn, the bastard raised his hand and the sound—like a whip crack—ricocheted through Hugo as Clevedon hit Olivia. Her head jerked sideways with the force of that blow and she slumped. Some deep, primal instinct surged to the surface as, yelling his challenge, he hauled on the reins and leapt from the saddle even before his horse stopped.

He was in no mood for talk or explanations. He grabbed Clevedon by the shoulder, hauled him around as his right arm, fist clenched, drew back.

And paused. Clevedon, in that split second, hefted Olivia to her feet and held her in front of him, his forearm crooked around her slender neck. Her beautiful silver eyes—always so full of sparkling life—were dazed and her smooth, delicate skin was imprinted with an angry red mark the shape of a hand. She looked horribly vulnerable and his heart clenched.

'Let go of her.'

His breathing came in hard, shallow pants. Fear clutched at his gut, but he ignored it. She was hurt, but she was alive. Nothing worse would happen to her now he was here. He vowed that his life from this point on would be spent protecting her. Loving her.

'You've failed, Clevedon. Let her go.'

Clevedon's lip curled. 'What is she to you, Alastair? You barely know the chit. And you were the one who suggested I court her in the first place.' He moved back a pace, dragging her with him. 'I need her. I need the money. She has to marry some time—popping out brats is all women are good for and she may as well pop out mine as anyone's.'

All the rage that had fired him up—that flaming, explosive rage—swirled tighter and faster, spinning around a point deep in his core where fury was coalescing into a cold, hard, solid mass. That fury was controlled, but it was a thousand… a million…times more deadly than all that hot, spouting rage. He took a step towards Clevedon and something shifted behind the Earl's eyes— an uncertainty…a shaft of fear…as he held Hugo's gaze.

Hugo closed the gap. Slowly. Relentlessly. Clevedon continued to shuffle backwards, hampered by Olivia as she sagged in his arms.

'Let. Her. Go.'

'What's it to you? What does it matter, if I have her?' Clevedon's voice quavered. '*You* don't want her. Or…is *that* it, Alastair? You fancy that huge dowry for yourself?'

Olivia's eyes had been half-open the entire time. Her drooping lids sprang open at Clevedon's words and her gaze flew to Hugo's face, a distinct question in her eyes, but he was beyond sending reassuring messages, his entire being now a mass of rigid, ice-cold fury. But he saw the instant that she dismissed Clevedon's accusation. She sent him a silent message…of reassurance…of intent… Then she dropped one lid in a wink and Hugo tensed.

Of a sudden, she surged upright and the shock caused Clevedon to momentarily loosen his hold on her neck. As Hugo leapt at them, Olivia jerked her elbow hard into Clevedon's gut and she twisted aside to allow Hugo to drive his fist into Clevedon's face—the solid thwack satisfying as knuckles connected with nose. He hauled Olivia clear as Clevedon sank to his knees.

The pounding of hooves penetrated the churning mix of fury and relief that still raged through him. He glanced back towards the town to see two horsemen galloping at top speed towards them. The Duke was in the lead, with Alex close behind—as soon as Olivia's note had been delivered to Alex, Hugo had guessed Clevedon was up to no good and had sent her brother to alert her father. Olivia, no doubt, would be relieved to be passed into her father's care while Hugo dealt with Clevedon.

The two horses skidded to a halt and first Cheriton, then Alex, jumped down.

'Hugo.'

He glanced down at Olivia's whispered plea. He still had hold of her arm, but one look at her—that handprint still livid on her cheek, stark against her ashen skin—and he forgot all about her father and her brother. She needed him. He released her elbow and opened his arms. She moved into his embrace and laid her head against his chest. As he folded his arms around her, holding her safe, he could feel the trembling of her entire body.

'Alastair—'

That one growled word of warning was cut short as Hugo's mother and Sir Horace hurried out from behind the barn.

'We came as quickly as we could,' said Mama breathlessly. She glared at Clevedon, who had regained his feet and was holding a blood-soaked handkerchief to his nose. 'You utter scoundrel!'

She advanced on him, her small hands clenched into fists. 'If I were a man, I should call you out myself!' She poked him in the chest. 'You should be thoroughly ashamed, plotting to despoil such a lovely young lady in such a despicable way.'

Sir Horace hurried to Mama's side and gently urged her away. 'Allow Hugo and his Grace to deal with him, my love. Come, let us take charge of Lady Olivia. That is why Hugo asked us to follow him, after all.' He shot a look at Hugo. 'You were right. We asked the driver of the carriage waiting by the barn and he told us he was hired to drive a couple to London.'

As Hugo had suspected, Clevedon's plan had moved on from simply entrapping Olivia in a compromising situation. He had now planned to remove Olivia completely from the safety and security of her family until she was so thoroughly compromised there would be no way out other than for the couple to marry. Even a man as powerful as her father would have to concede defeat in those circumstances.

Mama came to Olivia and coaxed her from Hugo's embrace. He wanted to object, but Olivia was better off remaining ignorant of what would come next.

Mama smiled at him reassuringly. 'We will take her back to the house with us. She will be safe.'

He watched them move out of sight, then pivoted on his heel to face Clevedon.

'I shall see you, sir. Name your—'

'Alastair!' Cheriton's hand was on his arm. 'She is *my* daughter. I shall be the one to defend her honour.'

Hugo steeled himself against the imperious demand in that silvery gaze. 'You are too late, Duke. The challenge is issued.'

Fury flashed across Cheriton's face, but Hugo did not care. He thirsted for revenge. He would prefer to beat the man to a pulp, but it was decreed that a duel was the way by which gentlemen of their world settled their differences and he would not behave as other than a gentleman in this matter. Olivia deserved no less.

'Your second, sir?'

Clevedon swayed on his feet, shoulders slumped. 'Sudbury. Yours?'

Hugo raised a brow at Alex but, before he could respond, the Duke astonished him by saying, 'I'll stand as your second, Alastair. Least I can do.'

He crossed to Clevedon and gave him a shove in the direction of the barn. 'Take your bloody carriage and get out of my sight. Have Sudbury call on me at six tonight to make the arrangements.'

As Clevedon stumbled away, Cheriton rubbed at his eyes before facing Hugo and Alex.

'Now, will you two tell me what the *devil* has been going on?'

Alex took a letter from his pocket and handed it to his father. 'Livvy sent me this. I've been staying with Alastair at his house on Sir Horace's estate. It is further along that carriageway.' He pointed.

Cheriton nodded and then unfolded the sheet of paper and read it, his brow furrowed. His chest rose and fell, and he closed his eyes for a second before fixing them on Alex.

'You are in debt again? After everything… all the promises?' He sounded weary, almost defeated, and Hugo's heart went out to him. He might be one of the most powerful and wealthy men in the country, but the estrangement between him and his younger son—which Hugo knew existed, but still didn't fully understand—clearly mattered a great deal to him. 'That, I presume, is why you did not inform me you were staying near Brighton?'

Alex's face flamed. 'It's a damned lie! I owe Clevedon nothing and if Livvy had only had the sense to *ask* me instead of believing that bastard's lies, none of this would have happened.' The corners of his mouth turned down. 'That's typical. You always believe the worst of me.'

Cheriton's lips thinned. 'Then I apologise. I do try not to do so.' Hugo admired the Duke's control of the temper that simmered behind his eyes and the effort it must have taken to humble himself in such a way, especially in front of a virtual stranger. 'Please continue.'

'Tommy delivered the letter and he told us Livvy hadn't gone on the picnic ride with the rest of the family, but had then decided to catch them up. That sounded like a ruse to go and race Clevedon and Hugo here guessed that Clevedon had some plan to either compromise or abduct her.'

Those silver-grey eyes narrowed as the Duke's gaze shifted to Hugo.

'I was aware Clevedon was getting desperate and that he had set his sights on Olivia's dowry.'

'Olivia?'

Cheriton's growl stirred Hugo's temper. He was damned if he would cower in front of the man. If he wanted to call her by her given name, then he damn well would.

'I have been looking out for *Olivia* ever since you dismissed my warnings about the man.'

'Perhaps you should have tried harder. Told me exactly what Clevedon was capable of.'

'Perhaps I would have, had I known,' Hugo retorted.

Alex cleared his throat. 'Alastair,' he said pointedly, 'has just rescued my sister and your daughter, and he *has* been looking out for her *and* helping me while you have been distracted by other family concerns.'

Again, Hugo felt sympathy stir for Cheriton

who, he knew, had been beleaguered by family affairs recently when his sister's half-Romany fiancé had been imprisoned at Newgate. Who could really blame the man for not realising what mischief was brewing in his young daughter's life?

'To continue,' said Alex. 'Tommy told me you hadn't ridden out with the rest of the family, so I rode to fetch you while Hugo headed over to the course to try to intercept them and stop Clevedon from whatever he planned. I don't know how come the Todmordens showed up, though.'

Hugo shrugged. 'That was luck. After Alex and I parted ways, I met Mama and Sir Horace coming back from town. When I explained matters, they told me they had seen a carriage waiting by the barn when they passed by earlier and I asked them to come with me to take charge of Olivia, to protect her reputation.'

Cheriton hauled in a breath. 'I appreciate your forethought and your consideration. I shall fetch Olivia now and take her home and I'll send you word once we have arranged where you will meet Clevedon.' His jaw firmed. Then he stepped forward and grasped Hugo's shoulder. 'Thank you.'

Chapter Twenty-One

Olivia held tight to her self-control until Lady Todmorden showed her into her private parlour and the butler had personally delivered a tea tray. But it took just one kind enquiry as to how she was feeling for her pent-up emotions to burst forth.

Her ladyship clucked sympathetically and sat beside Olivia, putting her arms around her to hold her as she cried. As the flood of tears subsided, she pressed a sensible, man-sized handkerchief into Olivia's hand and left her to mop up while she poured the tea.

'There now.' Lady Todmorden placed a tea-cup on the table beside Olivia. 'You no doubt feel better for a good cry. I know I always do. And a nice cup of tea will set everything right, I am sure. All's well that ends well, after all, my pet.'

Tears leaked again and Olivia dabbed her eyes with the now very damp handkerchief.

'It is all my own fault.' She gulped and then hiccupped. 'I was so certain I would be safe and win the race, and I thought I could save Alex.' She bowed her head as she twisted the handkerchief in her lap. 'Why didn't I listen? I am such a fool. A wicked, headstrong, conceited fool. Hugo warned me about C-Clevedon, but I thought... I th-thought...'

She felt the downward drag at the corners of her mouth as tears bubbled once again. She gritted her teeth hard and breathed strongly through her nose. She would not keep succumbing to bouts of weeping like some...some...silly milksop. But, oh, what a fool she had been indeed. When she thought about what could have happened... Sir Horace had pointed out the carriage that lurked unseen on the far side of the barn. She would never dare listen to that stupid, overly confident voice inside her head ever again.

How could she have made such a ridiculous mistake? How could she have, so mindlessly, taken such a stupid risk? No wonder Hugo wanted nothing to do with her. And on that thought, she promptly burst into tears again and Lady Todmorden once again took her in her arms.

'He thinks I am a s-s-silly little girl,' Olivia wailed. 'And he is right. I am a f-fool and he is quite right not to l-l-love me. But I—'

She stopped on a gasp as her brain caught up with her mouth and she recalled it was Hugo's mother whose shoulder she was drenching with her tears. She pulled away, the shock of having said such a thing out loud stemming her tears more effectively than any kind words.

'Now, now, my pet, I beg you not to work yourself into a lather over Hugo.' Lady Todmorden gathered Olivia's hands in hers. 'I assume that you are talking about that reprehensible son of mine?'

Olivia swallowed, willing her voice to remain steady. 'I am sorry. I should not have said that. I was distraught. Please, forgive—'

'Forgive you?' Through slightly blurred eyes, Olivia saw her ladyship tip her head to one side, a satisfied smile on her face as she scanned Olivia's face with her dark but bright eyes. 'There is nothing to forgive, my pet. Young love is—as I remember it—brutal and heartbreaking at times and then, at others—' her expression became wistful…nostalgic… '—it can make you feel as though you are soaring so effortlessly through the air your feet might never touch the ground again.'

Despite Aunt Cecily's constant reminders to Olivia to curb her curiosity, she could not help but ask, 'Was that with Lord Rothley, ma'am?'

Lady Todmorden started at her words and that wistful air dissipated.

'No. I am sorry to say that my father believed that girls should be biddable and marry whomever they were told to marry. *My* young love had no happy ending, my dear, and Rothley—my father's

choice—was not a kind man, either to his young
wife or to his sons. That is why, if you truly love
him, I advise you to fight for Hugo. Your papa
might disagree, but it is *your* life and you are the
one who must live it.'

Lady Todmorden's spirit kindled Olivia's hopes
until they were dashed all over again as she remembered the truth.

'It is hopeless. Hugo…' She gulped back another bout of tears. 'Hugo does not return my
feelings.'

A dull, hollow ache filled her chest. Then she
stared as Lady Todmorden laughed.

'Nonsense, my pet. Of course he returns your
feelings. I have known that since I saw you both
studiously avoiding one another's eye outside
Gunter's Tea Room *weeks* ago.' She took Olivia's hand again, patting it. 'Let me tell you, my
pet. I have *never* seen my Hugo put himself out
so much for anyone other than for one of his own
family. Do not despair. Although…' She paused
and Olivia waited with bated breath. 'I pointed
out Cedar Lodge as we passed, do you recall?'

Olivia nodded.

'Be very certain that you are prepared to live
in such a modest house. Hugo is not a wealthy
man and after getting into debt in the past, I know
he is determined not to do so in the future. He
stands to inherit Helmstone eventually—although
I hope not for a very long time—but you must be

absolutely sure your love is strong enough to live a much more modest life than that to which you are accustomed.'

'But I have a dowry—' She stopped speaking as her ladyship raised her hand.

'You have a very generous dowry, yes. I am aware of it. But my Hugo is a proud man and it can be difficult for such a man to accept a wife who both outranks him and is wealthier than him.'

'That did not stop Lord Clevedon from wanting to marry me. Although in his case it seems my dowry was the only lure.'

'Ah, but you see, my pet, Lord Clevedon is *not* an honourable man. But an unequal union…a disparity in wealth…*can* be most successful, even taking into account male pride. Only last year my niece—a wealthy peeress in her own right—wed the third son of an earl. Matthew had nothing of his own other than a business importing from the East and I have never known a couple happier and more content. Except for my Lucas and his Mary, of course.' She beamed with maternal pride.

Olivia pondered her ladyship's words as she sipped her tea and willed her tumultuous emotions to settle. Hope had once again been coaxed into life. This time, however, she would not allow it to run rampant, but she would keep it under control. She would not try to persuade Hugo to reveal his true feelings—although she prayed that her ladyship was right about them—but she would wait patiently for him to finally admit them to her. Then, and only then, would she do as Lady Todmorden advised and she would indeed fight with every fibre of her being to persuade Papa to accept Hugo as a suitable husband for his only daughter.

The sound of hooves outside brought both Olivia and Lady Todmorden to their feet.

'They will not bring Lord Clevedon here, will they?'

Olivia's stomach knotted—she did not know if she had the courage to face him, even if Hugo and Papa were both there.

'I am sure they will not bring him anywhere near you, my pet. But, just to make sure, I shall ask Sir Horace to check.'

She left the room and Olivia went to the window. Alex was outside, mounted on an unfamiliar horse, holding the reins of both Conqueror—Papa's horse—and Sprite. Olivia heard the low murmur of voices and then the door opened and she turned to face it. She had hoped Hugo might come, so that she might apologise to him and thank him again, but the doorway remained empty behind Papa and Lady Todmorden after they entered. Those treacherous tears threatened to erupt again, but she squared her shoulders and lifted her chin. She was a duke's daughter. She would take responsibility for her mistakes and stupidity, not attempt to avoid blame by crying.

'I am sorry, Papa.'

She felt she should say more but, really, she could find no words to excuse her actions. Papa shook his head at her and smiled ruefully. He opened his arms and she ran across the room and into his embrace, love for him flowing through her.

'Come on, minx. Let us get you home.' He pulled back and looked down at her. 'Are you up to riding, or shall I ask Sir Horace for his carriage?'

'No. I shall ride.' Olivia smiled at Lady Todmorden. 'Thank you—and I am sorry for all the trouble I have caused.'

'It was no trouble, my pet.' Lady Todmorden kissed her on the cheek and whispered, 'Courage, my dear. All will be well.'

They met no one else on their way out of the house. Papa lifted her on to Sprite and mounted Conqueror and then all three of them rode along the carriageway that led back to the Dyke road.

'I have everyone's agreement that the details of today will not be spread abroad,' said Papa. 'But I hope you have learned your lesson, young lady.'

'Yes, Papa.'

'You are not to go out without me or your stepmother, or your uncle and aunt, for the remainder of our stay in Brighton and I shall instruct two maids to watch you at all times. Is that clear? I will not have you take any further risks.'

His voice shook on those final words and guilt clawed at Olivia—she knew how he fretted over safety after what had happened to her mother, yet still she had put him through this.

'I understand, Papa.'

They rode in silence until they reached the neat brick house that Lady Todmorden had earlier pointed out to Olivia. It was set back from the carriageway in a forecourt bounded by stone piers and wrought-iron railings. A massive cedar tree dominated the neatly scythed lawn to the side of Cedar Lodge.

Hugo's home. Where was he? Why had he not come to her, to see that she was all right? That familiar ache swelled her throat again, but again she controlled her emotions.

'I shall leave you here.' Alex reined his horse close to Sprite and reached across to squeeze Olivia's shoulder. 'You're a troublesome brat, but I'm glad you're still here with us and not halfway to London with that bas—'

'Alexander!'

'Scoundrel,' he amended, with a wink at her. 'I'll come and see you tomorrow, Liv,' and with that he set his horse into a canter up the driveway to the Lodge.

Olivia scanned the windows, but the house was too far for her to see if Hugo was looking out. She swallowed, raised her chin and sent Sprite into a trot, back towards Brighton. Papa, seeming to sense her mood, trotted Conqueror alongside but, other than a few searching looks, he said nothing more until they arrived at the house. Thankfully, the rest of the family had not yet returned from their picnic ride—she was amazed that such a momentous event in her life had taken place in such a short time—and therefore had no idea of the drama that had taken place.

'I suggest—' said Papa, not unkindly '—that you go straight to your bedchamber and you remain there until the morning. That will back up your story that you were not well; the fewer people who know about this the better, even within the family. I shall ask Cook to send you a tray later on.'

Exhaustion and guilt and the need to just be alone robbed her of any argument or of any desire to question Papa about what had happened to Clevedon. She could not even think of him without a shudder. She climbed the stairs, pulled off her clothes and crawled into her bed, curling up into a tight ball.

There would be time to think later, when she was not so very, very weary.

Hugo paced the drawing room at Cedar Lodge, pausing only to look out of the window each time his circuit took him past it. Finally, he could see them: the Duke, Alex and Olivia. She was riding Sprite and respect for her courage filled him anew. Most other women would be swooning on a sofa after such an ordeal, even without that vicious slap. Fury erupted again, but he tamped it down. He would get his chance tomorrow and, by God, it would give him the greatest satisfaction to put a ball in that bastard.

After Clevedon had gone, Hugo's first instinct had been to ride straight to Helmstone to assure himself that Olivia was all right. The Duke, however, had made it abundantly clear he must stay away—and the more he thought about *that* edict, and the way he had meekly submitted, the fiercer his resentment grew. At the time it had seemed best to give Cheriton the time to sort his family out, but now…

He turned as Alex sauntered into the room.

'Is she all right? Will your father punish her?'

Alex crossed to an armchair and flung himself into it. 'Don't know. Oh, she's all right—Livvy always bounces back—but m'father…' he scowled, thrusting both hands through his hair to sweep it back from his face '…he seems unnaturally calm. He'll probably wait until after you meet Clevedon…he won't want anything to distract you.' He slanted a look at Hugo. 'Or maybe he's hoping you'll both get shot and save him a job.'

Hugo passed his hand around the back of his neck, rubbing as he tilted his head back. So tense. He felt like…he wanted to…he must…

He anchored his thoughts in place as he sorted

through them. The conclusion was—he could not bear to wait. He could not face Clevedon with this on his mind.

He swore out loud, softly and fluently. Alex flicked a brow. 'That's some inventive curse, my friend. Care to tell me what it's in aid of?'

Hugo strode for the door. 'I'm off to town. To talk to your father.'

An hour later—having first changed into fresh clothing—Hugo rode into Brighton. At the house on Marine Parade currently leased by the Duke of Cheriton he dismounted and beckoned to a young boy on the opposite side of the road.

'Here.' Hugo tossed him a penny. 'Hold him, will you? If I'm more than ten minutes, I shall pay you another.'

The boy's eyes brightened. 'Yessir.'

He was admitted without question and shown immediately to a back room.

'Lord Hugo Alastair, your Grace.'

The room—clearly in use as an office—was decorated in a feminine, floral style that was completely at odds with the furniture—a large mahogany desk set before the single window, several wooden chairs and a table piled with papers, where Freddie sat. The Duke stood on the far side of the desk with his back to the room, silhouetted by the light coming through the window.

'Leave us, Freddie, will you, please? I shall send for you when we are done.'

Freddie stood, tucked his crutch under his arm and headed for the door. He raised his brows and smiled at Hugo as he passed, but said nothing. Not until the door clicked shut behind him did Cheriton turn around. He gestured at a chair on the far side of the desk to himself and then settled himself in his own chair.

'You are here earlier than I anticipated.'

'I will not waste your time, Duke. I am here to ask for your daughter's hand in marriage.'

Dark brows rose, but there was no surprise on Cheriton's face. Merely, it seemed, a weary kind of acceptance. Hope germinated. He'd expected to be kicked out as soon as he uttered those words.

'You need to know that I have not declared myself to Olivia and she has no idea of the depth of my feelings for her, but I love her and I believe she loves me.'

Cheriton opened his mouth, but Hugo said, quickly, 'Please. Allow me to finish.'

The Duke inclined his head, and rose to his feet. 'Brandy?' At Hugo's nod, he crossed to a side table upon which there was a silver salver holding a crystal glass decanter and several glasses. 'Pray continue,' he said as he took the stopper from the decanter.

Hugo battened down a feeling of unreality. This interview was nothing like the one he had imagined as he had ridden into town. He gathered his thoughts and sucked in a steadying breath. He was determined to do this properly. Olivia deserved as much. After keeping her at arm's length for so long, the last thing he wanted was to raise her hopes only to have them dashed or—worse—for her to blame her father if he refused his consent.

'I know I cannot support her in the lifestyle she is used to, but I want to spend the rest of my life with her, if she'll have me.'

The Duke set a glass in front of Hugo, then rounded the desk to take his seat again. He took a sip and then placed his glass on the desk.

'Her dowry will go a long way to make up for any shortfall in her husband's income.'

The words were softly spoken, but there was a challenge in them, and in the silvery-grey gaze that pierced Hugo.

'I am not interested in her dowry. I will take her without any dowry, to prove my love is true. It is Olivia I want, not your money.'

His expression unreadable, Cheriton rose once again and turned to stare out of the window, his hands loosely clasped behind his back. Hugo waited. He had said his piece. Quite what he would do if the Duke refused his consent, he did not know.

'Are you prepared to wait for her?'

Here we go.

If her father refused his consent it would be three years before Olivia could wed without his permission. Unless they eloped. Hugo devoutly hoped it would not come to that. Now his decision was made—having denied his feelings for so long—he wanted no obstacles in his way.

'Yes. I will wait.'

Cheriton sat again, leaned his elbows on the desk and steepled his fingers in front of his face, his chin propped on his thumbs. He again scrutinised Hugo and then he sighed.

'Both Alex and Freddie have told me how you have helped and protected both Olivia and Alex over the past months, although they were both somewhat circumspect as to the exact details.'

Hugo sifted through his memories. They could not have told him about the necklace because neither of them knew about it. He doubted, therefore, that either of them would have told Cheriton about the visit to Vauxhall Gardens either. Having grown closer to Alex, Hugo now shared Olivia and Freddie's determination to help him achieve his dream of taking over Foxbourne.

'I shall embarrass neither of us by demanding those details from you,' Cheriton continued. 'Both my son and my daughter are—currently—safe and that is all that concerns me.'

He stood again and paced about the room. Hugo recognised that restless activity, the sign of a dilemma being grappled with. He waited until Cheriton sat again.

'I realise I owe you a great deal, Alastair, but that on its own is not sufficient to support your union with my daughter. However, I also see in you an honourable man attempting to put his past behind him—I remember how you stepped up last year when your cousin, Lady Ashby, was in danger and I have seen how you have supported your mother and stepfather since their marriage. I also—' his perceptive gaze again pierced Hugo '—remember your father and what he was like.'

Again he paced the room and Hugo waited. A man such as Cheriton could not be pushed or cajoled and woe betide the man who attempted it. This time he did not sit again, but came to a standstill next to Hugo's chair. Hugo rose to his feet. It was one thing allowing the man time to come to a decision, quite another to have him towering above him as he delivered his verdict. Hugo met the Duke's gaze and raised a brow. A smile flickered across the Duke's features.

'You may call upon Olivia and, if you still wish to, you may offer for her with my blessing. I do, however, have two stipulations. Firstly, you are not to call upon her or communicate with her until after the duel. Olivia knows nothing about the meeting and she will not know anything until the affair is settled. Is that clear?'

Hugo nodded.

'My daughter, as you may have noticed, is somewhat headstrong. If she hears the slightest whisper of your meeting then she would, I am sure, find a way to be there.'

Hugo shuddered at the thought.

'Now, Olivia is but eighteen years old and so my second stipulation is that a formal betrothal is delayed until Christmas with the wedding to take place in the spring. I want you both—but in particular Olivia—to be absolutely certain that this is what you want. In the meantime, you are welcome to come and visit Olivia at Cheriton Abbey whenever you can be spared from Helmstone.' He raised his dark brows. 'Agreed?'

Hugo shook his proffered hand. 'Agreed.'

Chapter Twenty-Two

Dawn the following morning found Hugo and the Duke high up on the Downs that surrounded Brighton, awaiting the arrival of Clevedon and Sudbury. Lord Sudbury had called upon the Duke the previous evening, as agreed, to finalise the meeting place and weapons. And Hugo learned that Sudbury had passed on certain information that shed new light on Clevedon's situation and his subsequent behaviour.

Clevedon's debt to Bulbridge was huge, but it had not been entirely due to gambling. Sudbury told Cheriton that Bulbridge and his cousin, Douglas Randall, were the feared and despised owners of Diablo's—both the gambling club and the linked brothel that prided itself on catering for men of various and unusual desires. Clevedon's sexual preferences—which had come as no surprise to Cheriton, evidently—had rendered him a victim of blackmail by the unscrupulous pair who had layered demand after demand on the Earl, pushing him to the brink of despair and leading to him snatching Olivia in a desperate attempt to gain her dowry.

Hugo's nerves had completely disintegrated at that information. The relief that he could now delope with honour…that he did not have to actually kill Clevedon…was enormous. Sudbury had assured Cheriton that, if Clevedon survived, he planned to leave the country and escape Bulbridge once and for all.

In their need to keep the entire affair as quiet as possible, it was agreed that Sir Horace Todmorden would preside over the duel and he arranged for a discreet doctor friend to attend in case he was needed. Hugo and Clevedon paced the required distance and turned to face one another, but sideways on. They took aim, keeping one eye on the white handkerchief held aloft by Sir Horace. As it fluttered to the ground, Clevedon aimed his pistol into the air and fired. He then turned to fully face Hugo.

Hugo sited along the barrel of his own pistol and then, quite deliberately, he, too, aimed into the air and pulled the trigger. As the puff of smoke dissipated into the cool morning air, he lowered the pistol.

'Let us repair to the Old Ship for breakfast,' said Cheriton as they rode into the outskirts of Brighton a little later.

Sir Horace had declined an offer to join them and Clevedon, shamefaced, had come to them to confirm his plan to go overseas. Once they were settled in a private room at the inn, Hugo found himself undergoing such a thorough interrogation about his life that he was eventually goaded into saying, 'I wonder you will contemplate a man such as me for Olivia, sir.'

Cheriton, having eaten his fill, leaned back in his chair.

'Even six months ago, I would never have done so. But this Season has changed my attitude to love and marriage. It has been a momentous time for my family with not just me getting married after having vowed never to wed again, but now both my brother and my sister have found love in the most unlikely of circumstances. And if there is one thing I have learned it is this. We cannot dictate where love will find us but, when it does, we must grab it with both hands. I am no longer surprised that Olivia has followed in my generation's footsteps and I now find myself watching Avon with some trepidation. I almost expect him to turn up with an actress upon his arm.' He grinned. 'But I might then put my foot down very firmly.'

'And Alex?'

'Oh, I suspect Alex will confound us all and fall in love with a princess at the very least.'

* * *

Olivia bent her head to concentrate both on her embroidery and on keeping her simmering anger and fear from erupting into fury. She eyed the two maids who had dogged her footsteps from the moment she emerged from her bedchamber. They sat close to the parlour door, a basket of mending between them, but when Olivia left the room not ten minutes ago—saying she was going to relieve herself—*both* of them had accompanied her.

She swallowed her *hmmph* of disgust at Papa's lack of trust in her.

She was forbidden from leaving the house—his Grace's orders, the maids had said, apologetically—and she was therefore condemned to simply sit and wait for news as she had done since first thing that morning. She had risen early, driven by a nameless dread that lurked deep, deep inside, setting her insides in turmoil, only to find that Papa had already left the house…and a part of her knew what that meant. Alex had regaled her often enough with stories about duels—that peculiar method by which gentlemen settled insults and arguments—and she had always imagined them as dashing and romantic, with the clash of rapiers in the early morning mist or deadly pistols at dawn.

Until now.

There was nothing romantic about it when someone she loved might be involved.

Was there to be a duel? Or—looking at the clock—had there *been* a duel? And was it Papa who had challenged Clevedon? Or Hugo? She could not decide which was worse, but she was certain of one thing—the very worst thing was that it was her fault and if either of them were injured, she could never, ever forgive herself. Dread and self-recrimination mixed with her other emotions.

At a quarter past nine—before any of the rest of the family had even arisen—the parlour door opened and Alex sauntered in. Olivia threw down her embroidery and ran to him, grabbing his hands and tugging him over to the window, as far away from the door and the maids' ears as possible.

'What happened?' she hissed. 'Tell me, please.'

Alex's brows stitched together. 'You *know*?'

Those two words confirmed her worst fears. 'Who challenged him? Papa? Hugo?'

Alex growled, deep in his throat. 'You bloo— blasted menace, Liv. You *didn't* know.'

'Not for certain, but I guessed.' She clutched harder at Alex's hands. 'Please. Tell me the worst. Is anyone hurt? Have they been arrested?'

For that was another worry and one that had only just occurred to her. Duels were against the law. There had been enough stories over the years of men forced to flee the country to escape justice.

Alex glanced at the maids, then put his arm

around Olivia's shoulders and manoeuvred them both so they stood with their backs to the room.

'Keep your voice down, do, Sis. The fewer people who know about this the better. Father will make sure the law doesn't become involved, never fear.'

'But why is Papa not home? He should be back by now.'

'Men never eat breakfast before they meet, Liv, so they've probably gone for a bite to eat. Devilish hungry work, staring death in the face as the sun comes up.'

'Did you not go to watch?'

'*Watch?* It is not a spectator sport, you silly gudgeon. It's serious business. Never fear. I'm sure Hugo'll come through all right—he's a tolerable shot, y'know.'

She swayed at his words, and he grabbed hold of her, supporting her. '*Hugo* challenged Clevedon?'

'Shhh. The last thing I want is for them pair to go gabbling to Father that I've been talking to you about this. You really have no idea of discretion, do you?'

'I will keep my voice down if you promise to tell me everything you know.'

'Such as?'

'Such as—did Hugo challenge Clevedon?'

'Well, of course he did. Haven't I just said so? Father was like fire that he got in his challenge first, but then he offered to stand as Hugo's second.' He hugged Olivia to him briefly before releasing her. 'Never fear, brat. Father would have been home long since had anything bad happened. They're having breakfast, you mark my words.'

Alex left soon afterwards and Olivia wore a track in the carpet, pacing around the parlour—terrified and furious in equal measures—as she kept her ears pricked for signs of arrival at the front door. Finally, she heard a murmur of voices in the hall and Grantham appeared in the doorway. First, intriguingly, he dismissed the two maids.

'There is a gentleman waiting to speak to you in the salon, milady.' He bowed, then favoured her with a rare smile. 'Lord Hugo Alastair.'

Olivia's heart skipped and jumped as she realised the implication of that announcement. But the fear and anger that had been brewing since she awoke still agitated deep inside her and Hugo needn't think she would simply fall into his arms because he had finally decided—presumably with her father's blessing—to make her an offer. Unless…

Her throat thickened. Did he feel it was his duty to offer for her, now she had tarnished her reputation? Had Papa put pressure on him and *forced* him to propose? She couldn't bear that. Resentment now mixed in with that volatile concoction of fear and anger.

She followed Grantham down the hall and he opened the salon door, standing aside for her to enter.

Her breath caught. Hugo stood on the far side of the room—utterly, mouthwateringly gorgeous—and, as Grantham shut the door behind her all that pent-up fear and emotion burst from her. She flew at him.

'You despicable cur!' She slapped at him, only for him to capture her wrist. 'You…you…misbegotten miscreant!' She aimed for his face with her other hand, but he caught that, too. Tears of pure frustration…and rage…and relief…flooded her eyes as she struggled to free herself. 'You swine! You…ch-churlish coxcomb!'

'You forgot sodden-witted lord.'

'Sodden-witted goat, more like. Why did you challenge him? *Why?* You could have been k-k-killed.'

'But I was not killed, was I, my sweet? Look at me. Nary a scratch.'

'But I did not know that! No one told me *anything*.' She fought again against his grip, but half-heartedly now as she gulped for air. Then the fight leached from her. 'Y-you didn't even come to see if I was all right,' she wailed.

And with that, he released her wrists to snake one arm around her waist, pulling her roughly, almost fiercely, to him. Her arms wound around his neck as their lips met with a savage intensity, his tongue plunging into her mouth. She returned his kiss with reckless abandon, meeting his tongue thrust for thrust until her lips were on fire, her body was throbbing with need and her lungs screamed for air.

She tore her lips from his. 'You could have been *killed*.' She could not let the thought go… she was compelled to say it again, to get him to understand how terrified she had been. She took his face between her palms and stared into his dark eyes, seeking his soul. 'Don't you *ever* do that to me again.'

She pressed her lips to his again but, as she did so, the realisation came from nowhere—this was *her* fault and, if they were to have a future together, she must find the courage to admit it. Again, she pulled away from their kiss and this time she wriggled free from his embrace. She inhaled and straightened.

'I am sorry.'

His brows knit together. 'Why are you sorry?'

'It is my fault you had to fight a duel. I should have listened to you. You only ever tried to help me, but I couldn't see further than what I wanted.'

His lips quirked. 'Which was?'

She bit her lips against her answering smile. 'You know the answer to that, Lord Hugo Alastair, but…very well—I shall pander to your ego. *You*. I wanted you. And now, because of my…my… stupidity—' she sucked in a shaky breath as she faced again the reality of the events she had set in motion and what could have happened '—you *could* have been killed.' She hauled in another breath, determined not to cry. 'I was mad with worry.'

'You were not *meant* to know anything about today. But... I find myself completely unsurprised that you do.' He opened his arms wide. 'Come here, Trouble.'

She walked into his embrace, the last vestiges of her panic and her anger melting away as his arms folded around her, holding her close to his chest. She slid her own arms under his jacket and around his waist, hugging him tight as the steady, reassuring beat of his heart echoed through her and his spicy scent curled around her.

'Papa knows you are here now?'

His chest jerked a little as he huffed a laugh. 'Of course he knows.' He tilted her face to his, his eyes solemn as they searched hers, igniting a flame deep, deep inside her. 'I came here last night to ask his permission to pay my addresses to you.'

Her breath caught. 'And he *agreed*?'

He nodded. Then he stepped back and took her hands in his, smoothing his thumbs across her knuckles. And before she realised his intent, he was on one knee, looking up at her with such love and devotion in his ebony eyes that her own knees threatened to buckle.

'Lady Olivia Beauchamp…'

'Wait!'

His eyes crinkled in amusement. 'I might have guessed you would not allow this to go my way.'

Olivia huffed. 'I only want to know if you are *certain*. You are not here because you now feel *obliged* to offer for me? Or because Papa has *forced* you to make me an offer?'

He laughed. 'Trust me, sweetheart. No one— not even your father—can force me to do anything against my will. I am here because there is nowhere else I want to be and there is nothing else I would rather be doing than kneeling in front of you waiting for an opportunity to actually propose to you.'

'But…you do not love me.' Olivia searched his features. 'And…' A memory was struggling to the surface. She frowned, concentrating to fully recall words barely noticed at the time they were uttered, but that now stung. 'You told Clevedon to court me. He said so and you did not correct him.'

A rueful smile tugged at Hugo's mouth. '*That* was a grave error on my part. I was so intent on retrieving the necklace for you that the suggestion was made before I could think it through. I knew Clevedon was capable of trying to compromise you, but I persuaded him that—if he persisted in using your necklace against you, it would only turn you against him. I didn't understand at that point just how desperate he was, how far he would go to get what he wanted…'

'And I am not very experienced. You said so yourself.'

'Olivia…?'

'Yes, Hugo?'

'I love you to distraction. I love you to the moon and back. I think I have loved you ever since the moment I heard you haranguing those youths with insults from the Bard. Now, will you marry me? Please?'

Her heart swelled so much she thought it might explode. 'Oh, yes!' She dropped to her knees, took his dear face between her hands and claimed his lips in a searing kiss. 'Yes! Yes! A thousand times, yes!'

Epilogue

Cheriton Abbey, Devonshire—March 1813

Hugo grabbed Olivia by the hand and ran, towing her behind him.

'Hugo? Where are we going?'

She snatched up the flowing skirt of her wedding dress to avoid tripping on it. He did not slow until he reached the foot of the imposing polished oak staircase. He looked up the stairs and then returned his gaze to roam her face, raising shivers of awareness wherever it touched. His eyes glinted.

'Hugo.' Her breath hitched. 'We *can't*.'

He raised one brow in that arrogant way of his—the way she still could not emulate no matter how much she practised.

'Of course we can.' His deep voice sent shivers of awareness, need and pure excitement shimmering through her until every nerve ending felt alight.

'But…what will people say?'

She saw him bite back his smile. 'Is this the Lady Olivia Beauchamp I know and love? Fretting over what people will say? Surely not?'

She went up on tiptoes and pressed her mouth to his. The merest touch of their lips sent heat pulsing through her.

'Lady Olivia Alastair, if you don't mind.' She smiled against his mouth and felt his answering grin. 'Or have you so soon forgotten?'

She stifled a squeal as he swung her into his arms, cradling her against his chest. He began to climb the stairs.

'Hugo!'

'Olivia?' He did not pause but climbed relentlessly, one step after another.

'What will they *think*? My family…your family…they will *notice*.'

'They will think, my sweet—' they had reached the landing and Hugo turned in the direction of the best guest bedchamber. He paused, and kissed her, long, hard and hot. '—that I have been remarkably patient for all these months and that my patience has finally worn thin.' He started walking again and Olivia tightened her arms around his neck, peppering his jaw and cheek with tiny kisses. 'They will think, my darling wife, that I

am making damned sure you are mine—at last—
and that no man will ever come between us.'

She nipped his earlobe between her teeth.

'Ouch!' He tightened his grip on her. 'You'll
pay for that, you little minx.'

She giggled and buried her face in his neck.
They reached the bedchamber door and he paused
again, waiting until she looked up into his beloved
face. He pierced her with a look of such hot intent
that her insides turned molten and her corset suddenly grew excruciatingly tight.

'They will think—' he pushed the door open
'—my utterly gorgeous, desirable wife—' he
kicked the door shut behind them '—that they
are unlikely to set eyes on either one of us again
until, at the very earliest, noon tomorrow.'

He laid her on the bed and followed her down,
taking her mouth in a scorching kiss as his hands
roamed freely.

It was full dark outside by the time she emerged
from the sensual haze that Hugo—her irresistible,
skilful, playful, *sexy* husband—had woven around
her. She snuggled up to his warm, hard body, trail-
ing her fingers through the soft hair that covered
his chest, down over his flat belly to—

She bit back a smile at his groan.

'*Again?* Have a heart, my sweet. I'm out of
practice.'

She kissed his nipple, then licked and, finally, softly, nipped at it.

'You owe me.'

She sensed he'd raised his head. '*Owe* you? What do I owe you?'

She wriggled to face him, draping her body across his, breast to chest, her nipples hardening at the rasp of his chest hair against them. She rested her arms on his chest and propped her chin upon her clasped hands.

'All these months and I had no idea what I was missing.' She shuffled, moving higher. 'All that time wasted. Why—' she bit gently at his chin '—didn't you tell me?' She licked delicately at his lower lip.

'Mmm...' His hum of appreciation sounded from somewhere deep in his throat.

She moved to straddle him and kissed him thoroughly.

'Well?'

His arms wrapped around her waist. 'You, madam, are insatiable,' he growled as he flipped her on to her back and covered her. 'A devious, manipulative minx. I didn't tell you because I know how curious and how persistent you are and I wanted our wedding night to be special.'

He bent his head to her breast, taking her aching nipple into his mouth. Olivia gave herself up to the sensation, smiling her satisfaction.

There were times when persistence most definitely paid off.

'I love you, Hugo.'

'I love you, too, Trouble.'

* * * * *

MILLS & BOON

Coming next month

THE WARRIOR'S BRIDE PRIZE
Jenni Fletcher

'I won.'

'What?'

'The game. I won.'

'Oh.' Livia stared at Marius blankly. Did he expect her to congratulate him? 'And you woke me to tell me that?'

'No.' His expression shifted to one she hadn't seen there before, as if he were uncertain of himself. He seemed to be having trouble finding words. 'There's more...about Scaevola.'

'Has something happened to him?' She felt a fleeting, *very fleeting*, moment of concern. If he was hurt in some way then it would explain his absence. Although it might also postpone their wedding, she thought hopefully.

'Not physically, but, yes, in a manner of speaking. He ran out of money.'

'You mean he was gambling?'

He inclined his head and she rolled her eyes scornfully. Of course he'd been gambling and now he'd run out of funds again, just as he had in Lindum. She was amazed he'd had anything left to play with in the first place. Then she tensed as another thought struck her. Was *that* why Marius was there? Because Scaevola owed him money? Had he come to ask *her* to pay the debt? Her mouth turned dry at the thought. Surely that couldn't be the reason he'd come to wake her and yet...what else could be so important?

She pulled her shoulders back, bracing herself for the

worst. 'If he's indebted to you, then I'm afraid I can't help. I don't have any money of my own.'

He drew his brows together so sharply they met in a hard line in the middle. 'I'm not here for money, Livia. Is that what you think of me?' His gaze dropped to her mouth. 'After last night?'

She tensed again as the low, intimate tone of his voice sent a *frisson* of excitement racing through her body, though she forced herself to ignore it. They shouldn't talk about last night.

'No. You're right, I shouldn't have said that. I just thought...' She licked her lips, trying to put her confusion into words. 'I *don't* think of you like that, but why are you here, Marius? What's so important about a game? Did Scaevola lose so much?'

'Yes, but it's not about money...'

'Then what?'

He muttered an expletive before answering. 'He staked you.'

'What?' Her body seemed to go into shock, though it took her brain a few seconds to catch up with the words.

'He had no money left so he staked you.'

'In a game of tabula?'

'Yes.'

'You're saying that he offered me as a prize?'

'Yes.'

'And that you won?'

'Yes.'

'So you won...me?'

Continue reading
THE WARRIOR'S BRIDE PRIZE
Jenni Fletcher

Available next month
www.millsandboon.co.uk

COMING SOON!

We really hope you enjoyed reading this book. If you're looking for more romance, be sure to head to the shops when new books are available on

Thursday
4th October

To see which titles are coming soon, please visit
millsandboon.co.uk

LET'S TALK

Romance

For exclusive extracts, competitions
and special offers, find us online:

f facebook.com/millsandboon

⊙ @millsandboonuk

🐦 @millsandboon

Or get in touch on 0844 844 1351*

For all the latest titles coming soon, visit
millsandboon.co.uk/nextmonth